RED FIST

JAMIEL JONES

D0713970

Dedicated to my dear friends,

who I wish to not let down because they believe in me.

Contents

Prologue

A Violent Encounter

Hushed whispers. That's all I could remember. I wanted to know. I needed to know. Knowing was essential. I was going insane.

"Devin, please," I pleaded to my best friend.

Devin continued to twirl around in my computer chair as if he hadn't heard a word I said. His shoulder-length dreads just kept helicoptering around and around.

Whispers of them: Red Fist. All day. And I knew nothing because I had lost my phone somehow.

"Devin, you're being an asshole, just tell me the number."

Again, he ignored me. He was pissing me off.

"Get out," I told him, pointing to my bedroom door.

Devin stopped his spin. He grumbled something under his breath, slid over to my laptop and began typing in the browser. I smiled. We switched spots, so I could see the screen.

The video started, and I turned the volume on my speakers all the way up. It was exactly four minutes and thirty seconds long. A cool graphic of blood splattering on the screen in 3D effect was shown, and then it began to slither down, disappearing.

The screen went black, and then a deep, unidentifiable voice began to speak. "This is a Red Fist installment. We are Red Fist. If you don't like blood or graphic and disturbing images, this video is *not* for you. But this is where the truth lies."

The blackness on the screen dispersed into tiny fragments that resembled broken shards of glass, and then the screen went starch white. After a second, recorded footage began. I leaned forward, and so did Devin, muttering something.

A man was tied to a metal chair with a black bag over his head. His head hung limply to the side. He was wearing a business suit that was no longer crisp, and it was flecked with dried specks of blood.

Beside him, to the right, stood a man that must have been six and a half feet tall. The man was brown-skinned, and he wore a mask over his head. Standing behind the bound man was a lean white woman whose face was also hidden.

The woman removed the bag, and Devin gasped. I was too absorbed in the footage to ask him what his gasping was about.

"This man right here is Senator Gregory Griffin of Arizona," the masked man said. "It took us a very long time to get our hands on him."

The man was smiling under the mask, and it sent a shiver through my soul. Something about him, even though he couldn't harm me, made me afraid, but the fear only lasted for a moment.

"We're going to kill him," the masked man continued, brandishing a wicked long knife that glinted in the lighting of the bare room they were in. The masked man plunged the knife into Senator Griffin's right thigh. Griffin immediately began shaking and wailing and cursing.

After all the videos, I still didn't know anything about Red Fist except that it was a terrorist organization, but the people involved always acted like they were justified in doing what they did. And who knew? Maybe they were.

"Levi?" Devin said.

Blood squirted into the air when the masked man yanked the blade out.

I smiled. Somewhere deep inside me, I found the video exciting, like some darkness within me was finally being fed. Devin punched me in the shoulder. I pressed pause on the video and stood up to face him.

"Turn it off, bro."

"Why?" I asked.

"These people are lunatics, that's why."

I shrugged and sat back down. Devin shook his head, breathing some remark that I couldn't hear.

I swung around. He was leaving. "What the fuck, Dev? Really?"

"You're a psycho. You're obsessed with a bunch of terrorists."

He turned the corner, and I got up to follow him. At the edge of the stairs, I grabbed his arm, but he yanked away from me. "What's your problem?"

Devin started down the stairs, and I grabbed him again. And again, he pulled away from me.

"Such a bitch," I said to him when he reached the bottom.

He looked back up at me, his shoulders bristling with rage. He opened the door and stepped out.

I stood at the top of the stairs for a couple moments longer, then went back to my room and pressed play.

You don't need that weakness in your life.

I pressed pause, looking all around. It sounded like someone had said something to me. I shrugged off the feeling and continued watching the video.

3

1

Fresh blood dripped from the blade as the man returned to his side. The woman behind Griffin lifted the senator's head, so his teary blue eyes were staring into the camera. Griffin looked ghastly. His five-o'clock shadow had not been maintained, and his wispy salt-and-pepper hair was soaked with sweat.

"Senator," said the woman, whose voice was also altered. "Tell the world, and especially your fellow Americans, about the sin you took part in, about the blood you agreed to spill."

Griffin said nothing.

The giant masked man punched him so hard his head snapped to the left with an audible crack. "Answer."

"I don't know…" the senator managed, tears running down his face.

The masked man and woman glanced at each other.

I laughed.

"Pathetic!" the masked man boomed. "You don't deserve to cry. You should be crying because you've helped take thousands of innocent lives."

The senator shook his head, mumbling. "Please..."

The masked man shook his own head as if disappointed. He cut the binding from the senator's limbs, and the weak man fell to the concrete floor. The camera zoomed in, then backed up, focusing on the masked man.

"That man..." he spat, his finger, like a smoking gun, pointed down at the groveling senator. "He is the owner of a bank passed down to him, called LG. Trillions of dollars go in and out of that place every day all over the US, UK, Australia, and other first-world countries. Senator Griffin here, to ensure his wallet is always fat, loans money to warring countries and groups for weapons that help kill innocent people and children. Examples: Syria. Afghanistan. ISIS radicals. Of course, big bad America knows about this and does nothing because the money's flowing and it would cause widespread distrust if it got out. Why are men and women continuing to lose their lives if we're technically aiding the very people we're supposed to be fighting against? Where is the justice? Ask yourselves. We are exposing the truth.

"I know some of you think we're scum—terrorists even—but we're fighting for ultimate peace, we're fighting for *you*. We are revolutionaries. We will destroy all nations that let the world crumble. We will take over and make the world better. We will not keep secrets from you the way your governments do. We welcome you all with open arms as our brothers and sisters. Together, we fight!"

The masked man made a dramatic pause, then clasped his heels together and pounded his chest with his right fist, his head held high, his eyes prideful, frightening, "We are Red Fist!"

The video blacked out, but it wasn't over.

The woman's voice came on. "Don't bother liking or commenting or even trying to subscribe. If we want you, we'll find you. We're growing ever stronger, and hopefully, we will have all your support to make this world a better place."

I was so excited. My heart was doing cartwheels in my chest. That was fucking exhilarating. Red Fist was astonishing. I didn't know if their videos were real, but I guessed they had to be.

I watched the video again. I tried to find some of their other videos, but they'd been removed.

By the time my mom came home that night, I had watched the video a dozen times. I thought about history class and how my history instructor told us all to always question everything and never just accept anything.

I thought about our government, all the scandals and half-truths, and all the presidents we've had that never seemed to fix anything entirely.

My dad was still MIA, presumed dead because of Bush. I hadn't seen him since I was a kid. It had been eight years. Thinking about him now, for the first time in a long time, I felt an old emotion. I fought back the rusty tears and concentrated on my computer screen.

I wanted some clarification. I needed *something*.

I did all types of research that night. I researched the world wars. I looked into our different presidents. I pegged some different radical groups. I just wanted to understand, not become an expert.

When my mom barged into my room, I was trying to dig up more information on Red Fist. She flipped on the lights, and I saw my wild and unruly reflection on the screen.

"Haven't you heard me calling your name?"

"Huh."

"Levi Rodriguez Cheveyo Conoway, shut that computer off *now*," Mom said in her thick Puerto Rican accent.

I groaned and slapped it shut. "Mom…"

"Don't mom me. How about you tell me why Officer Jefferson had to pull you over today."

I turned to look at her; she had one hand on her right hip. I always forgot she was a cop, and that shit like getting pulled over couldn't be hidden from her.

"I wasn't even speeding."

"Yeah, well that's not what I heard. See that it doesn't happen again," she warned and stepped out of my room.

I sighed, shaking my head when she peeked back in. "Come downstairs. Your phone's on the table and so is dinner."

When I got downstairs, I almost had a freaking aneurysm. Dickbag Darryl was sitting in the kitchen, smiling at me. I flashed my mom an irritated look, and Darryl laughed. He pulled her towards him as she walked by and stood to kiss her.

"Get a fucking room," I said.

"Go to yours, kid."

Before I could say or do anything, my mom turned to me, then back to Darryl. "You two really need to learn to get along. This is ridiculous. Two grown men acting like children."

"Get this piece of shit outta here, Mom."

"Eh, there, Alice, your son is real disrespectful." Darryl pushed past her and stepped to me. He was a bit taller than me, so I puffed up to try to match him.

My mom separated us. "I swear I'll arrest both of you."

I stormed away, pissed off. I really hated Darryl with a passion. I would've given anything to bash his head in.

I stopped at the bottom of the stairs and saw the two of them kissing again. I lashed out at the banister, running up the stairs, the pain not registering until I was back in my room. I spun myself around in the darkness in my computer chair until I grew dizzy. The only thing I could think about was smashing Darryl's face in. He always pissed me off so much. And Mom acted like Dad had never existed. I never saw her glance at his pictures on the walls anymore. Not even once since she'd met Darryl seven months ago. Fuck them.

Devin clawed his way into my mind, and I felt a pang of guilt. Maybe I should've tried to understand him a bit better. I couldn't wrap my head around why he was such a baby about the video. It was probably fake anyway.

I lay down on my bed and stared up at the ceiling, seeing nothing but pitch black. I felt silly for doing all that investigating. Most of it had been nothing but conspiracy theories. In that oblivion, I found my dad. I held on to his image, and memories surfaced from the puddles on the black ground in my mind. It was raining there, for some reason.

My dad always spent time with me when I was younger. He was a great dad. Eight years was a long time. I couldn't bring myself to believe he was dead. I wouldn't. I had this gut feeling that somewhere out there he was alive and breathing fresh air.

2

It was like some invisible force heaved me out of my sleep. I woke on the opposite side of the bed, still in the same clothes from the previous day. I sighed and rolled out of bed sluggishly, moping over to my light switch to flick it on. The sight of my room almost made me laugh. It was disgusting in there.

I headed for the bathroom and washed up with my mind on nothing in particular. I was on a roll that day, which was strange; by now, Devin was usually banging on the door for me to come out.

It was seven-fifteen when I left the house, surprised at the realization that on that day, Devin was not waiting for me by my car. I waited in my car an extra seven minutes before I realized that Devin's car was gone. He wasn't riding with me like usual. Whatever. Fuck him, I thought.

I ended up getting to my first class late, and I saw the professor write something on her green notepad, no doubt making a note about me. I shook my head. She would deduct points. I was already struggling in philosophy.

I thought community college was supposed to be easy. That's why I didn't go to university. I didn't know what I wanted to do with my life. I wanted to be like my father, but my mom was strictly against that, for obvious reasons. I was lost, and college wasn't helping me find anything but stress.

I sat through the boring lecture, thinking about more interesting things, things like Red Fist. I went through the entire day in sort of a daze, until it was time to drive back home.

I sat in my driveway for at least an hour. Finally, Devin showed up. When he parked his car, I got out and ran up to him before he could hurry inside.

He stopped and raised his eyebrows. "Do I know you?"

"Dev, listen, I'm sorry. You're my best friend. I was an asshole. I'll do better. I need you, man. I feel like shit without you."

Devin grinned so hard I thought his face would split in two. "Apology accepted."

"Really?"

He opened his arms, and we shared a hug, but he didn't let me go right away. "Dev?"

"Come with me somewhere."

I broke away from him. He had mischief written all over his face. "I gotta work later."

"Same, but let's call out."

I ran around to the passenger's side of his car and hopped in.

We ended up way out of our suburban area, about twenty minutes away, in the city of DC. Devin parked his car in a parking garage, and we got out. He stopped and typed in an address on his phone. He began walking.

"Where are we going?" I asked.

"Surprise."

"It's not my birthday."

Devin blew me off.

We walked out of the garage and down two blocks until we came to a huge factory. It was behind a high stone wall that had barbed wire on the top. The factory took up half the length of the block. I read one of the signs, on the wall: *Dan Fan Corporations*.

I groaned. "Devin?"

We reached the main gateway area, and Devin slid through the fenced-in area to the other side. I followed him. It was unlike him to do something like this. He was a cautious person, not so outgoing. But that evening was different.

He turned to me. "You know where we're at yet?" I cut my eyes at him, and he laughed. "Fight Club. It's our old friend, Brad. He's hosting it here. His dad is out of town on a business trip and told him to watch over the place."

"I'm not going in there."

"But"—he raised his pointer finger—"we're already here."

"He's gonna call me out."

"Levi, that was high school, he's probably forgotten you ever existed," Devin said, turning his back to me. The sun was beginning to set. Other people were sliding through the opening and passing us. He wrapped his arm around me and whispered, "Who's the bitch now?"

3

I got caught up in the cheering and screaming, and soon I was like everybody else, excited by the blood and sweat. The fight only lasted a minute and ended with a jock clutching his side. Brad helped him into the crowd, side-eyeing Jake. He used to be a theater nerd, but he'd been practicing martial arts.

Everybody was chanting, "Jake! Jake! Jake! Jake! Jake! Jake! Jake!"

Brad's voice came over the loudspeakers, cutting off the chanting. "This guy comes from far away. He says he's from Egypt."

The crowd hollered.

"He says he wants to fight!" Brad yelled.

The crowd roared.

"Step into the light!"

On my right side, stepping out of the mix was a guy with long dark hair identical to mine. I thought that was strange because not too many guys were rocking the long hair. I did it because part of my family is Native American. Tradition.

The guy hyped up the sea of people. He was about five-eight and had brownish-tan skin. He turned a full circle, beaming. He had that kind of dazzling smile that any girl would fall in love with, and his eyes were a moody brown, like dark tree bark. He was wearing a faded blue hoodie with the sleeves cut off, and dark jeans. He took off the hoodie and threw it to the ground. The girls went wild. The guy was cut.

Brad shoved the mic in the guy's face. "Say your name and call out who you're fighting."

The guy took the mic and scanned the area for a long time, taking in every face. When he got to mine, I felt an itch all over, and I began to sweat. Something was telling me to get away, but I was already crumbling.

"My name is Gary Conoway."

No fucking way. I wasn't breathing. Devin was shaking me. Brad was screaming something into the mic, but my ears weren't picking up a thing.

When I came to, Devin was yelling, "Fucking *run*."

I didn't get the chance. The mouth that was the hands of people who wanted blood swallowed me whole. Before I realized it, I was down the steps, in the light.

Brad smirked at me. "We have Gary versus Levi, an old friend of mine. *Fight*!"

The audience cheered.

I was looking at Gary. And he was looking at me. He was smiling. I wasn't. His skin was shining in the light, showing every bulge in his muscles. I knew he was going to demolish me.

"You gonna swing, baby brother?"

I was so dumbfounded by that odd question that I didn't even see his right hook coming. I fell to the ground, spitting up blood, my left

13

ear ringing. Gary was on me, beating at my back. I tried to protect my head as I took a barrage of bullet punches. Who the fuck *was* this guy who had long black hair like me, and the same last name?

I saw Brad out the corner of my eye; he was frothing at the mouth, my pain causing the fuck-face to go insane.

Gary picked me up by my shirt and slung me. All the air escaped my chest, and I was left squirming on the ground, looking up at the light.

Gary stood over me. "Dad said you might be weak. I'll go further and say you're a scrawny little bitch, really pathetic."

I heard what he said, and it instantly pissed me off. When Gary's foot smashed down on my stomach, I grabbed it and rolled to the side. He tumbled to the ground, but quickly recovered, pulling me in with his legs, choking me. I clawed at his ankles, gasping for air.

"Dad wants you, but you're nowhere near ready. You been on Xbox all this time, right?"

He let me go, and I jumped up, coughing, eating as much air as I could because the world was a blur, and when my vision finally became clear I found him right in my face. He had a cocky grin on his face that I wanted to rip off.

"Who are you?" I demanded, a dribble of blood leaking from my lips.

Kill him! Kill the guy! I shook my head, erasing that voice.

"I'm everything you're not," he answered, and gut busted me. I collapsed to my knees with my stomach feeling like it was being pulled out from the inside. With my head down, I didn't see the kick to the back of my dome coming.

I woke up in the back seat of a car, my head throbbing. I opened my eyes, and even that was painful. Where was I? I didn't know. I remembered getting that fist shot into my gut, but how did I end up where I was? I slowly brought myself up, and the world spun.

A familiar voice chimed, "I was worried you weren't gonna wake up."

In the front seat, on the driver's side, was Gary.

"What the fuck, man, why am I in your car?" I reached for the door handle and pulled. It was locked.

"I hauled your ass out of there, and that's the thanks I get?"

"Huh?"

"After I dropped you, I picked you up and carried you out. Oh, and your little boyfriend tried to stop me. I had to pound on him while carrying you."

I dug in my pockets. I needed to get out of there. "Where's my phone?" I needed to call the police, my mom, somebody.

Gary threw my phone back to me. Devin had sent me twenty text messages and called me eight times. I went for the door handle again, stopping short, remembering the door was locked.

"What the fuck, man?" My fingers didn't stop shivering, even as they curled around the door handle and pulled anyway. What did this guy want from me? Maybe he was some kind of human trafficker. "Let me go, please. My mom's a cop."

"I don't care about your mom, Levi. I'm here for you."

I almost pissed myself. What did the creep want? "I don't know you. You're just some fucking weirdo. Let me out," I said.

"Don't you think we look similar?"

"Let me out. I'm calling the police. I'll break your window."

"And I'll break your fucking arms." Gary moved unbelievably fast. He gripped my wrist, and I dropped the phone on the floor. I tried to free myself, but his other hand came out of the shadows holding a gun. At first, I couldn't see it in the darkness, because he had parked where the streetlights couldn't reach us. But I knew it was a gun because I heard the click of the safety coming off, something I'd heard many times with my mother when she would show me her weapon. I couldn't move because the barrel was threatening me. Threatening a bullet if I dared to move.

I glanced outside, wanting to yell for help. We were across the street from my house. How did this guy know where I lived?

"Listen, Gary—"

The gun kissed me on the lips. I still didn't move. "Cut that Gary shit out, kid. My name is Ali. I'm your big brother."

I didn't say anything. I couldn't. I was shitting myself.

"Your dad, *our* dad, is alive. He sent me to get you."

I couldn't think straight. Not with that gun in my face. Gary-Ali lowered the weapon. "Listen. Get out of my car. I'll be in touch. You can't tell anybody about this. Understand?"

I threw open the door and got out, wanting to dash away, to scream for help, but I didn't. I heard the window wind down behind me. "Hey, baby bro. I asked if you understood. You can't tell anybody about this."

I craned my head to look at Ali through the window. He was smiling, and I knew he had his gun ready in case I didn't understand.

"I promise you, if we find out that you're yapping, people close to you are gonna die. And by that, I mean your little boyfriend."

Tires squealing, Ali zoomed off into the night, leaving me brimming with questions, my heart beating to some silent dance with a fast tempo. I murmured to myself, "Devin's not my boyfriend."

Unable to think about anything coherent, I stumbled toward my house, feeling exhausted and drained, like somebody had taken a handful of my life and snatched away many years.

PART ONE

Changing Skin

1

Something inside me is sending adrenaline to every part of my body. Something is telling me to wake up right *now*. Not that I was really sleeping, I can't stop replaying in my throbbing head what had happened to me. I gasp and jump up out of bed. A shadow shifts near my closet and I freeze.

"Who's there?" I call out.

Ali steps out of the obscurity, smiling. I suck in a breath. "I came to talk, baby bro."

"My mom's a cop, she'll shoot you."

Ali laughs, drifting into the moonlight pouring through my window. "Do you want to know about Red Fist or not? Dad or not? Your computer says you're pretty curious."

"What?"

Ali backs into the shadows once again, and then opens my bedroom door. "Tomorrow, I'm taking you to our base." He steps out, disappearing from my view.

I want to stop him from leisurely walking around my house, but when I get into the hall, he's gone.

I hear the floorboards creak, and my mom comes out of her bedroom rubbing her eyes. "Levi? What are you doing up?"

My heart freezes for a second. "Uh, had to use the bathroom."

"You look startled."

I back into my room, "Yeah, Mom, you scared me."

"Okay. Well, I might as well tell you now, I'll be working late the next few weeks so we won't see much of each other."

"Okay, love ya." I close my bedroom door.

This is crazy. This is so fucking crazy. I can't believe that guy was in my house. My mom's a cop. Does Ali want to die? He has to be lying about everything. He can't know about my dad. He's been gone for *eight years*. How can Ali claim to be my brother? There's just no way. My dad wouldn't do anything like that.

I think about all the possible ways that I could have a brother. Maybe my dad had a kid before he met my mom and didn't tell her. I think back to our conversation in the car: Ali had said that "our" dad sent him to get me. He's alive! My dad is alive! I knew it.

Wait.

Red Fist.

Ali had asked me earlier if I wanted to know about Red Fist. No way is this real. I jump into my bed and flip over, burying my head in the pillow. This is a dream. It has to be.

Devin comes over. We sit on the couch watching an episode of *Futurama*. He's snacking on a bag of Doritos, and the constant sound of his hand

20

rustling in the bag is annoying. A commercial break cuts the episode, and his hand stops its assault on the chips.

"Eh, bro?" I look at him, and he continues. "You've been quiet since last night. Did that guy touch you?"

"For fuck sakes, Dev. *No.*"

"I tried to stop him."

"I know." I sit up.

He does, too. "What happened?"

I can tell Devin anything, but I don't know if I should tell him this.

He sees the doubt in my face and says, "We're brothers, right? I'm here for you, no matter what."

Devin is my only friend. It's always been this way. We grew up together. He's a passive guy, built sturdy. He looks like he could be a top athlete. He fits the description. Dreads. Dark skin. Stocky. Good looks. But he's a contradiction. He hates sports. He loves science. His voice is not deep or rugged; it is soft and humble. Anybody would trust him, but now, as we sit together, I don't know if I should tell him what happened.

"Okay." I shift uncomfortably. My mom's not home, so I don't have to worry about her hearing. "That guy said he was my brother and that my dad is alive."

"No fucking way."

I nod. "He's coming to get me today."

Devin drops his bag of chips on the floor. "You can't go with him."

"I have to, man. He has answers, I think."

"Answers to what? What do you wanna know from the guy that beat your ass in front of everybody then kidnapped you?"

I can't breathe. "It's my dad—"

Devin stands. "He would've walked through those doors if he was out there, Levi. Come on, let's just tell your mom what happened so they can find this guy."

21

I shake my head. "I shouldn't even be telling you this. They're probably listening." I feel sick. The living room begins to spin, and I have to get up. I need fresh air.

Devin follows me to the door. "They? They who? Levi, what the hell is going on?"

I'm twisting the knob on the front door when I get pushed back inside because somebody is pushing against the door on the other side.

Ali is smiling. "Us. Red Fist, Devin."

"Devin, you didn't lock the door," I snap.

"I-I-I did. What is this?"

Ali closes the door behind him, goes into the living room, and sits on the couch I was just on like this is his home. Devin stands by the TV, frozen in place.

I stand over Ali. "You can't just show up at my house any time you want. I told you, my mom is a police off—"

He stands, putting his face right in mine. "And I told you, I don't care about your mom. I want to know what your boyfriend was yapping about."

"Nothing."

"Something. You want him dead?"

My heart is beating so fast, it feels like I've run a marathon. "No," I answer.

Ali moves around me and grabs Devin by his shirt, pulling him close. He whispers something in his ear, and Devin nods vigorously, then leaves.

"What was that?" I say.

Ali pokes me in the chest. "You're going to come with me."

2

Ali takes me back to the bustling city of DC, to the Anglia district where the middle class and poor find their homes. He weaves through traffic until suddenly we're parked under a train rail, outside of a shabby apartment building, its brick walls cracked and plagued by green moss. Are my answers here? Will my dad be here? Is this a Red Fist hideout?

Ali tells me to get out. I meet him on the other side of the car. I look up at the gray sky, thinking that this might be the last time I see it if everything Ali has said has been a lie.

He leads me to one side of the building and up some side stairs. We reach the fifth story and enter a side door. I can't believe my eyes.

I watched that Red Fist video a gazillion times that night. When I see this mountain of a man with bronze skin, and tree-trunk-sized arms with tribal tattoos curling down them, I know for sure that it's him, the masked man. Beside him is a lean white woman with reddish-brown hair and pale pink lips. Her face is thin, her cheeks rosy. She's wearing sunglasses and an all-black outfit. It's her. It's the masked woman from the video.

Ali pushes me forward, and the enormous man holds out his hand. I take it, we shake, his grasp python-like. I do the same with the woman. Nobody says anything. The pair leave quickly out of the door, not even telling me their names.

The room is impressive. To my left is a small kitchen that is split off from the main room by a short wall with a countertop attached. To my right is a large living room with a sectional couch. There's a flat screen TV facing me, hanging on the wall, and under it, sitting on a stand, are video-game consoles. There's not much else in the room.

Ali comes out of the kitchen with a glass of water. "You should go sit."

I go to the sectional couch and sit down softly, finding that there's a person napping under some covers. I sip on the water, looking at Ali, who is back in the kitchen. I can't believe it. This can't be real. Red Fist is here, in DC. And I'm with them right now.

"What the fuck?"

I look to my left, where the mysterious person is lying. A dirty-blonde-haired girl with pale white skin and ruby green eyes is squinting at me. "Who are you?" she demands.

"Levi," I tell her.

"I'm Ghost. Thanks for waking me up." She falls back, covering her face with the blankets.

Ali comes over and sits away from her, at the other end of the couch.

The girl says from under the covers. "Ali, he's a pussy."

"I know," Ali says.

Ghost sits up again, snatching the blanket off herself and turns to me, her eyes shining. "Everything he told you is true."

I sit my glass of water on the floor and look at Ali. He stands, digs around in his back pocket and pulls out a picture. He flicks it towards me and sits down. I don't catch it. When I scrape it off the carpet and look at it, my insides become a tsunami.

In the picture is Ali, smiling ear to ear, with an arm curled around him. I follow that arm to a familiar face that calms my heart. It's my dad, with unruly black hair and a beard. He's smiling, and his eyes are glowing with happiness. In the background are pyramids and sand dunes, seemingly attached to a blue sky by the line that slices through the ground and the heavens as the horizon.

I give the picture back to Ali, feeling defeated. I don't want to believe this. I really don't. This must be a joke.

"That was six months ago before we all got tasked here," Ali tells me.

I breathe out. I need to calm down. I need to keep my emotions in check here. "So where is he now?"

"Classified."

"He's *my* dad." The lock I had on my emotions begins to grow rusty.

"Mine, too."

Ghost gets up and leaves the room.

I glare at Ali, and he gets up, stepping toward me. "I know it's hard."

That lock, so weak from bullshit raining down on it, snaps open. "You don't know *shit*. You've been with him this entire time."

Ali smiles at me. A burst of envy shoots through me, and my knee comes up into his stomach. He keels over and gasps, but recovers quickly enough to grab my hair. He falls to the floor, pulling me down with him, a fistful of my hair trapped in his hand. As we crash to the ground, he effortlessly flips me onto my back and mounts me. I can't move under his weight. His teeth are bared, and his eyes are cannons of furiousness.

"You've had it so easy. That photo was the first time I'd ever seen him. *Ever*. I grew up in a war zone. My mom got murdered when I was seven, right in front of me. I'm twenty-two, and I just met him. At least he was in your life. At least you weren't trained to kill your entire life.

You had a normal childhood. I didn't. So don't you ever tell me again that I don't know shit."

Ali gets off me and sits down on the couch. I just stay there, looking up at the white ceiling. I take a deep breath and close my eyes. This is too much. How am I supposed to accept all this information? Dad is alive? And he's working with this terrorist organization? Why? Why didn't he come back? Why did he cheat on mom? Why didn't he ever try to contact us?

I sit up. "Sorry," I mutter.

Ali doesn't acknowledge my apology. Instead, he asks, "What do you think about Red Fist?"

"It's cool."

"*Us*, not it. We're Red Fist through and through. Dad helped make all this possible," he holds out his arms.

"This apartment?" I ask.

"This entire building is ours. Our dad is one of the founders of Red Fist."

I don't know what to say. I don't know how to process this.

Ali asks again, "So, what do you think?"

"You guys are terrorists. I don't know what else to think." It comes out sharper than I intended.

"Revolutionaries. That's the correct term. This is real, Levi, and I promise you that I'm not lying. Alan wanted you in this with us, so I got you. What we do is real. Someday it's going to make everything better."

"You said he wanted me. Why doesn't he want to explain himself?" Heat rises within me.

"What is there to explain, little bro? I've shown you all the proof, and if you don't think that's enough, look outside, watch the news, hell, walk down the street. You can see all the proof you need. The world is going to shit. Dad and the other bigwigs in Red Fist are going to make everything like it's supposed to be."

"How?"

Ali stares at me, pondering for a moment. "We're going to melt the chains society has placed on everyone. We're going to break all these nations that have too much power. We're going to take over."

I laugh. "God, I feel like I'm in a movie."

"Well, you're not. And from this point on, everything gets very real."

"What do you mean?"

"We're gonna train you to be one of us. We're gonna mold you into one of us. Into a true revolutionary."

"I'll be a criminal."

"Don't you want a purpose? I've watched you for the past six months. You hate college. Your life is going nowhere."

I don't say anything. What is there to say? How can I accept this? "I can't—"

Ali walks over and helps me up. "America. Russia. Japan. France. Great Britain. China. Australia. Countries like those, they feed off the poor. They have so much money, but they don't even think to help the homeless. They all mistreat and misinform their citizens. They're leading this world in the wrong direction. All full of injustice and discrimination and mass shootings that go unanswered. All full of secrets and lies." He spreads his arms wide, gleaming at me. "This world was built on strife. We're going to crush them all and take over. We're here to build something new. Something better. That's our job as Red Fist members."

I honestly can't believe I'm hearing this shit. What should I do? What should I believe? Could all this really be true? Is my dad a part of this?

"Listen, I can't explain every detail to you, and I can't tell you that everything will be okay. I can't tell you that what we're doing is one-hundred-percent right, but I believe it's more justified than everything else. Alan wants you, Levi. Don't you want to make him proud? Don't you want the truth?"

3

Beep-beep-beep! I groan and turn off the alarm on my phone. I sit up, feeling like shit. Why am I even up? What am I doing? I lie down again, but my phone vibrates with a message. It's Ali, telling me he'll be here in twenty minutes. I close my eyes and exhale.

I remember agreeing to join Red Fist. What kind of idiot am I? How can I be a terrorist, a revolutionary, whatever? I get out of bed just as my mom slides into my room, flicking on the light.

"You can't just barge in here whenever you like," I say, covering my eyes.

"This is my house. I can go where I please."

I don't say anything.

She watches me as I put on some pants I find lying around. She laughs. "You're eighteen, almost nineteen, and you can't even put on a fresh pair of jeans?"

"I don't feel like it."

"Where are you going this early, anyway?"

Time to come up with a bullshit lie she won't believe. "Yoga. With some new friends from class. They said it's good for the soul."

She raises her eyebrows. "Oh. That's nice." She moves deeper into my room. "You're really going to try lying to a police officer?"

I deliberately go into my dresser drawer to find a fresh shirt so she won't say anything. "Mom, what else would I be doing?"

She walks up to me, pinches my face, and says something in Spanish before leaving the room.

I look at Ali's text again. Am I really going to do this? Go train with a bunch of criminals to take over the world? I smile. This is so insane, but this is also important. It's important because I need more answers from my dad. I need to know more. If Red Fist is trying to make the world a better place, then I should want to help. I should want to be a part of that.

College really isn't working out for me. I hate it. I don't see the point. It's not helping me at all. I still feel lost.

At least Red Fist will give me a purpose. A drive. But do I really care? Do I care about corrupt governments? Do I care about the needy? Do I care about race wars? Do I care about the world? Am I really that selfless? I don't know what I'm seeking in doing this. Validation possibly, or maybe just excitement.

You want to hurt people! You want to let loose!

I stop what I'm doing and look around. The voice sounds like me, so I know it's in my head, but I hear it as if I'm talking to another me, and he's saying these things right in my ear.

"I'm going nuts," I mumble to myself, heading downstairs to wait for Ali.

Ali takes me to the very top floor of the apartment building and leads me inside a pitch-black room. Once the door closes, I am blind.

The temperature in the room is significantly lower than it was in the hall, or any of the other rooms.

"Ali?"

No answer. I feel beside me. He's not there anymore. I can't hear his breathing. I can't even feel his presence. A voice slices through the obscurity. It is not Ali's. It's not even recognizable. It's altered, like the man's in the Red Fist video.

"This is going to be tough. You will hurt. You will bleed. We're going to break you. Mold you. Give you the conviction you need to fight with us. Get ready."

My skin prickles, and my heart starts beating five times faster. The darkness seems to get thicker. I don't hear a sound. I just feel a giant fist in my gut, digging into it, barreling through me. I cave and fall to the ground, clutching my stomach.

Somebody grabs my hair and starts dragging me. I dig my feet into the ground; it's hard, and my sneakers squeal as I try in vain to stop being dragged. The assailant stops, and a massive boot gets thrust into my chest. I grunt as the air flies out of my lungs.

The voice chimes in. "You can't see. Feel, with your being, and fight back. They won't stop until you fight."

Fists and boots rain down on me. I curl into a ball, trying to protect my head. A sharp jab to my back unfurls me, and I sprawl out, frozen in pain. I'm pulled up by the neck, fingers squeezing the air out of me. I scratch at the man's wrists and fingers, trying to pry them from around my throat, but nothing works. I feel my limbs growing weaker. Before I'm completely gone, he drops me to the ground, where I gulp in pockets of air.

"Stand up," the man says.

"Can't…not right now."

I'm pulled upright by the hair again, this time until I'm sitting on my knees.

A female voice hisses in my ear: "We're going to end up killing you if you don't fight. You can't be Alan's son."

I don't even have time to be pissed at what she says. My head gets thrown into the floor. I feel blood gush out my nose. I cough up more blood when I get kicked in the side. I try to crawl away, but someone takes hold of my foot and twists. I cry out, kicking out with my other leg. The pain is excruciating.

"Stop!" I yell.

My leg feels as if it is going to be rotated off. I try to go towards the attacker to get them off me, but that just causes more pain. I cry out again and again until eventually, I'm answered with a jab to the face and another layer of harsh darkness.

Water is dripping down my face. I'm soaked. I open my eyes. My head is throbbing, and I'm aching all over. I try to move and realize I can't. They have me hung on a wall, like a piece of meat. My hands are above me, shackled. My feet are free, and I kick the brick wall in frustration with my better leg. Where am I now?

All my clothes are gone except for my briefs. This isn't training. This is torture. Unlike the other room, this one is brighter. The wall in front of me is brick, and the ceiling is high. Light pours in from the window to my right, and I see the city skyline. We must still be in an upper story.

To my left, a black door opens and in walks Ali. With him are the big guy from the video, the woman with red-brown hair who was with him, Ghost, and another girl with a short, tomboyish haircut and glasses. They all come to stand in front of me. Ali immediately begins dying; he's pointing at me, holding his stomach, his face contorted in laughter.

He teases me with a shitty voice impression of me. "Stop!" he mocks.

He laughs some more and then stops abruptly. His face tenses. The atmosphere in the room changes and fear threatens to strangle me. I look at their faces. They all have the same steely expression. It pisses me off. I shut my eyes, rage boiling in my gut.

"Let me down."

Nobody moves.

"Let me fucking go!" I scream.

Ali finally stops being a statue and rushes forward, thrusting out his leg. His shoe hits me in my abdomen, and I wheeze. My vision grows bleary for a couple of seconds, but I regain focus. Ali is staring at me, his eyes shrouded in darkness.

He punches me in the ribs. I cough.

He hits me again, in the same spot. Again. And again. And again. And again. And again. And again.

I am swinging in and out of consciousness. Through my lapses, I hear one word, clear and crisp in my mind. Bold and full of viciousness: **Fight.**

I claw at the air, trying to swim upwards. I quickly realize that I'm not sinking, that my hands are free, and I'm on the ground. I manage to rise up, not moving my head too fast in fear of passing out again. I'm still in the same room, but this time everybody except for one man is gone. I laugh to myself.

The man towers over me. He's shirtless, and I see all his tribal tattoos wrapped around his body, stretching across his burly chest. I'm mostly naked, too.

"Stand. Grab the bat," he tells me.

I look around for the bat and see it right beside me. It's wooden and beat up. I bring myself to my feet, bat in hand, my legs shaking, practically spaghetti. There's only one guy in the room. He's shirtless. I have a bat. For fuck sakes, I have to fight this humongous motherfucker.

He sees me eyeballing him and reaches out his hand. "I didn't introduce myself last time. I'm Bear."

I shake hands with him; his hand eats mine. I smile. He seems nicer than everybody else. "Levi," I say to him nervously.

He nods at me, and his muscles ripple underneath his skin. I waste no time in aiming for his head, adrenaline coursing through me. He dodges, of course, so I swing again, and he avoids the headshot once more. I try something different and aim for his knee. He sees the attack and brings his leg up, absorbing the blow with his shin. I hear the wood crack, drop the bat, and back away. This guy's body is solid. He kicks the bat so that it rolls to me. A long split runs down the middle of the bat. Another run-in with Bear and the bat will be done.

Bear advances on me slowly. All I can think about is how much I want to run for the door. His presence alone is intimidating enough, but he actually wants to hurt me, too. I back up against the wall, and Bear stops suddenly, his eyes on me, hawk-like, ready.

"Why are you afraid?"

The answer is pretty obvious, but I reply anyway. "Look at you. Look at me."

Bear chuckles a little. "Fight. Use any means necessary. We don't have room for weakness here. We need you to be strong. I'm here to make you strong. The way you are now is no good."

He rushes me like a pro football player, arms outstretched. I have only one option. I throw the bat, and it flies, windmilling through the air, at the giant. He moves out of the way, but in this second, when he takes his eyes off me, his body is at a weird angle. I jump forward and send my right leg straight up into his groin. He grunts and falls to a knee, his eyes squeezed shut.

I feel horrible, but it was the only way I could win. I stand there and watch while Bear gradually but surely gets back onto his feet. His eyes are a dark, rich brown, and they glow with menace, the menace of a beast. I back away.

All Bear says is, "Good one."

I don't say anything. My heart is a ping-pong ball being ricocheted back and forth between players.

"Ali is going to take you home. Go find him. Your training continues tomorrow." Bear's face twists in discomfort as he takes a weird step forward.

Before I leave the room, I make sure to apologize.

Ali is waiting for me just outside the room. He raises his eyebrows and grabs me, not caring that his forcefulness hurts. "You wanna quit?"

I think about it. Do I want to get my face beat on again tomorrow? I ache all over, but something inside me craves this pain. I want this. Before I can finish thinking, I hear my mouth saying, "Hell, no."

Ali grips my shoulder, "Thatta boy. Now let's get you cleaned and fixed up some, so nobody freaks out."

I follow Ali into an elevator, and we go down all the way down to the third floor. He takes me to a room that resembles a doctor's office; it even has one of those comfortable hospital beds. I sit on the edge of the bed in the middle of the room while Ali digs through the cabinets for supplies, and a few seconds later, he's running a warm towel over my face. A few places on my face sting where hard knuckles have broken the skin. He pours peroxide on my cuts and stitches them up.

"We mainly go for the body," he says when I wince. "You're definitely bruised, but man up, little bro."

"Did you go through the same training?" I ask.

He shrugs. "Everybody is different."

"What does that mean?"

"I didn't have to get my shit pushed in like you because I wasn't weak." A grin creeps over his face.

I laugh. "So when do I finally become a full-fledged Red Fist member?"

"Whenever I think you're ready."

"When will that be?"

"Handlers decide when their recruits are ready. I have two tests in mind that I'm going to put you through."

"Cool."

"Oh yeah, before I take you back home, you need to understand something," Ali backs away from me and puts the peroxide away. "No more talking about Red Fist to Devin. Everything we do here must remain a secret."

"Got it."

"You better, because I'm looking for any excuse to kill him."

I gulp, nodding. He's still smiling, but I can feel in my heart that he isn't joking.

4

Alice sprints down the alley, her boots splashing through puddles of piss and rainwater. The man she's chasing is fast, nimble like an acrobat. He cuts a corner, his green hoodie flailing in the wind, sending dimes, quarters and pennies back at Alice. She pursues him around another corner, smiling. It's a dead end.

She pulls out her pistol, aiming at the man who finally turns around, pulling at his ginger afro with his bony fingers. His sunglasses slip from his face, his cold blue eyes ripping into Alice.

"You ain't gonna shoot me, lady."

"You know how this ends, Mason."

"You know that ain't my name, bitch!"

Alice sighs. "Turn around."

She's been trying to find Mason, aka "Robin Hood," for weeks now, and he wants to insult her. Mason's pink, chapped lips slice into a smile. He points.

She shakes her head, shifting her weight. Alice knows Mason well. The guy's a classic jokester, and he'll do anything to get out of trouble. He's just the kind of scum she wants her son to stay away from. "Turn around," she repeats.

"You might wanna do the same thing."

"Alice! Watch out!"

She spins, having only a split second to react. She jumps to the side, dodging a rusty pipe. Renzy, her partner, is chasing a man barely able to fit down the path due to his bulk. She hears movement behind her. *Shit!*

She turns, too late. Mason smashes the bar down onto her left shoulder and kicks her away. She falls into a puddle, kicking up at Mason as he advances on her, trying to bash her again. When Alice reaches for her gun, Mason almost breaks her hand. "Don't move!" he says.

She watches Renzy struggle to apprehend Mason's friend. The bulky man slings her partner into a wall and tries to reach for his baton. Alice can't see Renzy winning this fight. She must act.

She goes for her gun again, but Mason lurches forward, pipe descending down. Alice barrels forward, spearing him, taking thumps to the back. Mason continues to beat at her until she manages to knock him out with a quick jab.

She retrieves her gun and shouts at Renzy's opponent. "Put your hands up!"

Mason's large friend has the slim Renzy up against a wall, choking the life out of him. The man accesses the situation. Alice sucks in a breath. He throws Renzy aside and starts back down the path. Renzy stays down. Alice pulls her trigger twice, dropping the ogre, hoping her aim was true and that she didn't kill the guy.

Renzy is hospitalized; the psycho gutted him three times in the side. Alice has ice on her shoulder. She winces in pain as she continues her report.

"Girl, aren't you something."

It's Strong. The dark-skinned woman with a short cut bumbles up to Alice. "I heard what happened. Why aren't you home resting, honey?"

"You know what everyone will say. I don't have time for it. My injuries are minimum."

"Your father will be okay if you go home."

Alice stops typing. "He won't. Crime's been up. My father will want every officer physically available."

"You really want that promotion, huh?"

"I deserve lieutenant more than anybody except for you. I won't have everyone shaming my name just because I'm the chief's daughter."

Strong pats Alice on her uninjured shoulder, "That's why you're my best friend." She leans in, smelling like coffee. "But the chief told me to tell you to go home and have the report ready by tomorrow at noon."

Alice pushes through her front door. She's home earlier than usual, and it feels odd. Her shoulder is aching. She puts down all her things in the kitchen, not knowing what to do with herself. She heads upstairs to Levi's room, wondering if he's home. She's not seen much of him lately because of her schedule. Every time she arrests someone close to Levi's age in the city, she hopes her own son is not heading down the path as the rest.

She knocks. No answer. She opens the door and steps inside. She walks over to his desk; the familiar faces draw her in, and she picks up the photo. A young Levi, smile as bright as the sun with his father, her ex-husband, Alan. She places the picture down. A part of her wishes that Alan would come back, but she knows that he's dead. He must be. Alice would love to feel the warmth of his arms around her again, the security. She would love to see Levi actually smile. She can't remember the last time she saw her son smile. She knows he isn't fond of Darryl, but she had to move on. She waited for eight years.

Alice spots something in Levi's closet. She takes out his hamper of dirty clothes. Hanging off the side are a few shirts, each covered in blood. Where could all this blood have come from? She begins to search her son's room, her mother's intuition screaming at her. Under his bed, she finds books and magazines on guns and more bloody clothes.

Alice stands in the middle of her son's room after she has searched all over twice. She tells herself that she shouldn't be searching her son's room. She's invading his privacy. Despite that, she cannot ignore the blood on the shirts. Where did it come from?

Alice is worried. What is Levi up to?

5

"The pistol is the most basic and smallest firearm. It's used mostly to engage targets that are twenty-five to fifty meters away, but if you're a great shot, you can go greater distances."

Bear is lecturing me in my ear as I steady my breathing and continuously squeeze the trigger, popping off at the target, my grouping obviously too far apart. Bear tells me how to hold it, to picture any weapon I'm firing as an extension of myself. I level the gun again and focus on the paper target. I take a deep breath, and as I exhale, I tap the trigger five times in succession. From where I'm standing about fifty meters from the paper target, my shots look pretty tight.

"Weapon down. Follow me." Bear moves forward.

I drop the mag and pull the slide back, the round ejecting out of the chamber. I catch it, feeling like a cool guy.

Bear's massive frame is covering the entire target. He spins around, facing me. "Four out of five. Your fifth shot is off a bit, but we can proceed."

Pride courses through me as I see my grouping. I've shot before with my mom, but this is different. The reason why I'm practicing is different.

In the first half of the day, I get introduced to more guns in the Dark Room, the room I got my ass beat in when I first arrived. But the lights are on, so the panic screaming through my veins becomes a whisper. I rip rounds from an AK47, and I almost get my shoulder blown out by the force from the pump-action Remington 870. Bear told me it's the same model a lot of law enforcement agencies use.

By lunchtime I'm euphoric. I never knew guns could be so much fun. I eat a sandwich with my brother, Ali. He's sitting on the sectional couch chomping on fruit snacks and watching a show on Netflix.

"Hey, bro, how many more weeks?" I ask him.

He snickers. "Everybody in this building has killed. You think you're ready for that right now?" I dwell on that for a second, but Ali doesn't give me time to answer. "You're not ready, so stop pestering me. You can barely shoot, and you don't know the ins and outs of being out in the field alone. I'll know when you're ready."

"How, though? You gonna make me kill somebody?"

Ali yawns instead of answering me. That's not the answer I was looking for.

Bear comes into the room and motions for me. I shove the rest of my sandwich down my throat and get up slowly. My joints and limbs are sore from my previous beat-downs and workouts. We reenter the Dark Room. Bear leads me to the middle of the room, then the lights shut off. Anxiety shoots me in the heart with a flaming arrow.

Bear has told me that unless I can feel danger, I can't defeat it. He says he wants me to get to the point where acting on violence is instinctive. He says that once I get to his level, nothing will ever surprise me again.

Bear disappears, vanishing into cold oblivion. It's so quiet I can hear my blood traveling through my body. I focus on every sense. My ears pick up movement to my right, and I face that direction. I move back slightly, and I feel a tickle of air on the tip of my nose. The door slams shut, and I concentrate too much on that sound. A leg sweeps me, and I twist around, catching myself with my hands, pushing myself to one side before someone can stomp me. How many attackers are there?

My back hits the wall. I try to take a quiet breath to calm my nerves again. I have to follow my gut. I stand straight against the wall and close my eyes. Vision is useless here. I need to feel. I need to hear. I need to smell. I need to taste.

I become a statue.

The silence is so loud I want to scream just to hear something. I wait and wait and wait. Time doesn't exist in this room. Why haven't they found me yet? Are they waiting for me to come to them? That would be suicide because my combat level is nothing compared to theirs. I don't move. I won't. If they want me, they're going to have to come and get me. At least that way, I might have time to react.

My ears pick up some sort of mechanical sound like something is sliding open. It sounds as if it's coming from the other side of the room. I concentrate everything on my ears. Elevator doors? I feel the compression of air as something shuts, and then nothing.

Suddenly a flash of rude white light blinds me. I turn away. Obtrusive metal rock music begins to play. Harsh white light is blinking and bursting and flickering all around me. I bend over and clutch my ears, trying to plug them shut, afraid the music will make my eardrums rupture.

I straighten up, and a fist slams into my stomach. I keel over, but before I can fall, someone grabs my hair, slinging me towards the wall. I try to fight back, but one of my arms is twisted behind my back and yanked upwards as my head is forced against the wall. Hands pull me away from the wall and crunch me down into a chair. My hands are tied behind me before I can pull away. I kick up off the ground, and the chair goes sailing backward. As I fall towards the floor, I hope the wooden chair will break, and I can free myself. That hope is swiftly snatched away from me when the chair is stopped from its descent and put back on all four legs.

I'm blinded yet again when a light shines directly into my eyes. My legs are fastened before I can move them again. Now all my limbs are bound.

The light shines over me. Ali, Bear, Ash, and Ghost stand around me. They take off the dark sunglasses they're all wearing and unplug their ears. No fair.

I squint up at Ali, who has an ear-to-ear grin on his face. "You ready?" he asks.

I don't answer.

Bear moves behind me, grabs the chair, and drags me to the wall. He tilts the chair, so I'm leaning at almost a forty-five-degree angle. The rest of the Red Fist members melt into the shadows.

A few minutes pass, my vision adjusts. The others reappear, and someone hands Bear a bucket of what I'm guessing is water. Ash steps up to me and places a thick, already wet, towel over my entire face. My body is trembling in precognition of what's to come. I hear water sloshing onto the floor near me.

Then Ali says, "You better take a deep breath now."

Before I can suck in any air, water is poured down onto my face at a steady rate. Some of it gets into my mouth through the towel and I cough and jerk. The icy touch makes me squirm. The flow stops as I try to cough up the water from my throat.

A waterfall is yet again let down onto my face, and this time it goes on for longer. I close my mouth, but the water scurries up my nose instead. I'm trying to breathe, but I can't because every time I try to suck in some air, all I get is more water and the taste of the towel in my mouth. I shake my head, but that only makes it worse; the water that's lodged in the nooks of my throat yanks on my esophagus and makes me retch. The stomach acid and water doesn't go anywhere because of the towel, and most of it goes right back down into the cup that is my neck. I cough, hacking up my insides.

The towel is removed from my face, and fresh air enters my mouth. I suck it in as fast as I can, spitting and choking and cursing, and blinking frantically.

The torment doesn't stop. Ali's fingers wrap around my throat. "What's your name? Hurry up, *answer!*"

I begin to answer but am interrupted. The towel gets slapped onto my face again, soggy with water and puke.

"Answer," Ali yells again.

Before I can answer, I'm assaulted once again by the cloud that must be hanging over my head. More water shoots down my throat, twisting into both pipes, and my lungs cry out in pain. They thirst for air. I can't breathe. I try to, but I can't. The ruthless water won't let me. Panic rises sharply inside me. I buck in the chair, but I'm held fast by my restraints and the Red Fist members around me.

Fight. Fight. You have to fight!

I squiggle and flounder around, trying to escape. Nothing. My lungs are burning, feeling as though they're on fire in my chest.

"Stuuuopggg iggitt!" I manage to say.

I hear a faint cackle from Ali. He sounds far away, but maybe my hearing is starting to fail me because my body isn't getting the oxygen it needs. I'm drowning.

"He's not moving," someone says.

My lungs are like anchors. Sodden with water. The towel is pulled away from my face, and all I can see is blurry darkness. I can't feel anything. I can't even breathe. My body is too weak to take in air, so

I close my eyes and let the darkness take me away, down under, the mental waterfall pushing me deeper into the depths of my mind, where I see another me. He's trapped in a cage, but he's looking at me coldly, snickering at me as I lie on the dark ground, shivering uncontrollably.

Light descends down, grabbing me, taking me up to where I hear voices. Shouting.

"Fuck…"

"…far!"

"…little bro…"

I sit up, like a shot of adrenaline has been sent into me, coughing irrepressibly, water and vomit exiting my body. Somebody is patting my back as I puke into a bucket that's held out in front of me. My head is thumping. Where am I? I have to focus very hard to make my eyes move up just a little. A familiar brown face is in front of me, smiling. Who is this? A warm hand is still patting my back. Who are these people? Where am I?

"Levi, can you hear me?"

My chin is tilted up. Someone is checking my eyes.

I hear a woman's voice. "Flip him over, back up. He still has water in his lungs, he's not breathing right, and his eyes aren't clear."

I'm flipped over, and I try to struggle against these people that have me. What happened?

"Get…"

"Levi, calm down," I hear someone say.

A fist pummels my back.

"Why…"

Water jets up my throat. I cough, then throw up again and hang my head. My lungs feel a bit clearer. I close my eyes and try to make sense of things.

"Little bro, you all right?"

That question brings every lost puzzle piece back in order. I turn back over and sit up. Ali is standing in front of me, smiling sheepishly. "You piece of shit," I try to yell, but my voice is weak and cracking.

Ali doesn't stop smiling.

I squeak, "I almost died, motherfucker." I hear the dark voice inside of me: **Punch him. Bash his face in. Drown him in the sink.**

Bear steps beside Ali. "Ali understands that was a bit reckless for training," he says, stopping me from what would have been my weak attempt at assault. "Especially since this is all completely new to you."

"I need to go home," I tell them.

Ali reaches out his hand. "Come on—"

I smack his hand out of the way. "Not you."

I leave the room slowly. I feel as though there's a constant draft drilling into me, making me cold. Ghost follows me out and puts a hand on my shoulder. I shake it off, and we continue down the hall.

Ghost drops me home and pats me on the shoulder awkwardly before I can jump out of the vehicle. She smiles. "You did great today."

I don't acknowledge her. I feel her eyes on my back. I hear the car pull away and I shiver, remembering the cold. Remembering the darkness. Remembering that other me. Why was he trapped? Where is he? I make it to my blue front door and smile. This is happiest I have ever been to be back home.

6

It's been two entire days since I last saw Ali and the rest of the Red Fist members. Ali left me a dozen missed calls and ignored texts. Today is Tuesday, and for a moment I tell myself to go to class, almost immediately tossing the idea away. I flop around in my bed and sigh, wanting to scream, not knowing why I'm so frustrated. There's not one particular thing, just a lot of little things that have collaged and become a mass of derailment. Why did I gain all these bruises and scars? Why did I even agree to join Red Fist? They almost killed me.

Mainly, I'm angry with Ali. He's my brother, or so he says, but every time he sees me suffering, he's smiling. My pain gets him off, and that pisses me off. Some big brother he is.

Right now, I just feel cold. As cold as I was when I was waterboarded.

I want to feel warm, but I can't. I am freezing, and I am lost. I am lost because I don't know where I should be or where I should go.

Red Fist isn't for me. I don't even know what they're really about. All that shit about my dad being the leader could be bullshit. It all sounded believable, but I don't feel like I can trust them. I'm not in the right shape to handle that brutal training. This isn't a movie. I'm not going to be some super-cool spy or whatever in a few days. I'm going to lie here, and I'm going to quit.

I give up trying to be somebody I'm not. I *can't* be somebody I'm not because lately, I've been losing myself. I don't even know who I am sometimes. There's always that other guy, in the recesses of my mind, waiting and watching. Who *is* that guy?

I don't know myself. And honestly, it's scary. To be lost in your own body is truly disturbing. I want to cry, but tears evade me. They're locked away with the caged me. Like a hard knot of clay, stuck to the inside of my chest, sadness clings to me, chock-full of emptiness. I can't cry. I feel bitterness and rage, but I can't weep. I can't even move, for that matter. I'm a fly stuck on glue paper, trapped to my bed.

The sun peeks through my blinds, and I blink. I notice that my eyelids weigh far too much. The top ones haven't kissed the bottom ones in ages.

Time sails by and the sun is setting. Slivers of orange light shine through my window as the sun drops lower in the sky. My stomach is growling, my body is hungry, but I don't do anything. I feel this numbness within me. It's like static all over. I think I'm dying.

I hear the door open downstairs, footsteps on the stairs. My door cracks open. Devin walks in, smiling at me. When I don't smile back, his face goes slack.

"Bro, where've you been? I've barely seen you these past two weeks."

"Doesn't matter."

Devin stands over me, looking down at me. I don't look at him. "Levi? What's been going on? You haven't been in class, and some of the professors have been asking about you."

I shrug and flip over, turning my back to him. He grabs my shoulder and forces me to face him. "I've seen you leave early in the mornings. You always come back late at night, looking hurt, exhausted. What's your brother making you do?"

I stand up quicker than I thought I could and push Devin away. Ali's words haunt me. Devin needs to stay out of this. I can't talk to him. "Why don't you mind your own business?"

"What? Best friends can't check on each other?"

This stops me for a long moment. I have no words. I stare at Devin. His expression matches mine; he's somber, and exhaustion clings to his face.

"It's just none of your business, buddy."

Devin reaches out and grabs my shoulder. "Levi, this isn't you. Does your mom know?"

"Dev, leave it, man. Really."

"I won't. Something's wrong with you."

I ball my fists. "Goddamit, Dev. It's none of your fucking business." I grab his shoulders and look into his eyes, making sure he understands. "You need to stay out of this. For me."

Devin promises me he'll stop asking questions.

I call Ali once Devin leaves. "Yeah?" he says.

"I want one of my tests."

"You think you can just ignore us for a few days and then try to demand shit?"

"Ali, I want it. If I can't do it, I'm out."

"I decide when you're ready."

"Ali, if I can't do whatever it is you want me to do, then I'm not doing this…"

Ali is silent, giving none of his thoughts away.

"I need this. I need something, Ali. I need to find out who I am. Please!"

I don't even make it through half a day of my classes. I only came back because I had nothing else to do. Screw college. I've missed so much I don't know what the hell is going on. I'm failing every single course. I go out to the student parking lot and sit in my car. I decide to wait for Devin.

Rap-rap-rap-rap-rap! I awake, accidentally honking the horn. It's Devin.

"Took you long enough," I say as he gets in the car.

"You skipped?"

"Of course." I bring my car seat up and twist the key in the ignition.

"You're going to fail your second semester."

"I don't care anymore, Dev."

Devin looks at me. "What wrong with you, man?"

My phone vibrates. It's a text from Ali. I grow excited and turn to Devin.

"You're coming with me to fight club tonight."

"Uh, sure. I guess. Wait. Remember last time."

"That was brotherly love."

"Are you fighting?"

"I hope so," I say with a grin.

The place is exactly how I remember it: dark, with the one light in the middle. Globs of people are everywhere. Ali, Devin and I make our way to the edge of the circle, pushing and shoving to get to the sidelines where we can see the brutality up close.

Devin looks nervous.

"What's up, bro?" I ask.

He turns to me. "Nothing. I just have a bad feeling, I feel like everybody can see me here."

"Relax, man, everything will be cool."

Brad jumps into the spotlight, the white light making his hair look frosted with gold. "Are you ready, ladies and gentlemen, for tonight's beat-downs?"

Everyone cheers.

The speakers squeal, causing me to wince.

Brad continues. "We have five fights set up tonight. Remember, after that you can call out whoever you want. All right! First up is Hillary Spencer versus Jeanna Grayyyy. Somebody stole a boyfriend."

Everybody begins chanting: "Fight! Fight! Fight! Fight! Fight!"

Two slim, average-height girls come into the light. One has blonde hair and a splash of freckles across her nose, and she's beautiful. The other has brunette hair down to her back and round, hazel eyes. Both girls take the time to tie their hair up in ponytails.

"FIGHT!" Brad yells into the microphone.

The brunette lunges at the blonde, and both fall to the ground, rolling around grabbing hair and trying to dig into each other's faces. The blonde manages to get on top of the brunette and pin down her arms. She smiles down at the girl and immediately starts to whale on her. Her fists rain down on the poor girl until Brad runs in and pulls the blonde off. He starts to raise her bloody hand but stops when the brunette stands, fresh blood trickling out of her nose.

"Come on, bitch," the brunette says. "This isn't over."

The blonde rushes her, and the brunette steps deftly to one side and trips her. Before she can fall, the brunette grabs a handful of the other girl's hair and yanks her back, quickly putting her into a chokehold. It doesn't even take four seconds for the blonde to tap out.

Brad announces the winner. "By tap out, Jeanna Gray wins!"

People start yelling Jeanna's name, and some boo her. Either way, before she leaves the light, she helps Hillary up. They merge into the crowd together.

"Next up…" Brad begins.

Finally, on the fifth fight of the night, I grab Ali, who hasn't said a word to me. He looks at me, confused at first, but then his eyes light up.

"Oh yeah, hold up." He runs off, shoving into the crowd.

Two hairy men are on the floor in the light, grappling each other, each one trying to find ways to outmaneuver the other. Drops of blood are splattered on the floor and even more sweat. I see Ali reappear next to Brad on the other side of the room from Devin and me, and speak into Brad's ear. Ali shoves a thumb my way.

Brad notices me for the first time tonight. He gives me a wicked smile and nods at me and then at Ali. I'm so ready to pound Brad's face in. I told Ali that's who I wanted to fight. I don't take my eyes off him. I remember all the times he fucked with me. All the times he fucked with Devin. All the times he threatened me and pushed me in the hall. I see his face in my mind, and I let the years of hate balloon inside me until I take a mental thumbtack to that balloon.

I focus everything evil and vicious inside me on Brad. He's going to be so surprised when I break his arm. I'm not saying that two weeks has been enough to make me unbeatable, but it is enough for me to hurt Brad. I want to watch him squirm in pain.

I watch Brad walk into the light. He's staring right at me, smiling. What a cocky smirk he has. He doesn't even know he's about to get his face beat in. He puts his lips near the mic, and I almost jump on him right then and there, the anticipation almost too much for me to contain.

"We have a returning fighter: Levi Conoway versus his best friend, Devin Jonesssssss!"

People shout and rage. I don't move. Ali reappears beside me and nudges me forward, but I'm a rock. I stare at him pitifully. "I'm not."

He gets close. "I thought you were ready."

"He's my best friend!"

"Tonight, he's your punching bag. You wanted this. I'm giving you the opportunity."

Everybody is bloodthirsty.

Brad is looking right at me. "Don't keep these people waiting," he says.

I look at Devin, whose eyes are full of something I can't discern. "Dev…" He doesn't look at me.

Ali gets in my ear. "Get out there. This is your first test. Do you want this or not? Do you wanna see Dad or not? It's up to you."

I don't want to hurt Devin. I don't even make the decision to; I just move. It's not me in control here. It feels like I'm watching myself from the back of my mind. I see my legs walking into the light, and then I see the people on the sidelines, forcing Devin into the arena.

Brad is looking back and forth between the two of us. "Better make this worth everybody's time."

Devin has a lost look on his face. I don't even think he knows where he's at. Brad is spewing bullshit into the mic, pumping up the audience. Devin finally looks up at me, and all I can think of is that he reminds me of a cornered lion.

I nod at him.

Devin balls his fists. I can tell that he's blaming me already.

Brad hollers, *Fight!"*

We don't. Empty beer cans are being tossed at us when Devin steps towards me and decks me. I fall to the ground, he jumps on me, both hands wrapped around my neck, yelling, "You knew about this."

I'm starting to run out of air. I don't blame Devin for being pissed. He didn't know this was going to happen. But neither did I. Devin punches me in the face, but somehow I don't feel a thing. The rational part of myself is retreating with every punch. I block out everything. I hear Ali's words.

Then that other guy inside of me tears free, bending the bars to his cage: **Crush him. Crush him.**

I see my father's face in the liquid darkness. I need to do this. I jab Devin in the throat, his hands weaken around my neck. I thrust my hips upwards and throw him off me. When I stand up, he's on his hands and knees, gasping for air.

I don't know what's going on. It's like I'm not me right now. I take a cluster of Devin's dreads in one hand and make him face me. With the other hand, I raise it high, my fingers curling into a fist. I hit him. Everybody goes insane as the hammer that is my hand continues to ruin Devin's face. I don't even know how many times I hit him. I just know that when I let him go, he drops to the ground with blood all over him. He's looking up at me, his eyes cloudy.

Guilt hits me like a wave. I sink to my knees and cradle his head, repeatedly saying, "I didn't know, I didn't know, I didn't know. I'm sorry, I'm so sorry, Dev, I'm sorry."

There's a commotion around us. I look up, and everybody is swarming, trying to get to the door, screaming and pushing and shoving. I hear one word, and my heart drops. *Police.*

Ali runs up and grabs me. "You pass. We gotta go."

I rip my arm away from him. "Not without Dev."

He spits. "Fucking—all right, whatever, you're carrying him. I know a different way out. Follow me."

7

We sneak pass two officers who have taken down a fleeing man. Ali leads us through the shipping area, and we make our escape with no problem. I lay Devin in the back seat, my legs and arms tired from carrying him.

It takes me some time to realize that Ali is not heading for any hospital. "What are you doing? He needs a hospital," I say.

Ali doesn't look at me. "I've already contacted the doc. We're going back to base. She'll make sure he's all right."

"His face isn't gonna heal by tomorrow."

"You did a wonderful job." Ali compliments me on my handiwork.

He makes it sound like beating your best friend to the ground is an achievement. I don't know what happened to me in there. I couldn't control myself. I shut my eyes and think of the voice inside my head whispering to me, saying awful things.

This is Ali's fault. He set up the fight. "You did this. You made this happen. This is your fault."

"You passed. Why are you so angry?"

"Look at Devin. He'll never forgive me."

Ali laughs. "It won't matter. He's going to forget the past twenty-four hours."

Oh no. I can't let this happen to Devin. Ali showed me a video of our government using a drug on prison inmates to make them forget for a set period of time, depending on the dosage. The video showed the drug being administered one day, and the results the next day. The men couldn't remember their own names.

The drug had failed. It was meant to calm people who had been through traumatic experiences, but the side effects were too detrimental. The FDA has not sanctioned its use. And yet, when the CIA doesn't want someone to talk, and they're not worth killing, they use that drug.

"So Devin could end up in a mental hospital. That's not happening."

"You don't get to decide." Ali faces me. "You made your decision. Your boyfriend will be fine."

There's no way out. I can't escape this. I have to accept it. I can't save Devin. I have no words. I sit back and think about Devin. I picture him in a mental hospital, not being able to remember anything, not knowing his mother or father's names. Not being able to recognize me.

I clutch my stomach. I feel sick. I open the window and let the brisk night air smack me in the face, wondering how much I'm willing to lose to continue with Red Fist.

The next morning is Saturday, and I don't wake up until around nine-thirty. I have two missed calls from my mom and three text messages. One text message is from Ali, telling me to get an update on Devin ASAP. The second is from Devin, asking me what happened last night and why he woke up in his car. He said his parents are taking him to the hospital because he's been nauseous and damn near throwing up his life. Fuck.

The third text is from my mom, telling me to call her back immediately. I start to spaz out. I text Ali: Parents taking him to hospital.

He responds with angry emojis, telling me they would get all the information they needed on their side. I call my mom, my stomach lurching around before she even picks up.

"About time, son," she says.

"Yeah, Mom, what's up?"

"Devin's parents called me this morning to say they're taking him to the hospital. Do you know what happened last night? What were you guys doing?"

"We went to the McDonalds in the city," I lie.

"You guys came back really late. Devin's parents said they didn't get a text from him, letting them know where he was. They said they found him passed out this morning in his car, unable to remember anything. He had a cut on his face and a busted lip."

"Okay," I say, not knowing how to respond.

"Were you guys at the fight club we busted last night? Were you doing drugs, Levi?"

I vacuum in a hard breath and cough. "Fight club? What? Drugs?" I try to sound completely clueless.

"Levi, I found those bloody shirts in your room. There are ten people down here, and I'm sure one of them will tell me if they saw you. Please don't lie to me."

She knows. I don't know what to say. "I need to get to the hospital to see Devin."

"Levi—"

I hang up.

This is becoming a shit storm. The police showing up really blindsided everyone. Devin is in the hospital. They're going to find something of that drug in his system. Fuck. There are so many things that can really cut me deep here. If I get blown, there's a chance Red Fist will get blown, too. To top off this delightful ice-cream sundae, there are ten snitches down at the station. If any one of them mentions my name, I'm royally fucked. Of course, I can deny it all to hell, but my mom would never believe me.

I call Ali and spend five minutes on the phone with him. I tell him everything that my mom told me. He's coming to get me.

I run downstairs and eat some cereal; the silence in the house is too much to bear. Damn, how did the police get wind of the fight club? I look over at Devin's house. If his memory loss persists, it will all be my fault because I'm the one that involved him. What a piece-of-shit friend I am.

Ali pulls up, and I rush out to the car. He pulls away as soon as I get in. He doesn't speak to me; he just drives. In the time it takes us to get to the base, I grow more and more nervous.

I walk into the room with the sectional couch. I feel a bunch of eyes on me. It seems to me like somehow this is all my doing. In the room are Ghost, Bear, and the lady with the fall-colored hair who is almost always with Bear. There are three others. One of them looks familiar, but the other two I've not seen before.

Ali speaks up. "Everybody, this is Levi. I know not all of you have gotten the chance to meet him yet, but we don't have time for formalities at the moment. There's is a strong possibility that our entire op could be blown."

I lean against the wall as listen as Ali goes into further detail, telling the story about the fight club, how the police showed up, and everything up until now.

"I know some of you have already been working hard on this development, but I wanted everybody to have a say in this matter. What do we do now?"

A formidable-looking dark-skinned man speaks. His name is Solomon but insists on being called Sugar. His African accent is heavy, his voice powerful. He is bald, and his eyes are smoke colored. He rolls a piece of candy around in his mouth and crunches loudly. "From what I've heard, it seems that the biggest problem right now is the detainees down at the station."

Bear's partner, the lady with hair that reminds me of autumn, agrees. Her name is Ash.

"If they mention they saw Levi fighting, it could lead to them investigating you, Ali."

"What about his friend's parents, and what about the whole drug situation?" Ghost says.

"All right, all right," Bear says, holding up his hands, silencing everyone. "Myla, are there any new developments on Devin?"

The girl that I thought looked familiar is already on her tablet, her fingers skiing over the screen. She was there when Red Fist had me hung on the wall. She's a small Hispanic girl, thin…**breakable**. No! What? *Not* breakable. Her hair is cut short, and it's spiky, dark. She glances up at me briefly, giving me a tight smile. In moments she has the information on Devin.

"He's been released. I'm going to check their phones, but it seems like they're heading towards Levi's mother's police station."

Fuck. I bang the back of my head against the wall. They're going to demand information from my mom. My mom is going to want information from me. "Can the hospital get an idea of what you've had to eat in the last twenty-four hours?" I ask everyone, something nauseating dawning on me.

Before anybody can say anything else, my phone rings. It's my mom. Ali tells me to answer it. I put my cell on speakerphone. "Hello?"

"I'm sending a squad car to come pick you up."

"I'm not home, Mom. I'm out with some friends."

"Just be home in twenty minutes, Levi or things are going to get more complicated than they need to be. You're not in trouble. I just need you to clarify some things for me."

"I can do that over the phone."

"Obviously not," she says with indignation, "since you lied to me about being at McDonald's. Levi, I want you at this station in the next hour. Be home in twenty minutes."

"Mom, I can't." I hang up and turn off my phone, looking around.

Bear steps up to me and rests a hand on my shoulder. "You need to make a choice, right now."

I stare up at him, then around at everyone else. They all are giving me this look that worries me.

"What do you mean?" I ask.

Bear holds out his hand, eyeing my phone. I place it in his palm, and he tosses it back to Myla, who immediately begins dismantling it.

Bear takes a step back, near everyone else. "We abandoned everything we used to love for this. We became a family. Will you do the same, Levi?"

8

Darryl is standing over the kitchen table digging into a sandwich. I lean against the wall in the entryway. "Of course a bum like you would be freeloading food out of somebody else's fridge," I say.

Darryl swings his head around and sees me. The waste of space scowls at me. "Your mom wants you down at the station. The police have already been by looking for ya, kid. Always knew you were worthless."

I laugh dryly. "You're one to talk."

Darryl steps towards me, a vein bulging in his red neck. "Alice ain't here to stop me from knocking some respect into ya."

He's in my face, and for a moment I reconsider everything. I wonder if I should go through with all this. I hate Darryl, but maybe this is going too far. Darryl moves past me, smiling as he shoulder-bumps me. He heads into the living room.

I need to do this. I told Ali I'd handle it. Everything is for the greater good. This is my second test. I'll abandon everything, right here.

I follow Darryl into the living room. He's bending down to pick up his phone. "Yo, asshole," I say.

He looks back at me.

"Put down the phone."

"Or what?" he says, turning to me but ignoring my instruction.

I headbutt him, and he falls on the couch. I throw the gun in front of him. "Let's play a game."

Darryl holds his bloody nose as he stands, eyeballing me, then the gun. "You fuckin' psycho. I'll beat the livin' shit out of ya."

He rushes me and tackles me to the ground, the blood from his nose dripping onto my face. He's over me, a dark rage embedded into his ugly, unkempt face. He punches me, and blood sails from my mouth. I smile up at him; inside me, I can feel evilness enveloping my heart.

"That all you got in you, fucking pussy." I spit up into his face, and he veers back, wiping my crimson saliva off him and bombarding me with three punches, then standing.

He stomps on me. "Kid, I will kill ya. I'll tell Alice you attacked me. You got some balls thinkin' you can beat me. Bringin' that peashooter in here." He picks up the pistol that's lying behind him and waves it at me. "What was you gonna do, huh?"

He kicks me again. This is fun, this pain. I can't control myself. I sweep Darryl's legs, and he crashes to the ground. I jump up and pin down the hand that's holding the gun.

I send my other foot towards his face, but he manages to block my assault with his free arm. I put more pressure on his hand until he lets go of the gun. We both eyeball the gun and move at the same time. We roll on the ground, wrestling for the weapon. His bony elbow flies into my jawbone and freezes me just long enough for him to kick me away and get the gun. He stands, aiming at me.

I pick myself up off the ground, swooshing around the blood in my mouth. I let it waterfall out, and as I do, I let the other me come out for some fresh air. It's not me talking. I hear the words he's saying to Darryl though, the encouragement. "Go on. Do it. Shoot me. I want you to."

"Crazy kid. You're crazy. Get out of here, go on." Darryl sounds shaken. I realize he's afraid.

I step forward. I feel unstoppable. The dark part of me is hungry, starving for blood, for Darryl's blood. I'm going to feed this other me. I'm going to let him pig out. I'm enjoying every single second of this.

Darryl's hand is trembling. "Stay away from me, son."

I don't know if I can smile any harder. I grab the gun from Darryl's hand and backhand him upside the head with it. He crumbles to the floor. I think of the way he's always acted and dressed, like some country white boy who was born and raised on beef and gunpowder. What a fucking joke. He's a phony. A fake.

"Listen now, boy put it down. We can work things out."

I can hear him trying to make amends, but the other me doesn't care. He wants blood. I can see Darryl's tears glide down his face. I can see him shiver. He knows death is knocking at his door. I can't do this. I can't take his life. He's not worth it. I begin to back away when that voice, that *me* who has been there by my side, sounds off in my head: **I got this. Take a break.**

I freeze. What will my mom think? I hate Darryl, but I don't want to hurt my mom. I raise the gun anyway...

And I squeeze the trigger.

9

Alice is barely breathing as she steps through the doors to the police station. She couldn't believe what Strong had called and told her. She was one of the officers investigating the scene at the fight club, and upon hearing what had happened, she took off, tears fleeing from her eyes. Everybody is looking at her as she zooms through the station towards the interrogation chambers. Her son is sitting there in handcuffs, watching the door, waiting for somebody to come in. It's a one-way mirror, so he can't see her through it, but she can see him.

She puts her hand over her mouth, afraid she's going to scream. Tears roll down her cheeks, and an arm slides around her body, pulling her in. She closes her eyes and leans into the embrace, the build and smell of her comforter all too familiar. It's the chief, her father.

"Everything's gonna be okay, baby. We haven't heard from him yet. We don't know the entire story."

Alice sniffles and pulls away, looking at her son. He doesn't look shocked. He seems bored and indifferent. She grows concerned. He just shot a man, killed a man, he should be showing…something. She turns to her father, "Can we go in?"

He shakes his head. "We have to wait for a third party not related by blood. Jefferson's coming."

Jefferson arrives moments later and pats Alice on the shoulder. He looks at them both and smiles. "Ready?" he says softly.

The chief nods and reaches for the door, holding it open so everyone can enter. Jefferson pulls out a chair across from Levi for Alice. He sits next to her, while the chief takes a seat at the end of the table.

Jefferson breathes out, nodding. He's a lanky white man with slicked-down, dirty-blond hair. His face is round and almost babyish, but at the same time rugged, with a hint of stubble on his chin and neck. He looks at Levi. "All right, man, everything okay?"

Levi nods.

"Okay," says Jefferson. "I want you to start from the top. I want you to understand that everything you say is being recorded, and can and will be used against you. Can you tell us what happened between you and Darryl?"

Levi cuts a glance at his mother before he speaks. "I went home to get some food, and Darryl was in there pigging out in our fridge. He started complaining about me being there, so I told him to fuck off, and he got in my face. I told him to back off again, and he didn't, so I pushed him."

"So, you touched him first?"

Levi doesn't confirm or deny the question; he just makes eye contact with his mother.

"All right, please continue."

"After that, he pushed me back and said he'd beat my ass. So I told him to try it and walked out of the kitchen into the living room to get away from him. I don't know, I think he was drunk or something. He followed me and grabbed me by the back of my shirt, and that's when we got into a wrestling match on the floor. I saw his gun—"

The chief cuts him off. "You know I hate liars, right?"

Levi doesn't acknowledge, but the two lock eyes.

"Answer me, boy."

"Yeah."

"So, before we ask any more questions, I want you to tell me right now. Did Darryl really have a gun, or did you bring it with intent?"

"Why would I have a gun?"

Alice is confused. She looks at Jefferson, who is gazing around the room in his own world and not really paying attention. She rolls her eyes at him. How could he act so carefree?

The chief clears his throat. "All right, everyone. We have the ringleader of that big fight club bust we did recently. He seems to know Levi very well."

Levi shifts uncomfortably in his chair. Alice shares a brief glance with him, and she sees the flash of shame in his eyes. She has a brick in her chest. When her father gets up and stands over Levi, Alice knows she needs to leave. She knows her father's temper all too well. The chief is a stocky man and has his hair gelled to keep it professional. He may look out of shape to some, but they've never seen the man move on a foot chase. His mustache bristles along with his anger, his brown eyes ablaze.

"Brad says you were in a couple of fights at this fight club," the chief says. "He said you beat up your best friend, and before that some guy nobody knew gave you a good beating. Is this true?"

Levi nods, and the chief slams his fist down on the table. "Speak!"

"Yes," Levi says, annoyance laced in his voice.

"Who is this mysterious guy that beat you up?"

"I thought we were talking about my case."

"It's *all* your case, son. You have been actin' shady. Alice told me about the bloody shirts, boy. You can't lie to us."

Alice sees the disbelief on her son's face. "This is bullshit—"

The chief pulls Levi close to his face by the scruff of his shirt. "You know what's bullshit? You. You're a disgrace. How dare you sit here and lie. Shame me, your mother—"

Alice interjects. "Levi, we want to help you. Please tell us what's going on and what you know."

"I'm in a gang."

Alice can't believe her ears. In her own mind, going back, she was negligent. She saw all the signs that her son was acting differently or in something dangerous, and she just let him be. Let him lie to her when she knew something was wrong. She can't believe it. She's done so much for him, tried to give him a good and honest life.

Alice doesn't want to hear any more. She gets up and steps out of the room, once again with her hand over her mouth, afraid she might scream.

10

I'm faced with my grandfather's steely gaze. He rubs his temples with his fingers and sighs. He sits down where my mother was. "Why?"

I play it exactly how Ali said I should. "They forced me to. They forced me to do a lot of things, Grandpa."

"It's sir, here. So, they gave you the gun?"

"No. I told you that was Darryl's."

My grandfather shoots upright. He's frozen. He looks like he wants to burst, but before he can say anything, he breathes out loudly. I want to laugh; I can almost see the steam coming from his body.

He touches Jefferson's shoulder. "All right, I'm done here. Find out who this gang is and who their top members are. I want names and a location. Question him some more. I'm losing my mind dealing with him. When you're finished, let me know immediately."

"Roger, Chief."

After my grandpa leaves, I'm left with the one called Jefferson. His arms are long, but kind of skinny compared to the rest of his body, so his hands appear large as he cracks his fingers. He smiles across at me, his silver eyes gleaming with mischief, and then goes over to the wall and flicks a switch. He comes back and undoes the cuffs. "I know those cuffs hurt."

"Not really." He takes the cuffs off completely.

"You can cut the tough guy act. I know who you are." He sits back down across from me.

I smile. "You're it?"

He reaches below the table out of my line of sight. When his hand comes back into view, he's holding his gun. "You sure you can do it?"

I reach out my hand, and he slides the gun across to me. Grinning, he leans back and puts his hands behind his head. "I'm really looking forward to seeing what you're capable of."

It's time for my final test.

***

Alice is twiddling with her fingers, looking down at her hands. She's lost a boyfriend, and her son is a mystery. She wants to believe Levi, but something in her gut is telling her that he's way off. He's different somehow, and she can't really put her finger on what it is.

She sees her father walk into his office, close the blinds, and slam the door. He's pissed. He's a man that holds his reputation to a high standard, and she knows that to have his own grandson in trouble for something like this must be weighing on him.

On top of that, the fight club bust had the police department working extra shifts, to patrol and to keep people off the streets past a particular time of night in that area. Alice knows that mayor came down earlier to meet with the chief, but she doesn't know what for. Maybe the mayor thinks her father is losing control and that his own family might be the cause.

Alice doesn't notice the smoke because she's so deep in thought. She doesn't even smell it. Nothing registers until someone shouts, and she glances up. A gunman is waving an assault rifle in the air, and he starts shooting at the ceiling. She jumps behind her desk for cover and takes out her pistol.

Nobody has to give the order: bullets start flying over her head, and Alice stays down, behind her desk, trying to work herself up to defend the station and her fellow comrades, but all she can think about is running for Levi.

***

Jefferson jumps up. "And the party has started." He opens the door. "Get into the chief's office."

I move through the door and out into the hall, which is filled with smoke. Jefferson grabs my shoulder, directing me forward. "Turn right, take fifteen steps, then left, head up that flight of stairs and the chief's office will be right there."

He forces me to the right, and then his hand is gone. I turn back and see only thick gray smoke. I cover my mouth and move forward, squinting my eyes when they start to water. The smoke is a monster to deal with, and I can't tell where I'm going. I just count my steps and feel in front of me for stairs.

I can hear screaming and gunfire, and my gut twists when I picture my mom on the floor, maybe bleeding out. I almost stop and turn around, wanting to find her, to make sure she's safe. But Ali reassured me my mom would not be targeted. I have to continue. After this, I'll be with Red Fist officially, and I'll get my mark.

I walk carefully up the steps, the alarm in sync with my thundering heart. I grab a doorknob and rush through with my eyes closed. I'm instantly thrown backward; a hand is around my neck.

"Grandpa, it's me. It's *me*."

The vise grip around my neck relaxes, and he steps back. "Get behind my desk. I've called for reinforcements."

"Grandpa, who are these people?"

He joins me behind his desk. "I don't know. Terrorists."

"Jefferson told me to come here. That I'd be safest with you."

"He shouldn't have done that. He should have guarded you until this is over. You could've been shot." He reaches for me and begins to run his hands over my body. "Are you okay? Have you been hit? Let me check you."

I scoot away from him, not wanting him to discover the gun on me. "I'm fine."

He looks at me a moment longer, then stands. "I'm going out there. You stay put. Don't you leave this room until I come back." He turns his back to me.

Let me do it. I won't miss. Promise.

I shake my head, slowly reaching for the gun in my waistband. A million thoughts are racing through my head. I watch Grandpa reaching for the door. What if I miss? I aim the gun at his back. My hands won't stop trembling. He's opening the door. I only have a few seconds left before he's out, but those seconds are agonizing.

Shoot! Shoot! Shoot!

He hesitates for a moment and turns around abruptly. His face is instantly stricken with horror. He is swift, swifter than a man his age should be. His gun is up and aimed at me now.

I slam my eyes shut and open them, cursing myself. It's a standoff. "Levi?"

I can't do this. I can't do this. This is blood.

My grandfather drops his gun to his side and looks at me with saddened eyes. "What is this?"

"Grandpa, I'm sorry."

"What are you caught up in?"

"I have to."

He turns his back to me, his shoulders tensing up. "They want you to shoot me?"

"Yes. In the shoulder."

"After this, you run. But let me tell you this, the next time we cross paths I will not hesitate. If you do this, there's no turning back."

"What if I kill you then?" That dark part of me creeps out again, taking over. I try to push it down, but it stays level with the me who knows that what's going on right now is very wrong.

"Son, I don't think you can kill me. After this, you no longer have a place in my heart."

Those words strike me through the chest like a frozen sword, and I can't breathe. My world will never be the same. My grandpa has always been there my entire life. He's taught me so much. I can't do this.

Then Ali's words cut through my self-doubt. I've come too far to back down now. I have too much to lose and too much to see through just to give it all up. I will do this.

I steady my aim and take a deep breath. I block out everything; the noise of the gunfire and the yelling are now nothing to me. All my doubts and fears vanish, and my mind settles on the task at hand. I focus on my grandfather's right shoulder. **We got this, Beta.**

The other me stops me from shuddering.

"Sorry, Grandpa," I say, and pull the trigger.

There's no going back now. I've officially broken everything that's ever loved me.

The pistol fires, he falls to his knees, and I step past him. I reach for the door handle and begin to open it, but he grunts and yells my name through his pain. I cower, not wanting to look at him, but the other me inside powers through, not afraid to see the damage he's done. My grandpa is breathing as if he has weights trying to drag his lungs down, but he makes sure to reach into me, his eyes lava pits blistering with hellfire.

"If you ever even think about hurting my Alice," he says, with so much malice and steel that the world seems to shake, "I will hunt you down and skin you from the inside out, boy. You better run far and run fast with your friends. If I find you first, I won't be so nice next time."

I take in his words, harbor them as I duck out the door, disappearing into the dark smoke, the dying sounds of gunfire and the wailing alarm, my heart so broken that when it thumps in my chest, I can hear glass shattering.

11

My grandfather's last words to me slice through my brain in the darkness of the room. They filet me over and over and over again with no respite. The space around me is a shade of swirling black, and nothing comes into focus. There is one window beside me, the sill a few inches above the bed mattress. The blinds are halfway up, and I can see that it's raining outside. I had been staring at the ceiling for the past two hours, unable to sleep, but now I focus on the droplets of clear water traveling down the window, each drop making an audible thumping sound as it makes contact with the glass.

I battle with my grandfather's words in my mind, trying to convince myself that I am the good guy. I tell myself that what Red Fist is doing will help the world in the long run. I wish more people could see this. The world is covered with layers of secrets, and governments don't want their general populations knowing the truth. Every government wants control and their piece of the pie.

My grandpa's face blows up inside my head. His eyes pierce me. True and utter disappointment. I see it all in the replay of his face in my head. And now he hates me. He has every right, and I will take his hate on my shoulders until I can convince him that I'm doing the right thing. He thinks I'll try to hurt my own mother. I don't think I have that in me. I don't *want* to have that in me. If I ever come to that point in my life, I will shoot myself in the head.

I get up and check my phone, a new one that Red Fist supplied with me after we got back from the mission. It's eleven-thirty. I can't sleep.

I open the door and go out into the living room of Ali's apartment. He's snoring on the couch, an Xbox controller dangling from his hands, the flat TV screen idling through events, games, and friends online. The kitchen is bare. Actually, the entire apartment is pretty barren except for the couches and a couple of stools in the kitchen area. Ali said we must keep things like this in case we get burned and have to leave in a hurry. He also let me in on an important detail: if we ever do get found out and have to leave, precisely two minutes after we leave someone will put in the code for the sleeping bomb in this building to go off. Pretty cool, in my opinion.

I get onto Grand Theft Auto 5, an old game now. I go on a killing spree. Ali's character is overpowered and seems to be impervious to all the bullets flying his way.

On the couch, Ali lashes out, his foot jamming into my side. I glare at him, but he's still sound asleep. I get up to pour some cereal into a bowl, thinking about my mom. No doubt she's heard about what happened with Grandpa and me. I wonder what she's feeling. I've never really thought about making her proud, and right now I know she is the exact opposite of that. One day, though, she will understand. I'll make her proud of me.

I want to contact her right now and say sorry and tell her that I love her, but I know that's the wrong thing to do. Ali would beat my ass for being an idiot.

After finishing my cereal, tiredness does hit me. I head back to my room, checking my phone. It's now one in the morning. I lie down and somehow manage to fall into a restless sleep.

A pillow smacks me in the back of the head. After the second hit, I hear the third coming down and move.

"Get up, sleepyhead, it's time for your ceremony."

Ali continues hitting me with the pillow until I roll out of bed.

"You look like shit," he says, "get excited." He swings the pillow at me again, but this time I block it. I reach back with my other hand to grab mine, but he knocks me off balance. I shove back, and we get into an escalating pillow fight. I finally manage to push him out of my room and slam the door shut.

He bangs on it. "Hurry up!"

I slide down the door and sit on the floor, smiling. It does feel nice to have a big brother. A memory of Devin and me having a rambunctious pillow fight in my old room comes to me. Damn, I sure do miss my best friend. I can't talk to him at all. The last time I saw him was when I left him knocked out in his car after we drugged him. I regret letting that happen to him. Did his memory return?

Ali punches my door again.

I'm amped for my ceremony. I'll receive a code name. Getting a code name means I'm officially recognized as a member of Red Fist. Ali told me that sometimes names are given through personal events that people remember, or by ability, and sometimes agents even get to choose their own names. He also said that not everyone has a code name and a lot of agents decide not to have one.

We leave our apartment on the fifth floor and go down to the third, heading for the main meeting room with the sectional couch. Bear is standing in the kitchen. Ghost is on the couch playing on her phone, and Myla is sitting near her on a laptop. Walking in right behind us is Sugar and a brown-skinned woman with dreads. I never caught her name last time. Ash comes through the side door, from outside, followed by Jefferson, who winks at me.

Ali claps. "All right, looks like everyone is here." He turns to me quickly, leaning in. "This is everyone plus the doc"—he looks around—"who's not here."

Bear is chopping something up in the kitchen, and the sound of the knife hitting the counter rapidly seems to annoy Ali. "Bear, we're about to start."

Bear turns around, smiles bashfully and nods at me.

Ali continues. "I know we've all been swamped, but today is a good day. We get to welcome a new member into our family. Levi is my little brother, and at first, I thought he wasn't going to make it, but he managed to grow a pair. He's changed so much since I first met him." Ali pauses to look around. All eyes are on him. "So today I just want to give him the honor of receiving a code name. Any suggestions?"

Ghost raises her hand from the couch first. I know she's going to say something stupid. I now know that she loves to joke around. "We can call him Crybaby."

Ali and Ghost die with laughter, but no one else finds the joke funny. Ali stops when he realizes only the two of them are laughing. He shrugs and looks around, waiting for somebody to make another suggestion. Everyone looks perplexed, lost in thought.

After a couple of minutes of silence, Bear speaks up. "How about Toko?"

"What does that mean?" Ali asks.

"It means sibling or brother in Tongan, my native language. Levi is our newest member, and he's family now, our little brother."

Smiling, Ali looks at me and raises his eyebrows.

I nod, unsure. It's not like I really have a choice.

Ali claps. "All right, everyone, I like Bear's idea, but I don't think it really fits." He nudges me. "Any suggestions for your code name?"

I get a choice? I've been thinking about a cool name for the longest time. I know Sugar has his name because he always has candy in his mouth. Bear has his name because he's ginormous and ferocious. I don't know why Ghost has her name or Ash. I rub my arm and look around at everyone; their eyes are on me, waiting. Something odd clicks together in my head, but it seems so cheesy.

"Well, Ali, you said I've changed a lot," I say, feeling stupid, "so…"

"Spit it out, man." Ali crosses his arms.

"Chameleons. They change. They adapt. I've done that, and I'm still changing."

Everyone is stuck behind a door of silence; I'm waiting for them to laugh. I watch Ali out of the corner of my eye and to my surprise he nods, then snaps his heels together and pounds his chest with his fist. His body is steel. He's saluting me, honoring me. This is the Red Fist way.

"Let's welcome the Chameleon," he says proudly.

Every single Red Fist member snaps to salute me.

Then Ali tells me to hold out my right hand. I'm about to receive my mark. His fingers curl around my wrist. "Don't cry now."

I level my eyes with his. He smiles. Everyone has made a circle around us. His grip tightens around my wrist.

"Do you promise to use your body, your mind, and your soul for all those who cannot fight for themselves?" Ali says.

"I do."

He produces a knife and sends its sharp end into the palm of my hand, making a straight line down. I do not flinch.

"Do you promise to spread the truth, and break everything unjust and impure?"

"I do."

The second cut stings more. There's now a bloody *P* carved into my palm.

Ali grins. "Do you, the Chameleon, promise to give your life and undying loyalty to Red Fist, to the ones that want to make the world just, true and free?"

"I do!"

Ali slices my skin a third time. On my palm is a scarlet *R*.

"Salute my brother, the Chameleon."

I smash my heels together and bang my bloody fist to my chest. My brothers and sisters give me a round of applause. Ash takes my hand and pours on a solution to keep the mark fresh on my skin as it heals so that my oath will never be forgotten.

During the celebration, I'm raised on top of shoulders, and everyone congratulates me on the success of my first mission. It reminds me of why I am here. This is where I belong. I am a secret fighter for the greater good.

After an hour, everyone returns to their duties. Ali tells us that the techies are handling deterrence measures from yesterday's mission.

When Ali and I return to our apartment, he goes into the bathroom and starts rummaging around. I plop down on the couch, feeling content. My right hand throbs, but I smile. I know that everyone has the mark of the Red Fist on their right palm.

I hear the hum of an electric razor behind me. Ali is slowly walking towards me, smiling. No. No. No. He stops and stands over me, laughing.

"We have to," he says. "Your face is already all over the TV. If anybody sees you, you're gonna get canned. The Feds want you because you're their only link to us."

"I can put it in a ponytail."

"You already look enough like a girl. I'm cutting it, so go sit on the stool." He points to the kitchen and stands there like a mother waiting for her defiant child to start acting right.

I got my hair from my Native-American grandmother. I've been growing my hair for years. "Cut yours, too."

"I have before." He grins down at me. "You're the Chameleon, right?" He points to the stool again.

I groan.

This is bullshit. I'm being stripped of everything, including my friends and family. I can't go home. Ali was wrong when he said they were going to mold me, make me better. Red Fist is completely erasing who I was.

I sit down, and Ali starts. I see the first strands of hair float off my head. I close my eyes and desperately try to concentrate on something else. I think that maybe being a chameleon is one of the worst things ever because I'll never be the same. I'll never be original. I'll never be comfortable in my own skin. Not without my hair.

Not with this…other guy inside of me.

Not after all I've done.

I mean, how can I be?

12

Alice has to steel herself when she enters the whitewashed room in the hospital. Strong follows her in. Her father is asleep in the bed, and all the machines and monitors around him are zipping and beeping in a constant and ordinary rhythm. He is okay. He is alive, and that's all that matters. She walks up next to him and smiles down at him. His face is contorted. He does not look peaceful. He is frowning. Her smile falters, and she rubs her fingers across his hairy arm. The light touch wakes him, and his hard, brown eyes soften when they stare up at her. Her smile that was hesitant now beams.

"Father. I'm so glad you're okay."

"My Alice…" His voice is weak.

"Glad to see you're looking strong, Chief," Strong adds, making the man in the bed rumble with laughter.

The chief shakes his head and holds down a button at his side. The bed comes up, so he's sitting slightly upright. "I need to get out of here. It's just a flesh wound."

"You need to rest," Alice says.

"How's everything at the station?" he asks them. "I hope Johnson hasn't let the power go to his head."

The two ladies look at each other and laugh.

"Ah, I see," the chief says, joining in on the laughter. "I'll be back soon, ladies, don't worry." Then he realizes that his daughter is on the verge of tears and is barely holding herself together. Right now, he needs to be there for her. "Strong, could you leave us a minute?"

Strong heads out, shutting the door behind her. Alice lets the waterworks go and grabs onto the side of her father's bed railing so tightly that her knuckles turn white.

He caresses her face, saying, "My baby, everything is going to be okay. Stop crying. I'll make sure everything gets back to normal."

He realizes his reassuring words are not getting through, and it pains him so much to see his blood, his child, crying so deep. She is hurting immensely. Her internal pillars have crumbled and become chalky dust. Her child has gone rogue with some unknown terrorist organization.

The attack on the station couldn't be called a common gang crime. The chief has a good idea of who had the balls to attack his police station, but what he's wondering is how his grandson got involved with such a notorious and dangerous organization.

Alice is sniffling, but her tears fail to ease her grief and anger and guilt. She's already cried far too much. She looks at her father in total disbelief, "Father, I'm so sorry. I've failed you and the station. I've failed as parent…" She starts to sob again, her words breaking up. "I'll make this right. I will—"

Vance Cheveyo Rodriguez, chief of the DC Metropolitan Police Department, uses all his strength to reach out, wrap his arm around his daughter and bring her into a tight embrace. She lets herself melt into him. The chief feels the wetness from her face on his shoulder soaking through to his skin. He doesn't let go. He doesn't want to. He just wants his daughter to be okay. How could his grandson cause so much pain? He never thought he would come to hate any of his blood, especially not his only grandson.

He fortifies the walls within himself at this very moment and for all the future moments. He will not hesitate again. He will make sure Levi pays dearly. He will make sure his grandson is full of regret for the rest of his life for cutting his own mother so viciously. Any person that can turn his back on humanity and his own blood has no place in the chief's heart.

The door swings open and Strong pokes her head in. "Excuse me, Chief, the FBI is here. They need to talk to you and Rodriguez."

"Send them in."

Alice wipes her face, trying to regain her composure. An average-height black man wearing a crisp black suit and dark slacks walks in, followed by a slim, white woman in formal wear of the same color. The man has short curly hair, and his eyes are a chocolate-caramel color. He looks trustworthy, with his broad face and smile, but his stocky physique says he's not someone to be taken lightly. The woman looks rather small next to the man, but she holds her head high with confidence and walks as if nothing can stop her. Her hair is a cinnamon color, her eyes alert, warm like honey.

The two walk up to the bed and nod simultaneously.

"Our condolences, Mr. Rodriguez and Ms. Rodriguez," the man says. "It's like you've lost a family member."

Alice swallows, taken aback by the man's rudeness in bringing up her son so casually.

The woman smiles at Alice, silently acknowledging her partner's obliviousness. She grunts and holds out her hand for Alice to shake. "I'm Agent Grant, and this is my senior, Agent Frazier."

Frazier also holds out his hand and shakes Alice's.

Both Grant and Frazier look at the chief, but Agent Frazier is the first to speak. "Mr. Rodriguez, we want to wish you a swift recovery, but let's not waste a second. We need to ask you both some questions."

The chief sighs softly. "You want to know about my grandson, Levi."

"Precisely, sir. Right on the ball."

"And?"

"We want a detailed report on him and his actions during the days prior to this attack. Any and all information you can give us about him will be appreciated. Everything will be recorded."

"So, you think you guys with your fancy suits are just gonna waltz in here and take this from under us," the chief says. "He's our responsibility."

Agent Frazier takes a step closer to the bed. "You're bound by law to cooperate. This terrorist attack is bigger than what you guys can handle."

The chief's face turns red. He despises being looked down on. He stretches his neck as far as it will go. "You guys just want a direct connection to them."

Alice looks at her father, a question mark written on her face. "What do you mean?"

Agent Frazier turns around and takes a deep breath, facing Alice. "We have reason to believe that your son has gotten himself mixed up with a terrorist organization that calls itself Red Fist."

Alice's next heartbeat racks her soul, and she has to gulp in air to keep from falling over. She thinks about her son. She remembers when he was just a baby, stumbling around in his Pampers. There is no way he would ever be a part of something so hideous.

"There's no way he would do such a thing." She looks around at everyone in the room, and all of them shy away from her gaze.

Agent Grant clears her throat. "How can you defend him? He shot your father. He's obviously a part of something much bigger than a gang. The gangs of today don't have the means to carry out an attack on a police station that smoothly."

Alice whirls on the woman. "He is my son. I don't care what you people say about him. He is a great young man. If he's doing these things with these people, there's a reason behind it."

"A mother knows best," Agent Frazier says snidely.

"Exactly, and that's why if you guys want to find him, you'll need me."

The chief almost chokes. "Alice—"

"I'm the only one that will be able to get through to him if they've done something to make him act the way they want."

"Ma'am, we just want answers, not your physical assistance," Agent Frazier says, holding up his hand.

"We all know about Red Fist," Alice says. "If my son is a lead to them, a lead to stopping another attack, a lead to protecting this country, I want to help."

"Ms. Rodriguez, you are not qualified to assist us in operations regarding this matter," Agent Grant states matter-of-factly.

"You can train me. I'll do whatever you guys ask of me. You want to find my son, I'm the best shot you got."

Frazier whispers in Grant's ear.

"Can you excuse us," Agent Grant says, "we have to make some phone calls."

As the two leave the room, Strong enters. "What's the deal?" she says to Alice and the chief.

The chief is already bursting his lid. "Alice, you will *not* work with the FBI."

"I have to do *something* to help my son."

"He's beyond help."

Alice wants to slap her father but refrains from doing so. "I will do everything in my power to make sure he comes back safely."

"My dear, there's no safe place for anyone who has turned his back on his blood. You're not thinking rationally."

"They're brainwashing him."

"I don't want you any deeper in this," the chief says. "What if you get hurt?"

"I will not sit back and let Levi become an enemy of this country when I have the power to save him."

The FBI agents enter the room again.

Agent Frazier is smiling. "It seems you're in luck, Ms. Rodriguez. With your current training as a police officer, you can assist us temporarily, but we'll need to run you through some training to bring you up to speed on the current situation. You will be directly under Agent Grant and me, in a partnership with the FBI, since this is a special case and Red Fist is a major threat. Do you accept?"

For the first time today, Alice smiles because she is happy. She can actually do something. She can save her son from these terrorists who have gotten their hands clamped around his brain.

13

In the mirror, I rub my fingers through my now short hair, feeling the unevenness of my head. It's painful for me to look at myself, and I want to cry. To me, I'm no longer who I used to be. I've changed into someone else, something else. My hair was a substantial part of who I was. I shake my head and walk out of the bathroom.

Sugar is standing in our kitchen, talking to Ali, whispering. I walk by slowly, trying to eavesdrop but failing. Sugar cuts his eyes at me and stops whatever he's saying to lay into me. "You look harder now. Not like a woman."

I don't know what to say. "Uh, thanks?"

Sugar says to Ali, "Maybe you shouldn't have chopped him up, he could've been useful as a girl."

Ali dies laughing, falling against the wall.

"The Chameleon, perfect name for you." Sugar applauds.

I turn around and leave the apartment. I go down to the main area, where everyone usually meets. The woman with the dreads is standing in the middle of the room, motionless. Her body is loose. I sit down softly and watch her, studying her for the first time. Her dreads are shoulder length, black and glossy. She has a slim, fit, and tight body. She's short, but somehow, I just know she's dangerous. Her face is round, and I can't really tell how old she is. If I had to guess, I'd say mid-twenties. I focus on her dreads, envying her to the fullest. She's lucky; she gets to keep her hair. The woman is insanely beautiful. Her skin is the color of cocoa beans and glows in the natural light that squeezes through long, sliding blinds.

I jump a little and look away from her when she suddenly snaps at me. "You bring negative energy with you."

"I can leave. Sorry."

She turns towards me and sits down, right where she's standing. "Come over here. Sit with me. You need to relax."

I follow her instructions. She has a slight accent. Kind of like Sugar's but different; I think she might be Haitian. I sit down in front of her, exactly as she is, with my legs crossed. Her eyes are closed, and she's breathing softly. She's only wearing a black tank top and jeans, and the rise and fall of her breasts is kind of distracting.

She giggles and my eyes find hers, dark and starry, glimmering all over; might as well be the night sky. "It's okay. Men are always curious."

I must be blushing because her eyes shimmer with even more amusement. "Give me your hands, Levi." I send out my hands. She interlocks her fingers with mine. "I want you to close your eyes and take a few deep breaths. Think about something nice and calm, like the ocean or a blue sky."

Her voice is serene, and her touch is soft and sensational. She is sliding her fingers over and under my hands, pressuring specific points repeatedly. I take a couple deep breaths and think of a night much like the dread-head's eyes: a black night with countless stars and a full moon.

"Now, if you have your place," she says, "I want you to go there. Be there. Sit there. Relax. Breathe."

I pull the image in my mind closer, dragging it into something physical, something real. I drag that image until I'm sitting on top of a hill on a warm night. A light breeze is blowing through my once-again long hair, and each star in the sky is twinkling. The stars are playing a silent, elaborate symphony. I watch their song in the sky, and I let the breeze slide around me, hearing the woman's voice.

"There we go, Levi. You're good at this. Keep it up."

In the stars, I start to see faces. At first, I think they're constellations of the greats, but when I really look, I see my mother crying. I see Darryl's dead eyes glaring at me. I see Devin, banged up and dazed. I see my grandfather, shame engraved into the entire sky.

The stars stop singing. Somehow, I feel like I've been cheated out of a beautiful song and left alone to sit on this hill in silence. The sky curves downward, as though it's ashamed of me, and the stars don't gleam anymore. Instead, they become a fist. I guess the constellations want to punish me. I don't deserve to bask in their glory. The billions of luminous balls of gas and hydrogen swarm down towards my isolated hill, a massive fist of righteous punishment raining down to crush me. I'll take it. I deserve it—

"Come out now."

I open my eyes; my chest weighs a ton. The dread-headed woman leans in and touches my knee. "Never ever bring others inside your zone. That place is yours, and foreign intruders from your mind are not welcome there. Understand?"

"Yes, ma'am."

She laughs and stands, reaching her hand out to me. I grab it. "Call me Asha, not ma'am. I'm only twenty."

I drop her hand, and my phone vibrates before I can say anything else to her. It's Ali. "I have to go. Thank you."

Asha waves me away, and I find Ali waiting for me by the door. He motions for me to go into the living room. He looks me in the eye for a moment and then finally speaks. "This is gonna suck for you, little bro."

What could suck more than losing my hair?

"You're all over the news," he says, "and social media. You're the hottest thing on the web right now. The Feds really want you because you're a link to people like me, Bear, and Dad."

"Okay…"

"You have to lay low for a few months. We're gonna make you go dark. You can't leave this building under any circumstances. That means no outside calls—to *anyone*. Understand?"

I nod. "How long is a few months?"

"Long enough for people to stop caring." I shake my head, and Ali reassures me. "It'll be okay, you need way more training anyway. We can work on your body, make you bigger and stronger."

I nod. I feel trapped. I can't leave this building for a while, and I don't know when my sentence is going to be up. I go to my room and lie on the bed, thinking about all the time I was going to spend staring up at this ceiling, regretting my choices and remembering hurt faces.

***

The Federal Bureau of Investigation Headquarters

The man is fat, with flappy cheeks. His blond hair seems to be untamable as he bumbles inside the door, staring at the Executive Assistant Director of Counterterrorism and Counterintelligence, Marco Welch.

Welch smiles kindly at the man, who looks like one of those guys who only sees daylight to go to some nerd convention. Welch notices how pasty the man is. His blue-gray eyes are full of skepticism. Welch wants to frown. *Why is he wearing shorts and a T-shirt to a job interview?* Welch's men said this man was the best of the best.

The overweight man's name is Alfonso Gordon, and in the past year, he was the top graduate at Harvard with a degree in information technology. He is said to be a genius when it comes to computers and their systems. He bested everyone in the hacking test and got top scores on the IQ test. His teachers and friends vouch that he is up to date with every system in the technology world.

Brilliant minds like Gordon's are a rare find. The only thing Welch wants is exceptional aptitude. He wants people he knows he can rely on. Welch knows that this man right here may be the bureau's only hope to catch Red Fist.

"Mr. Gordon, nice to meet you, finally. I've heard great things."

The young man's rosy cheeks jiggle when he tilts his head in some form of a nod and smiles as politely as he can without trying to come off as weird.

"How old are you again, Mr. Gordon?"

"Twenty-two," Alfonso wheezes, still trying to catch his breath from hurrying up the stairs. The elevators were full, and he did not want to be late.

"My God, and so smart. Well, let me tell you, you will not be disappointed. We need minds like yours now more than ever."

"I'm happy to help, sir," Alfonso says this a little more loudly.

"Do you know about Red Fist?"

Alfonso confirms that he does with a shake of his head, Welch noting that he's a man of few words.

"Can you find them? The ones in DC?"

"Of course. Everyone leaves a trail."

Welch picks up on the man's cockiness, smiling. "We have a team ready for you, our very best. Let's start now. Follow me, Mr. Gordon."

14

Three Months later, in Washington, D.C.

Ali can't stop himself from staring at Ghost as she sifts through the jewelry, looking up at him and smiling every now and then when she finds something she likes. Ali has never been the type for relationships, but for some reason Ghost makes something inside of him sing a little song, and whatever the song is, it makes him dance closer and closer to her every day.

Ghost saunters up to him, putting a hoop earring near his ear.

"Damn, girl," Ghost teases.

Ali swipes her hand away. "Fuck off."

In the back of his head, Ali beats himself up because Levi is back at the base, suffering, while he's out here enjoying the day. Ali refuses to let anyone, even his own brother, ruin this operation they are planning. He is the one who ultimately decides when Levi's time is up.

Ali sighs as they leave the jewelry store and puts his arm around Ghost. This leader thing is not all it's cracked up to be. His handler got reassigned, which pretty much forced Ali to be in charge of this team, even though there are at least three individuals that are more qualified than him. Bear has been a part of Red Fist almost from the beginning. Sugar has been on so many different special operations for the government he worked for and against that he could write three books about it. And Ash, she was trained by Bear, so that speaks for itself.

Ali feels small compared to them. Whenever he isn't sure about something, he always goes running to these three for answers. They are always his first picks for advice and his go-to people for planning missions. Without them, this family they've created would be in shambles. He respects the three of them for sticking with him, even though they could easily do his job better.

Ghost shakes his arm off. "I think we're being followed."

"What?" Ali stiffens for a moment, but then he quickly loosens his body, knowing that if anybody is following them, they'll notice signs of being blown.

"Where?" Ali asks.

"They just crossed the street and got about fifteen meters behind us. They were looking too hard at us when you wrapped your arm around me."

"Description?"

"Both female. One has dark hair, light brown skin, probably Spanish, and the other is a white brunette. Both in business casual."

"There's no way," Ali tells her.

"Drone, maybe? Some new tech?"

The two reach a corner, where they have the option to cross the street and continue, or turn right. The numbers are counting down at the crossing before everyone streams to the other side.

Ali grabs Ghost's left wrist and pulls her close, whispering something in her ear with a tight smile.

She smiles back, her cheery attitude a facade, and kisses him on the cheek softly. "See ya, babe." She waves, and peels off to the right, mixing in with the pedestrians on the sidewalk.

Ali reaches into his pocket, fingering out his phone. He makes a show of dropping it behind him. He retrieves his phone, scanning the area behind him as he rises. He sees the two women, off to the right, about ten meters away from him. Both females avert their eyes when he makes eye contact with them. When people start walking across the street, Ali makes a split-second decision and heads back the way he and Ghost came. If they really are tailing him, they'll turn around and follow him.

He puts his phone to his ear and talks to no one. "Yeah, bro, I can be there…I can't hear you, there are a ton of people…yeah, sure…"

"Sir?"

Ali's skin crawls. They know.

The two ladies are on either side of him, and both have a hand in their small purses.

He looks at each of them, confusion on his face. "Excuse me, is something the matter?"

"We need you to come with us, please," the brunette says.

Ali wants to laugh at their directness. This no-discretion thing means that they definitely know who he is, and they're prepared. "What?"

"Sir, we need you to come with us. Please do not make a scene." It's the brunette again.

Ali glances at the other woman, immediately realizing she's Levi's mother. He stops himself from showing surprise. This complicates things.

People are starting to give them glances. He has to do something.

"I don't know what—"

"FBI," the brunette says. "Put your hands behind your—"

Ali gut punches the brunette with his right hand and moves behind her, pushing her towards Levi's mom. By the time the two recover he's sprinting down the street. Alice pursues immediately. Agent Grant calls for backup, then follows suit.

Ali pushes people out his way, cursing under his breath. He hears the women screaming behind him.

"FBI!" Get out of the way!"

He looks back for a moment. They're struggling to keep up with him in the crowd. He ducks into the jewelry store he and Ghost were in earlier. The middle-aged saleswoman, skin like chalk, is sitting behind the counter, reading a magazine. She stands, jittery when she sees the raised gun.

"C-can I help you?"

"Back entrance, where is it?"

The lady screams, and Ali shoves the gun in her face. "I swear I'll fucking shoot you. Shut up. Answer me!"

Words spill out of her mouth in a rush, and Ali runs to the back of the store. He can hear the lady still yelling for help. He makes it to the back alley and books it down the narrow path, coming out into a clearing. He stops for a brief second to collect his breath and dials a three-digit code in his phone to alert every Red Fist member on his team that he's blown and that he's in trouble. Protocol.

He checks frantically around the clearing, trying to find an escape. He glances up at the sky and grimaces. He can't tell how high it is, but there's a drone above him, almost invisible, hovering, watching his every move.

He squints, aims his gun, and shoots it down. He watches it crash to the ground. It's so small he could take it with him, but he doesn't have the time. He snaps a picture of it and heads toward a ladder he spots in the corner that leads to the rooftops. He hears footsteps shuffling down the alleyway and climbs as fast as he can. He's almost to the top when there's a shout below.

"Stop your escape. Come down now, or we will shoot."

He pauses a few rungs away from the ledge and looks down. "Why are you guys chasing me?" He does his best to sound innocent, even though he really wants to laugh. He wishes he could just kill them, but if Levi ever found out Ali killed his mother, that would ruin everything he has planned.

"Come down, *now*," the brunette yells up at him. "You have five seconds."

Ali sees that both women have their handguns pointed up at him. He's going to have to risk a bullet if he wants to escape. He takes in a sharp breath and then lets it go. He acts as if he's coming down, but as his hand reaches to grab the lower rung, he clutches it tightly and takes out his own gun, rapidly popping off shots down at the women, being sure to focus on the brunette.

The women return fire while moving to cover behind some dumpsters, and Ali continues to shoot until he's out of bullets. He scrambles up the ladder as bullets whiz by him, impacting with the stone walls and ricocheting off the metal ladder. Ali doesn't freeze, not even for a millisecond. He has scrambled through war zones full of debris and ashes from dead bodies. This is nothing.

Just as he's about to climb over the edge of the roof, he's hit in the right leg, in the calf. He closes his eyes briefly as the pain burns through his entire leg. He rolls onto the roof, reloading as he does. Ali sits up and rips off a part of his shirt to make a tourniquet above the wound. He bites his lower lip as the pain flares up and down his leg. His vision tilts, and he clamps down on his tongue to concentrate on a different pain.

He gets up shakily, and moves, stumbling, his body is failing him. Ali's phone vibrates. It's Bear.

"Where are you? We can intercept."

"On a roof. I'm tagged." Ali glances down at his bloody leg. They could have killed him if they'd wanted to.

"Find a way down, we're two blocks away from you."

"It's my leg."

"Ali. Come on, push, brother."

Ali stops, listening. He doesn't hear the FBI agents following up behind him. At least they're not stupid; they know he would kill them. He won't let anybody get in his way. He pushes himself forward, across the roof, trying to keep his breathing steady.

"I need someone closer, to make sure they aren't netting me in."

"On it."

Ali hears the distant blades of a helicopter in the sky. Off to his west, just a black speck in the blue. He sees the metal bird chattering towards him, and curses. "Hurry, they're bringing out a bird!"

He finds another ladder, and slides down into a quiet, remote clearing, keeping as much weight off his right leg as he can manage. He limps off, his right leg tingling with numbness.

15

Alice and Grant curse under their breath. The perp has gotten away. The two run out of the alley and onto the busy street, weapons out, pedestrians keeping clear of them and giving them worried looks.

"Everything's okay, please go on with your day," Grant reassures them as she gets on her phone. "We need a pickup now. Clear the roads and tell the heli to keep an eye on the perp, he's tagged."

Moments later, a glossy black Ford Explorer with tinted windows stops in the middle of the street. Grant and Alice run for the vehicle as people stop and stare, all seemingly mystified. In the driver's seat is a wiry blond-haired man with droopy eyes that make his expression that of permanent boredom. Sitting beside him is a stout older man; his brown hair is going gray, but his cloudy blue-gray eyes remain sharp.

The older man looks back at the two women. "The pilot said he's jumped into a red Ford Focus. Seems like he's got help, two blocks ahead of us. I'm Agent Ross, and this is my partner, Brandon."

"Did you clear the roads?" Grant asks.

"Red lighting currently. And the police are putting up roadblocks where they can as quick as possible."

Brandon floors it, weaving in and out of traffic, slamming his palm against the steering wheel, so jaywalkers know not to cut their lives short. He cuts to the opposite side of the road, maneuvering around traffic, siren blaring, blue and red lights flashing; the vehicles ahead of them stop so that he can merge back onto the correct side of the road and continue the pursuit.

"They're just up ahead," Agent Ross says.

Alice draws her gun and checks it, making sure she's ready for a fight. She checks her phone. The tracker is only centimeters away from hers. The perps are trapped in traffic.

"All right, Brandon, we're getting out and moving up," Agent Ross says, "you stay here."

"Roger, sir."

Ross turns back to the women. "All right, ladies, on me." He jumps out of the vehicle, racking his Remington.

The three move up, hunched over in a crouched position. Alice follows ten meters behind Agent Ross. Grant is on the other side of the vehicles.

Agent Ross holds up a balled fist, notifying them through their comms to halt. "Smoke, coming from the red Ford Focus."

Alice sees smoke climbing over the slew of automobiles and along the length of the street, thick and heavy and gray. It consumes her, and all she can think about is that she doesn't want to miss this chance to capture the ones responsible for her son's fall into terrorism. "We need to go in, sir."

"No way," Agent Ross says, "we haven't got a clear line of sight."

Grant cuts through on the mic: "B104, we need a status on the red Focus."

The pilot from the helicopter hovering above the scene sends immediate feedback. "Three perps from the Red Focus are on the move through traffic on foot. One of them is being carried."

Not a second later, Alice hears a shriek up ahead and a car horn.

"Move up *now*," Agent Ross orders, running into the smoke. "They're stealing a different car."

Alice shoots into oblivion behind him. More screams and a gunshot. She trips over something. She jumps up immediately. Somewhere near her, a woman is calling, "Blake! Blake! Where are you, baby? Blake!"

Alice has tripped over the boy. She turns back, getting down to feel the body for any moistness, any blood, soon realizing that she's fallen over a grown man and not a boy. "Sir, are you all right?"

Wheels screech and then a couple of loud bangs from a shotgun thunder in Alice's ears, followed by pops from a pistol.

"Shoot the tires!" Agent Ross yells.

The man underneath Alice moans, and she informs the group, "We have a man down over here."

Agent Ross grimaces. He lowers his shotgun and gets on the mic. "B104, follow that car. Brandon, get your ass up here. Call an ambo. We have a man down; I guess he tried to help the mom and the boy. Agent Grant, make sure those two are okay, Agent Rodriguez, I'm coming to assist you."

The smoke finally begins to clear. People are getting out of their cars, watching, and some are recording. Grant tells them to back away and to stop recording or be arrested.

Alice sweeps the man's body with her hands, finding a gunshot wound on his left side. She applies pressure and assures him everything is going to be fine, smiling into his eyes, which are growing dimmer with every second.

The senior agent kneels beside her, and she reports, "Gunshot wound to the left abdomen." She curses herself and then feels his backside for an exit wound. "No exit wound."

"Brandon, bring that first aid kit. Run!" Agent Ross screams into his mic.

Seconds later, the wiry man is with them, stuffing gauzes into the wound and applying pressure. "Brandon, stay here, make sure he doesn't die. Rodriguez, Grant, on me."

The three run back to their vehicle, and Agent Ross jumps in the driver's seat. He syncs into the truck's Bluetooth as he pulls out, roaring down the road. News crews and paramedics arrive as they speed away from the scene. "B104, update," Agent Ross says.

They can all hear the reply. "They've parked the vehicle and have proceeded inside Providence."

"Fuck!" Agent Ross slams the pedal to the floor, heading for the marker on the truck's GPS.

Alice watches the dot pulsate on her phone. She hopes that what she thinks isn't true. She grips the headrest of the front seat, finally noticing the drying blood that's changed the color of her hands. She closes her eyes, praying, as the metallic smell of iron drifts up her nostrils. She doesn't want to fail. She doesn't want to lose these terrorists.

Alice jumps out of the truck as soon it slows down enough so that landing on her feet won't be a problem. She hightails inside the hospital's emergency entrance and cuts off an elderly couple at the front desk.

The receptionist gives her a disgusted look. "Ma'am, the couple behind you were before you, can you please—"

"FBI," Alice says, shoving her ID in the woman's face. "Have you seen any suspicious people enter? A man with a gunshot wound to his leg, with long dark hair and brown skin. He may have been with a Caucasian woman, blonde hair, green eyes."

"Ma'am, if he was injured, it's likely he was brought in by the paramedics. I wouldn't have seen him."

"No, these people…" Alice stops herself, realizing she's losing her calm state. She excuses herself, heading back for the vehicle. "Agent Ross, we may have a problem."

"Nothing there, huh?"

Before Alice can answer, Grant shouts, "Guys! The marker's moving away from the building right now."

Alice hops into the Explorer, and Agent Ross burns rubber.

Alice whips out her phone. "I believe they have connections in the hospitals," she says as Agent Ross drifts around a corner.

"Most likely."

"I think they stole an ambulance."

"Rodriguez, did you see something we didn't?"

"No sir, I'm just starting to get a sense of how this group operates. They always have a plan."

"So, what else do you think?"

"I think they'll take the bullet out and get the tracking device. I also think that wherever we're headed is either a trap or a diversion."

"Hmm, you may be right. We're almost there."

The drive had only taken a few minutes. There's an ambulance sitting in the middle of the road. The three agents clear it. It's empty except for the trail of fresh blood.

"The tracker says they're inside," Agent Ross states, and leads them inside a bar cramped between other businesses and apartment suites.

It doesn't take them long to find the tracker buried in the trash, the bullet wrapped in some rough paper. Alice was right. Agent Ross curses and Grant sighs. Alice questions a couple of bartenders she finds cowering behind the counter.

Agent Ross calls Alfonso. "We lost them. You have all our locations marked for today?"

"Yep."

"We're gonna head in for the day."

Alfonso grunts in reply and hangs up.

Agent Ross shakes his head. "All right, ladies, we're heading in. There's nothing more we can do today. We'll have to question these people more before we go, then write our reports."

Alice will not take that. She points to the two bartenders. "They said they ran out the back. We need K9s."

Agent Ross shakes his head. "We'd be chasing them all over the city all night. For today, we're done."

Alice breathes in deeply. She was so close. So close.

It's been three days since Red Fist outplayed the FBI. Alice lies awake in pajamas on top of her silk sheets, staring up at the ceiling. The air in her empty house is brisk, and goosebumps are rigid on her skin. Once again, she can't sleep. It's only nine, but she had tried to tuck in early in hopes of getting sleep for a change.

She gets up, and feet gliding across the soft carpet of her bedroom. She knows where she's going. She's been doing this every single night, in a desperate attempt to feel him out there somewhere, to smell his sheets and blankets, to look around at everything that made her son the person she remembers.

She sits on Levi's squeaky mattress and rests her head on his pillow, closing her eyes. Tears flow down the crevices of her face and the lonely woman sobs. All the pain she's felt since she realized her son was with Red Fist has never left her chest. It's a ball of turmoil, unrelenting, black and impenetrable.

She thinks about the man who broke her heart long ago. She remembers the man who had the best eyes to lose herself in. The man who made her feel safe. The man who made her son's smiles the brightest. The man who always knew exactly what to do; who would know now how to fix her pain, and how to fix Levi. Alan Conoway, her ex-husband, MIA, presumed dead.

Alice cries more deeply, the grief she felt back then at the news of his disappearance coming back in waves, mixed with the pain of her son's affiliation with terrorists. She cries until her tears dry up, and she can barely breathe. Her body is exhausted from grief. She settles down on her son's bed, where she eventually finds sleep.

Alice's body shakes, and she jumps awake, her instincts making her keenly alert. She looks at the door, which is open a bit wider than she had left it. She sits up and listens. The door opens, revealing someone she's been aching to see.

She stands up, joy filling her chest, "Levi!" she gasps, moving towards him, before being told to freeze. Levi has jammed a gun in her face.

She pauses, and her breathe retreats. She smacks herself. This must be a dream. She shakes her head and closes her eyes, backing up against the wall.

16

shut my eyes when I see my mother's expression. She looks at me in confusion, as if she doesn't recognize me. I shouldn't have come here. I shouldn't have snuck away. Why did I come here? I lower my gun a bit and take a step towards her. "Mom…"

Her eyes dart around my room, hazy and questioning, bewilderment etched into her face. "This isn't real. Wake up, Alice, wake up!" She pulls at her hair.

I let my gun hang in my hand by my side, a mixture of emotions battling inside of me. I look at what I've done to my mom. She's losing it. "Mom, it's really me, Levi."

I watch her rush forward, and before I even know what's going on, I'm crying into her shoulder, and she's crying into mine. "I'm so sorry, Mom. I'm sorry I hurt you. I didn't think it would be this way."

"It's okay, baby." She grabs my face, wiping away my tears with her thumbs. "We can fix this. No matter what, I will protect you."

I shake my head. Her mouth opens, but I slowly force her away from me. She has a tight grip on me. She doesn't want to let go. Her hands are clamped around my arms now.

"Mom, let go."

"No. You can't just leave again. I won't allow it."

"Mom, please," I beg. She doesn't listen. I use more force and push her up against the wall, my arm against her throat. The dark side of me dances to the frontlines.

You're weak. Just let me have some fun.

I push the other me down and focus on my mom. Determination rages in her eyes.

"You don't understand," I say through clenched teeth and back away, aiming my gun at her once again.

Her determination seems to deflate, and she sinks to the floor. "Well, help me understand."

"I can't tell you everything, Mom. I just came here to say sorry for making you hate me."

She jumps up. I don't even stop her from swiping her ten-ton hand across my face. "I will never hate you. You are my *son*."

I wince from the sting and rub my tender jaw. "How can you not? I'm not coming back. I can't. Not after what I did."

"Why, Levi? Just give me a reason."

I look down, and I contemplate for a second if I should really tell her what I know that she doesn't. How will it affect her?

"Tell me," she pleads.

Should I tell my mom what I know? Would that make me a traitor?

I manage to face her. I gaze into her eyes, and I tell her: "Dad's alive."

***

106

Alice has to find something to lean on, somewhere to sit. She plummets onto her son's bed, the news so shocking she can't breathe for a moment. She can't even speak.

She hears her son say, "Mom, I love you."

She watches him back out of the room as her heartstrings grind against each other in some new profound way that makes a weird sound, making music that only hurts.

She chases her son down the stairs. She grabs his waist and puts her lips to his ear. "You can't leave. Please don't do this to me."

He powers down the rest of the steps, dragging her with him. He reaches for the doorknob, and she still doesn't let go. His hand falls from the doorknob. He turns around, and for the first time, in the gloom, she sees how much he's grown in the four months since she's seen him. He looks so different. His long hair has been replaced by a much shorter cut, making him look older. He is taller now.

She backs away from him. *He...looks like his father.*

"Join us." He reaches out his hand to her.

Alice looks at his hand and then at her son's face, and the fleshy mound of tissue and blood and cells in her chest becomes glass that shatters. She slowly shakes her head and steps away even further. "Levi, what you're doing with these people is not right."

"Dad thinks it's right."

She swallows hard and asks, "He's with those terrorists too?"

"We follow him, Mom. Please, join us. We're going to see him soon. We're going to make this world a better place."

Alice is becoming nothing, nonexistent. She can't believe her ears. "You're a *terrorist*. A criminal. You helped take innocent lives at the police station. Do you not understand how that is wrong?"

Levi hangs his head. "Yeah, it may be wrong now, but in the end, it'll be better."

"If your father had been alive all this time, he would have come and seen us. A real father would have come home. I don't know what it is these people are planning, or what your father has to do with it, but you are my son. *Mine*. You can come back home, and we can fix this. They could be lying, Levi. Have you even seen him?"

"I won't. They're not. And I will." He turns his back to her.

Alice's heart is so crushed right now that she feels as though it's been trampled by an elephant. "You need to grow up. You're eighteen. You don't need him."

He whirls on his mom, his gun aimed at her head. "You're the last person to know what I need. All these years and you never knew. That's why we're in this situation. That's why I am what I am."

She watches him for a moment before he turns back to the door. She grows afraid. This person in front of her, who just aimed a gun at her head, is not her son, not her Levi. She puts a hand over her mouth and lets him open the front door to leave, abandoning Alice once again.

She feels empty. She has lost. She feels like dust, like nothing at all. She has failed her son all this time, and she never knew it. She has let him fall into darkness, be brainwashed by people who could be lying. Everything is her fault. The realization is so sharp it pierces her soul. She knows she has not been stabbed, but she feels the edge of an invisible knife in her heart.

Depleted of energy and life itself, she crashes to her knees. Tears drip onto the floor. She doesn't know what to do. She can't escape this agony, this pain. It's eating her alive, from the inside out, a parasite, one she can't get rid of.

17

I pull away from my house, not looking back. The clock reads nine-fifty. The summer air is ablaze. I'd much rather have the windows down, with the breeze blowing away the congestion of negativity and life-draining thoughts in my head, but I can't risk being seen.

The tint on the windows is just below the level where a cop might decide to pull me over. Once I get out of my old neighborhood, I let out a breath of relief. I checked all around my neighborhood for surveillance before entering my old home. I'm sure the FBI is watching my mom, but I don't know where to look. It would be just my luck to have gone in there and come out to a bunch of Feds, guns drawn. It's a risk I had to take.

Doubt needles into the back of my mind. Will my mom stitch on me? Will she tell her buddies that she saw me? I dismiss the thought. If she had done that, I would be getting pulled over right now.

The image of my mom's wounded expression is plastered to the inside of my eyelids. I can't go back to that life. Not now, not ever. This is what I'm meant to do. I have a purpose now. And after all the studying I've done over the last few months, I truly believe that Red Fist's ideology is just. There are a lot of problems and secrets and lies that need to be addressed head on, but the government is sure to keep a lid on their boiling pot of bullshit. The media is no different, spinning the tale that will fit the right person's agenda.

The American people are focused on the wrong things, not realizing they have strings attached to them and are doing exactly what the men and women who control everything want them to do. My brother and the rest of the Red Fist members have taught me so much, showed me so much evidence that I can't just sit back and not help the cause. I'll be the vigilante for now, if it means I can do something for the greater good.

All the world governments claim they're fighting for the people; that each one is doing everything it can for their people and their nation. But it's just a bunch of old men and women fighting for personal gain and glory. They don't really care about any of us. They never did, and they never will. Red Fist wants to eradicate them all, and that's something I will stand behind.

I look in the rearview mirror; my eyes are lightless. Evil. I swerve. The chill I feel is momentary. I blink and peer into the back seat, then smash the brake pedal and pull to the side of the road.

Cold and keen, glinting even in the dim, yellow moonlight, a blade licks my throat. I freeze. Damn, I've really blown it.

My eyes meet his briefly in the rearview mirror. Those familiar eyes are pits of swirling disgust and rage, and, for a moment, a cloud of absolute confusion.

"Who are you?" he asks, digging the knife deeper into my neck, but not breaking the skin.

"What? Why are you here, Dev?"

"Who are you?"

"Devin—"

He punches the back of the seat, and the knife nicks me with its lethal tongue. Blood slides down my neck.

"I'm the one asking the questions!" Devin roars.

"Levi. You know who I am."

"You're not the Levi I remember."

The knife drops from my neck, and I twist around to see someone I hardly recognize. Something inside me splits open like a coconut. A crushed shell, my head diverges in two halves. My brain pulses and I understand something, and that knowledge of what I'm seeing shanks me, letting loose a realization, a consequence that I had forgotten.

Devin looks frail, and a lot smaller than I remember him. His dreads are gone. He's a skinhead now, and his head seems much larger now that I'm seeing it for the first time. I don't want to ask, but I need to know if what I'm seeing is my fault.

"What happened?"

He finally looks up at me. His brown eyes are sunken and sleep deprived, boiling like dark coffee.

"A lot. Ever since you disappeared, ever since the hospital. I can't remember *anything* now." He knocks himself upside the head with his free hand as if he's trying to knock his own brains out. "But sometimes when I think this potato can't remember anything. It remembers…it sees you…it says your name: *Levi*." He spits out my name through his teeth like it's a bad omen.

I feel obliterated. I don't say anything.

Devin claws at his skin. "I don't know what that means. I don't even know who you are anymore. I saw your face on TV and the police still come to question me on the good days."

I don't know what to say. What *can* I say? I did this to Devin. "Dev—" I begin.

"Don't you *dare* say that to me. You've said it a billion times, and you've never meant it."

"I didn't know—"

"Yeah, well, none of that matters now. Whatever drug was in my system causes temporary and occasional memory loss." He smacks himself in the head again. "And hair loss." He begins cackling like a deranged hyena. He notices my short hair. "We've both lost our hair. How ironic."

"Dev—"

"Funny thing, Levi. I was up in my room thinking about you. Something told me to look outside, and there you were, sneaking towards your own house. I couldn't pass up the chance." Devin leans forward and grips the back of my seat, his lips close to my face, so close I can feel his breath whip me. "You ruined my life. Some friend. Some brother. And for what? Give me a reason."

My mind and thoughts are so jumbled up that I can't come up with a concrete answer. All I say is, "You have every right to be angry, but I can fix you." I try to grab his wrist, but he snatches it back and looks away. "Devin, I promise."

He turns back to me, his eyes twinkling with something like satisfaction, his lips curved into a smile. "Too bad promises don't do you any good where you're going."

Before I can react, before I can even think, Devin has his arm curled around my neck. Headlights flash into my eyes as I struggle to free myself. White light glints in the rearview mirror. I'm jerking, but Devin's hold is too tight.

Kill him! Kill him! Kill him!

The window on my side is busted. Glass sprinkles into my lap and I feel a prick in my leg. I glance down; in my thigh is a dart. Devin releases me. My head drops. I can't move. My legs are pudding. I'm stuck in quicksand.

I hear a voice outside the car. "Good job, kid. We told you to use anesthesia. You didn't have to do that. He's your friend."

"Well, he's not the friend I remember. Maybe you guys can bring him back."

It's Devin. What does he mean? Who are these people? Brutal cold grips me. I'm locked in an ice cube. I crash into a malicious void.

18

The cold feeling has been replaced by an unknown hurricane of darkness, and my thoughts are running rampant, untamed, savage and vicious, words echoing in my head, bouncing off the inside of my skull like ping-pong balls. I surface in murky water, but I don't feel wet. I can't feel anything. All around me is intense blackness.

I stand up. An orange glow flickers ahead of me, calling me. I take a step, the water almost like sludge now, not wanting to release my feet. A barrage of thoughts swoop down on me, like seagulls plucking fish from the ocean.

"Bad friend. Mistake. Why did you go? You messed everything up. Let me take the wheel. I'll make sure everything goes the way you want it to. You're weak. You're useless. I can be strong for you."

I don't think these are my thoughts. Worry slides through me; fear seizes my soul. I hurry through the sludge, the orange light becoming brighter and brighter, almost blinding. My entire being feels like dead weight. Suddenly I feel even colder, but the hollow, empty area around me is muggy and hot. I have to get out of here. I have to get back before something I'll regret happens. Something I can't fix.

"You already messed up because you're weak."

I grab my head and shake it, but the thoughts aren't coming from inside it. They're coming from above me like missiles. They annihilate me.

"You cannot escape me this time."

"Who are you?" I speak into the oblivion, searching for an answer. I step up in front of the orange light, covering my eyes. The answer comes sooner than I expect. An invisible blow to my stomach takes the wind out of me, and I crumble. When I look up, I am faced with a giant mirror. A chill races down my spine when my eyes set on my reflection.

My doppelganger is laughing, mocking me because I'm in this pathetic state.

It leans in closer, placing its hand on the mirror. **"Come."**

"Who are you?" I back away from the mirror. I know who it is. I know that voice.

"You know the answer, Levi."

"I have to get out of here."

"You can't."

I keep moving away from the mirror, my heart fluttering like the wings of a hummingbird in my chest, yearning to escape.

"Why should you be in control? I am what you want to be. What you need to be."

"You aren't me!"

"I am you! The you that can do the right things."

I shake my head. The other me laughs and sticks his arms through the mirror, reaching out for me. I look up into his eyes, so vicious and power hungry.

"Come."

He's starving. Almost begging. But at the same time, I know that this me isn't a beggar. He isn't asking. He's commanding.

I stand up. Something inside me is attracted to this idea of power and fearlessness. Maybe this is what I've been waiting for all along. Maybe this is who I'm supposed to be. I shake my head again.

"No!" I scream, my legs moving on their own.

"You want what I have. You need it. You crave it."

I clutch my head and look down into a black void, willing my legs to stop moving forward towards the mirror. Dark Levi keeps calling me, coercing me forward. I need him. He is strong. I am weak. This is a simple equation. He's gotten me this far.

I get sucked into the mirror, the glass like an unbreakable see-through wall.

Dark Levi turns around and smirks at me, waving, and I feel helpless and weak. He vanishes into the orange light that burns viciously now, leaving me in the depths of my mind, alone and freezing.

19

Devin is, once again, stuck in some phantom zone, some other realm of the world where people go when they just seem to disappear entirely. He has a blank expression on his face, indistinguishable from any emotion; it holds no substance. The young man is peering out of the window from his bedroom, looking at nothing in particular. He doesn't hear the frantic knocking at his bedroom door. He doesn't move a muscle, not even a single twitch.

Devin, the poor boy, is locked in his land of nothingness because he forgets things constantly. He can't remember why he was so pissed earlier that night. He can't remember what he was doing ten minutes ago. He can't remember his purpose in this world.

The hollow shell that is now Devin Jones, the forgetful husk of a young man that has lost everything, moves. He moves, he blinks, and a weak, almost crying thought reaches out for him inside his head, saying a name that he has forgotten, a name with significant weight in his life. He remembers, for a split second, that he was saying this name earlier for some reason.

He rubs his hand over the skin of his skull and gets up from his chair by the window to open his door. Devin's mother and father burst in, hysterical, grabbing him and hugging him.

"Devin," his mother cries, "we told you *no* locked doors."

"Sorry, Mom, I forgot."

The frightened woman looks at her husband, a worried expression on her face.

"Darla, honey," Devin's father says, grabbing his wife's shoulders, "he probably forgot to take his medicine again."

Darla looks at her son's blank face. He is lost in illusions, and his once beautiful mocha eyes are trapped behind a smokescreen of side effects from whatever drug that delinquent boy he used to hang out with got him into. She moves away, covering her face, tears escaping her eyes.

Devin's dad rushes to her, turning his back on Devin, who is standing as still as a statue. "Baby, go sit down. I'll take care of this," he says.

He guides her out of the room and shuts the door, turning back to his only son, a somber expression on his face. He never imagined such a thing would happen to his son. Devin was always such a bright young man.

Maurice walks over to his son's dresser and grabs the pill bottle, immediately feeling the emptiness that is inside.

He snaps his fingers in front of Devin. "Devin! Devin! Where is your medicine? Why is it empty already?"

Devin doesn't answer. He hears everything. Sees everything, but all he wants to do is remember. He wants to remember who he was.

"Devin," his father yells, shaking him. "Answer me, son." Devin smiles, and his father, still anxious, gives him a nervous smile back. "I am here, Devin. Please talk to me."

A bit of clarity shows in Devin's eyes. "I want to remember, Dad."

"Yes. But you need your medicine."

Devin's smile turns upside, and he pushes his father away. "I don't want it."

"What did you do with it, Devin? You can't get better if you don't take it."

Scattered memories swarm the inside of Devin's cobwebbed mind, and one recollection glows brightly for a moment.

"I am broken," he spits. "I can't remember anything. That medicine isn't going to help. There isn't a cure for it. The doctors said so. All these pills *might* help me. All those therapy sessions *might* help me. The doctors don't even know what kind of drug I was exposed to, so everything about the medications and the treatments is bullshit if they don't even know the reason why my brain is so fucked up."

Maurice Jones, a man who has worked so hard to get to where he dreamt of being many years ago, a man who has put countless hours into bettering himself only for his family, a man hell-bent on making sure his son and his wife have the very best life he can possibly offer them loses face, right here, in this very moment, and breaks down, in front of his son, falling into his boy and hugging him tightly.

For a moment, Devin feels a firm yank on his heart, like someone is inside him, trying to pull his heart down from its throne. The stone embedded in his skin cracks and begins to crumble so he can dive into the embrace. "Dad, it's not your fault. I'm sorry. I really am."

Maurice looks his son in the eyes. "You will get better. I promise. Whenever you forget, you have to remember us. The people you love."

Devin nods, and his father backs away, putting a hand on his son's shoulder. "I will go get you a refill first thing tomorrow morning. Do you want anything from downstairs?"

"No."

Maurice turns around slowly and heads for the door. He stops in the doorway and looks back at Devin. "No. Locked. Doors. Repeat that to yourself so you don't forget."

Devin nods. His father flashes his son a grin and leaves him in his own mind, searching for all the answers to the questions he has.

Devin sits down in his chair and looks out the window onto the dark street below. He takes his dad's advice and thinks of his parents. He keeps their brown faces hanging in the smoky darkness inside his head until finally, memories pop into his mind's eye. Memories of when he was a kid. Memories of family dinners where he's laughing, his parents on either side of him. Memories of unfamiliar faces. Memories of vacations. Memories of smiles. Memories and memories. Devin stays in this bliss for a long time, happy that he can remember things. Ecstatic that he isn't as broken as he thought he was.

**

Darla Jones is outside enjoying the fresh summer's night breeze, drinking a glass of wine and smoking a cigarette. She usually doesn't stay up past midnight, but stress is stopping her from sleeping. And she's smoking, something she hasn't done in years. With everything that's happened, she needs something to take the edge off. So she resorts to blowing some of her worries away with the smoke she lets drift up towards the moon. She keeps reminding herself that her boy will be okay. That he will get better. She has prayed so much and for so long every night for her son to heal.

Darla has never been a religious woman, but lately, she's been screaming to God for help, for healing, and for guidance. She knows it's wrong to begin worshipping and asking for things from such a being of greatness only when her perfect little life starts to not be so perfect anymore. Darla knows, though, that she needs something to believe in. Someone.

She finishes the last of her wine and puffs on her cigarette, listening for her husband. Maurice would be furious if he opened the back door to see her smoking again. *To hell with him.* She blows into the sky, keeping her eyes on the shining stars, wondering if God is watching her right now. She decides that he is, and snuffs out her cigarette, then putting it in her pocket.

She begins to pray. Her mother was a church-going woman and always dragged her along with her when Darla was younger, but as Darla got older, she refused to keep going, so praying has always felt very odd to her.

She closes her eyes. "God, I know I'm not the greatest person. I'm going to keep apologizing to you every time I talk to you. I'm sorry for not being a better person. I just want you to help me through this tough time, and please, I would give anything from myself, from this earth, if you would just heal my baby." She stops, her emotions getting the better. She sniffles and continues. "Please take care of my son, God. Please bring him back to me. Please touch his mind with your…holiness, God. Please. Amen."

Darla opens her eyes and lets out a breath. She feels a bit better now after the praying and the cigarette and the wine. She begins to head back inside when their dog, Mel, who she was supposed to be watching use the bathroom, starts barking. Mel barks again, and then begins whining.

Darla rushes off the patio, into the backyard, "Mel, Mel, come here, girl."

Darla is standing in the light shining from the patio, and that light is keeping the darkness from engulfing her. Tall bushes push up against the high wooden fence that surrounds their entire backyard.

"Mel, you better not be playing around. Come here!"

Darla doesn't ever remember having a raccoon problem. Against her better judgment, she pushes out of the light, towards the bushes, searching for her little dog. "Mel! Mel, girl, where are you?"

Darla becomes concerned. An odd chill scampers down her spine. She touches her chest. Her heart is panicking. "Maurice!" she yells, "Mel isn't com—"

A hot and fiery pain shoots through her right thigh, and she falls to the ground. She's confused. She's unable to see the cause of the sudden injury. She can't feel her thigh. She thinks she's been bitten by a snake and reaches down to check. Her hand comes away smelling of blood, and she screams, "Maurice! Maurice!"

A dark shadow moves from the bushes and stands over her. She looks up at a tall, mysterious man. She continues to stare at his face until the moment he places a gun to her head. Then she turns away and tries to crawl towards the patio, screaming for her husband and son to run, the pain in her thigh bellowing now, ripping through her, sucking the life out of her.

Sugar lets her get to the patio steps, and then he crunches down on the peppermint in his mouth, breaking it into pieces. Killing always leaves a distinct, terrible taste in his mouth, so he never forgets peppermints whenever he's on an operation. He lets the minty candy hotbox his mouth and then points his silenced pistol at the crawling woman. Her desperate attempt to get away is futile because her life was over the moment Sugar saw her.

He puts two bullets into her. She slumps on the steps and lies still. He walks over to her, closes her eyes and says a prayer for her in his native language, asking for her soul to be at peace, and asking for forgiveness.

*****

Devin runs out of his room and down the steps when he hears his father cry out. Near the bottom of the stairs, his gaze falls on a ghastly sight, and he freezes. His father is sprawled on the floor of their living room, mouth wide open, eyes staring up at the ceiling. Devin can't speak, can't call out; can't do anything.

There are people standing around his dead father. They look at him, standing frozen in disbelief. One of them smiles, and Devin knows that he's seen this ugly curvature of lips before. He digs into the banister for support, but his legs won't move.

"Why?" he screams.

The door to the patio opens, and a dark man wearing a fancy-dress hat walks in with his thumbs up. Devin doesn't know how he knows this, but it means that his mother has been taken care of, too. Devin wills himself to move, to run. He has to call the police. He has to tell them that his parents have just been murdered by thugs.

The smiling man is staring directly at Devin. He's leaning on a crutch. He reaches up with one hand and takes off his pizza-delivery-boy hat. Fireworks of memories explode inside of Devin's head, and he rushes down the last few stairs, his fist cocked. Synapses buzz to life in his head, and he recalls an image of Levi passed out over this guy's shoulder. He remembers this piece of shit's voice as he threatened his family that day in Levi's living room. He remembers seeing the man's face, eyes smiling, as a Levi that Devin never knew existed beat his face in.

The others don't move; they don't need to. The guy with the crutch deftly, with one fluid motion, brings the end of his crutch up into Devin's groin area and he collapses onto the floor, crying.

"You finally remember?" Ali grins.

"Why?"

"I told you what would happen. You've caused trouble for Levi. I know he snuck home earlier. I know you saw him. You fucking scumbag, we know you're working for the government. Some friend."

"I had to. I want to help him." Devin can't look any farther into the ground. He wishes he could just fade into nothing.

Ali's pupils contract and he jabs the end of the crutch into Devin's side. "What do you know? You're useless. You don't know anything."

Somebody grunts loudly.

"Yeah, yeah," Ali says. He desperately wants to enjoy ruining Devin. For some reason, he hates him. He hates this kid who will soon be just a memory to his little brother. Ali points his pistol at Devin's face, looking down at him coldly. "You did this to yourself. You should've stayed in your place."

Ali pulls the trigger once, hitting Devin in the side, and a smirk flashes across his face as Devin whimpers like a broken pup. Then Ali points the weapon at Devin's head and pulls the trigger one more time for insurance and for good luck.

20

Alice jolts awake, instinctively grabbing underneath her pillow for her weapon, but hands force her to keep still.

"Let go of me," she yells.

She bucks and resists until a familiar voice lulls her into calming down. It's Grant.

The hands of the men in body armor leave her body, and she sits up, rubbing her eyes. "What's going on?"

"Something tragic," Grant tells her. The men leave the room, and Grant sits beside her. "Have you seen your son recently? Tell me the truth right now."

Alice remembers how she begged Levi not to leave, but still, he left. The worst envelopes her mind and tears burst from her eyes. "Please, no, please don't tell me…"

Grant rests a hand Alice's shoulder. "We have your son in custody. That's the good news. The bad news is, your neighbors next door and the team we had posted here are all dead."

Alice regains herself. She figured the FBI had people watching her house. "You already know the answer to your question."

Grant nods. "Yes, you saw him last night. But some are wondering why you didn't report it. You can't be trusted to act selflessly."

"He's my *son*. What would you do? See your child murdered before your eyes?"

Grant looks down at her hands for a moment. "Listen, Rodriguez, Red Fist just killed an entire family, most likely in retaliation for us having your son, and they must've figured out what went down."

"What exactly went down?"

The agent gets up. "I want you to know that you're still my friend, and if anything comes up, or you ever need someone to talk to, I'm here for you."

Alice is in disbelief. "You guys can't do this. What am I supposed to do? Where are you keeping him?"

"Alice, this job requires you to put your feelings aside to get the mission done first. This was not my choice, I would prefer to keep working with you." Grant quickly turns away from Alice.

Alice leaves the bed and hugs Grant from behind. "I understand how you feel. I don't need you to feel sorry for me. But please—"

Agent Grant sniffles and turns to give Alice a proper hug. "You stay safe and keep your head up. It was a pleasure working with you. They told me that your pay has been handled."

"Thank you," Alice says, smiling, and then she adds, "Agent, can you promise me something?"

Grant knows that making promises in her line of work can be deadly, but she nods.

Alice continues. "Can you promise me that my son will be okay? That you will protect him? That I will be able to hold him in my arms again?"

Grant gives Alice a tight smile. "Sure thing. I will do my best. For you."

"Thank you," Alice says again, and watches the agent leave her room.

The mother of a young man that many assume is an evil terrorist, a maniac, sits down once again, newfound energy settling over her. For some reason, Alice feels free, like she has no restraints. Nothing can hold her back now. Not the police. Not the FBI. Nothing. She is not going to stop pursuing her son. She is not going to give up on saving him from those monsters.

21

Out of the darkness, I come, awaking blurry eyed and thirsty, my mouth feeling like sandpaper. My hands are restrained behind my back, and I'm sitting in a metal chair in the middle of a gray room. I try to move my feet, but they're tied around the legs of the chair. I jerk my entire body, but the chair is nailed to the floor.

The room has no color other than gray; it is just cement walls on all sides with a single humming light on the ceiling. To my left is a large gray door with no door handle. In front of me is a black window, no doubt with one-way glass. Somebody is watching me; I can feel it. There doesn't seem to be anything behind me, but there's a camera in the right-hand corner of the room, so I'm going to assume there's another one behind me.

I take a deep breath and smile. I have to stay calm. I am the strong one, after all. They want information, so they aren't going to do any real damage to me.

What kind of information will they want? They want important names. Names to go with faces. And they want targets. They want to know Red Fist's next target, and whether it's a person or place. Whatever they want to know, it doesn't really matter because I don't know anything.

By now Ali is probably raging. Red Fist is probably already moving to try to figure out where I am. I won't be here long. I trust Red Fist. They are my family.

I hear a click, and the door is slowly pushed open. Three men walk in, all dressed in suits. One man stands to my right. He's a bald black man with a thick head and beady eyes that somehow manage to pop out a bit too much from his eyelids. He's sturdy, a brick wall of a man, towering over me, staring down at me in disgust.

Another man stands in the middle of the room. He's a bit shorter than the black man. He has dark hair, graying on the sides. At the corner of his blue eyes are crow's feet, and when he smiles down at me, the wrinkles in his face really show. He's important. I can tell because, unlike the other two, he holds an air of confidence. He's smiling; he's happy he has me here.

The third man is around the same height as the one in the middle. He is Asian, with jet-black hair slicked back. All his features look too small for his face, which holds an expression indifference. He's staring past me.

The man in the middle reaches out his hand. "I'm one of the FBI's executive directors, Marco Welch." His hand lowers, and he smiles wider. "Nice to meet you finally."

The cockiness coming from this man is irritating. I want to bash his skull in.

Welch jabs a thumb to his left, at the black man. "This is Dragon." He points to the Asian man. "And this is Jung."

I shrug, and Welch continues. "You do know why you're here, right?"

I say nothing.

Welch looks up and clenches his fists. He breathes in and then out. He gets close to my face, his pointy nose inches from mine. "I know you think you have some sort of shield with your mother's position, but let me connect some dots for you. You are a terrorist, an enemy of this country, and if push comes to shove you can be eradicated."

Eradicated? Yeah, right.

Welch regains his composure and stands over me once more. He lifts a single finger. "Dragon, I give you permission to harm this man until he speaks. Understand?" He goes into the corner and leans on the wall and begins picking at his nails.

The brick man looms over me, cracking his knuckles, breathing out slowly. He raises a giant hand in the air and brings it down, smacking fire into my face, sending my head flying to the right.

"Oooooh." It's Welch in the corner, inspecting his hands. "That sounded bad."

I don't feel any fear. I just feel pissed. When I get out of these restraints—Dragon smacks me again—I'm going to stick—and again—my foot so far up this guy's ass—and again—he's gonna wish he was never born. Dragon backhands me on the other side of my face and blood trickles out of my mouth. Shit. I'm a leaky fucking faucet. I manage to smile up at the man.

Dragon's reptilian-like eyes are possessed by some psychotic force, and I figure he gets off on beating on someone who can't fight back.

"You think this is funny, little man?" Dragon croaks at me.

He smacks me again, and this time, I think I feel my brain bounce inside my skull.

"You think taking innocent lives, betraying your country, and being a murderer is funny?"

His pitiless hand doesn't stop coming for me. I don't know how long he keeps hitting me before I can't hold my head up anymore.

Welch moves forward, lifting my head up so he can stare at me. He bursts out laughing. "I respect your balls, kid, but you look like shit. You sure you want permanent face damage for the sakes of your little friends?"

"This is againiss the luhhh."

"Oh, you wanna talk now? I want a location. Names."

I let the blood steadily leaking from my mouth be my answer.

Jung, who has been standing in the exact same spot since he came in, speaks up. "What we're doing to you is perfectly justifiable, Levi. You're a terrorist. Don't you get it? You're down there with the worst, and nobody cares about you except your delusional mother."

For some reason, that line sparks the match inside me. I spit blood in Welch's face and he veers away. He's replaced by Dragon, who begins punching me, his knuckles my lullaby.

A splash of water pulls me from my knockout, and I lift my head up, looking around wearily. Dragon and Jung are absent. Welch is sitting in front of me with his arms crossed, staring at me curiously. He perks up when he notices I'm awake.

"Oh great, you're awake. Maybe you've had a change of heart."

I shake my head, feeling my swollen cheeks ache.

"Shame. Red Fist is using you, you know. They don't care about this country, this world, or anything at all. They want power. They're ruthless murderers, and that should be enough for you to know that they're wrong."

I lock eyes with Welch. I smile at him and wince. My lips are busted, and my face aches.

He jumps up and takes out his phone, pressing a single button. "Seriously, you sure you don't want to talk? My friends are a nasty bunch, they are wayyyy meaner than Dragon."

"I'm sure. Fuck off," I tell him slowly, making sure he can hear me say those words clearly.

Welch shrugs and sits back down, staring at me once again. "I have a nephew around your age. What are you, eighteen, right?"

I don't answer.

Welch rambles on. "You're awfully boring, kid. Such a loyal little dog, too."

I tilt my head all the way back, looking up at the ceiling. This guy is pissing me off big time.

"What's your story? How'd you encounter that organization?"

I guess Welch finally gets tired of his losing battle because he says, "Oh, well, kid, time's up. I'm not really one for violence anymore; those days are behind me. You will talk. We've brought in the specialists of interrogation: the CIA."

My body tenses just a bit. I smile as I bring my head back up to sneer at Welch. "I ain't scared."

He gets up and opens the door with his card. He looks back at me, a weird expression somewhere between smugness and solemnness on his face, and he says, "You will be."

22

I'm blinking in and out of consciousness; time doesn't exist in this cement jail. I don't know how long Welch has been away, but if I'm starting to lose myself to sleep, it must be nighttime. Strapped down still, I'm shrouded in darkness. My arms ache from being tied behind my back, and I can't feel my fingers. My eyelids feel like there's a ton of bricks weighing on them…

Sneaky hands wake me. I buck, jumping up out of my restraints. Three men are now standing in front of me, near my chair, their faces covered with ski masks. They inch towards me.

"Calm down," one of them says.

I'm fidgeting around, ecstatic that I'm free, that my body isn't pinned down anymore. I subdue my joy and focus on the men, grinning. The CIA?

"Who are you guys?" I back away, adrenaline making a trip throughout my entire body. I can hear my heart pulsing inside my chest. No one answers.

My eyes don't adjust to the murkiness, but I know there's no way to escape. The three men are still creeping towards me, hands outstretched, arms tensed.

I back myself up against the window that I can't see through. "Who are you?"

"You must calm down," one of them says.

It's too gloomy in here. That son of a bitch, Welch. "Answer my question!"

"Stay still. Don't move."

I see that the one in the middle is holding a syringe or something, and I freak out a bit. That old bastard really must have called the CIA.

The three men are about five steps away from me now, slowly sliding their feet forward, encroaching upon me, lions cornering their prey.

Four steps away.

I breathe in. I need to calm down. I'm the strong one. I'm in control of this party now.

Three steps away.

I breathe out.

Two steps away.

I pick my target.

One step away.

I don't move.

Their arms are all just a few inches away from grabbing me. I propel myself off the window, attacking the one on my left. I jab a fist into his jugular, twist his arm behind him, and push him towards his buddies, making my way past them.

"Open that door," I growl.

None of them move.

I'm going to have to power my way through all of them if I want to get out of here. Bear taught me a lot about fighting at a disadvantage in close quarters, and all that time spent in the Dark Room, getting my ass delivered to me helped a lot. Right now, I need to establish control of the situation.

I try to heave the chair up, forgetting that it's nailed to the floor.

The guy in the middle and the one to his right come for me at the exact same time, hopping forward into fighting stances. "Get down on your knees, hands behind your head!" the middle one says.

"Fuck off." I jump over the chair, making them both jerk to the side.

I dart to my right and go for the guy that was in the middle, but he's ready and blocks the blows I aim at his face. I feel the other one move in, so I lash out behind me with my foot, making contact with something. I turn to exchange blows with him, not seeing the third guy I got the best of earlier coming for me. He shoulders me, knocking me off my feet and onto the ground, and before I can get up a boot is slammed into my stomach.

"Stay down!"

I'm not a pussy like the other Levi. I smile and grab his foot, twisting my body so it rolls underneath me, but he brings his other foot to his aid before I can bring him down and smashes it into my side, making me let go. Boots rain down on me, striking me from all angles. I protect my face and head, but one of the guys keeps kicking me in the back of my skull, breaking the skin on my fingers. I try to hold on, but a sharp jab in my side again steals all the air from me, and one of the boots finally lands a clean hit on the back of my head. My face slams into the floor and the syringe is jammed into the back of my neck.

Sweat is sticking to my body like a fly to flypaper. It's all over me. I turn the knob in the shower and let cold water tumble down my body, battling the heat away from my soul. I spin around a couple of times and then turn the water up a bit. It becomes colder. I back away, out of the stream, my body shivering. I dart back in and turn the knob all the way up. I want warmth now.

The shower stops. No water comes out, and all I can hear, other than the shrieking silence, is the steady drip from the showerhead. I open the curtain to step out, and there's a loud bang behind me, causing me to trip. The showerhead has flown off, and a rush of water is jetting into the tub, filling it quickly. I stand there and watch until it overflows until freezing water swallows my feet. My naked body is trembling.

I open the bathroom door to escape and shake my head in disbelief. A violent storm and ocean are before me, and a massive, mountainous screaming wall of waves looms over me before beginning to make its brutal descent.

"His fingers are moving boss, he's up," I hear over my pounding headache. I don't want to lift my head. Actually, I can't, my neck feels like a limp noodle.

Hands grip my head and force it up. Blood drips from my nose. My eyes meet a man wearing an eye patch over his left eye. His visible eye is as black as an abyss and unwavering.

"Keep your head up," he tells me.

He sits down across from me. I'm in a different room now, and my hands are shackled to a wooden table. The three guys that beat my ass are standing against a dark wall, all still in ski masks. I flash a smile at them, and the man with the eyepatch clears his throat loudly. I pay him no mind.

He gets up from his chair and comes around the table to me. He chokes me with one hand. His grip is tight, and he pushes into it, tipping my chair off balance and onto two legs. He pushes so hard that my hands, locked to the table, feel like they're being ripped off.

He speaks to me through clenched teeth, "Boy, you listen here, and listen good. You keep your eyes on me. You don't look at my men. You don't smile at my men. You don't talk to my men. You speak when spoken to. You will answer all of my questions. Understand?"

I can't really answer when my lungs aren't getting enough oxygen. He lets go and my chair slams back on all fours, the wood protesting its rough treatment with a loud crack. I take deep gasps of air while he sits back down, keeping his one eye on me.

"Answer my question."

What? Oh, yeah. Do I understand? No, I don't. I smile at him. "Are you a pirate?"

The one-eyed man gets back up, rushing around to smack me upside the head. "Let's play a game. I call it you answer my questions, and I don't remove body parts."

"Pass," I say to him casually. The trick is to not let these guys feel like they're in control.

You're going to get me killed!

I block the weak part of myself out and continue staring at the pirate man as he stares down at me. He has brown hair shaved down to the skin, and the right side of his face has an old jagged scar. Typical-looking badass.

He pulls a little knife from his pocket and with a sudden motion and to my surprise, hammers it into my left hand.

I scream.

Shut up, Levi. Shut up, Levi. Shut up, Levi.

He yanks it out. "Answer!" His one eye is full of violence. He's like me, thirsty for blood.

I'm trying to hold on to my placidity. If I show weakness, I lose the mental battle against the weaker me, and this prick in front of me. There's a heartbeat in my hand, and the blood is streaming, mixing with the dust on the wooden table.

Tell them what they want. Red Fist can handle it.

Shut up.

"Tell me who the leader of your little circus is."

I shake my head. The man punches me. My jaw is still raw from Dragon. "Tell me!"

"How about you just kill me already. I don't know *shit*."

"You want nerve damage in your hand? I'll stab away."

"I just told you to fucking kill me." I'm not afraid to die. Not right now.

Mr. One-eyed Asshole punches me dead in the nose. Blood gushes out my nostrils.

"You think we don't know about your dad, kid? We know."

I tense up, then immediately loosen myself. I'm not getting put through any of this because of my dad. I'm doing it for the greater good.

"We know about your brother. He's the one the FBI chased, right?"

"Good observation," I say.

"Where's your hideout?"

"Even if I told you guys, they're gone by now."

Willy, the one-eyed dickhead, punches me in the nose again. Blood flows out of it faster and faster, and I part my lips, tasting the glory. Tasting the victory. I'm winning!

He punches me in the face again and again and again.

When I come to, his hand is reaching for my throat. I feel his python grip, his fingers wrapping around my neck. "This ain't a game, son."

He must see that I'm fading and lets go. My head hangs. This is a game I'm not going to lose.

He lifts my chin with two fingers. Blood is everywhere. I manage to say what I know he's going to think is a joke through the pain. "I'm the good guy. You just don't know it."

"Yeah, and I'm Barack Obama, you little shit." He reaches for my nose, and his fingers toy with it roughly. I wonder if I can die from excessive nose bleeding.

"Tell me where your base is."

"Up. Your. Ass."

Mr. One-eyed Asshole takes my nose into his fingers, and with a crude yank and twist, he breaks it, the crack deafening to my ears. I almost pass out. It throbs with so much pain I can't even scream. Instead, I pant, trying to take in a decent breath, finding even that task uncomfortable and gruesome. I try to just shut my eyes. I try to just fall, but he doesn't let my head hang. He takes the back of my head and slams my face into the table so hard it bounces back up.

A wall of blackness descends, and dark spots flicker and sling into my field of vision. My face is a punching bag, a thing that absorbs the pain, people's insanity. I hurt all over, ache in places I'd never thought of. This is hilarious. Red Fist will come for me. They will. We're the good guys.

I let my head hang, watching the blood from my face drip into my lap. Gut-wrenching dizziness slips around me, hugging me.

I hear Mr. One-eyed Asshole say, "Don't die, you cesspool, we'll be back."

23

Four Days Later

Alfonso's phone will not stop ringing. He finally loses his patience and grabs it off his nightstand. It's Welch. Alfonso groans, wondering why this man is calling him at three A.M. when he didn't leave work until eleven last night. He slides his chubby finger across the screen and breathes into the phone, so Welch can hear that he's there.

"Oh great," Welch says, "I thought I'd have to send a team over. Anything suspicious happen?"

"What?"

"You sound grumpy? Were you asleep?"

"Welch, I've been busting my ass trying to find Red Fist all night, so of course I was sleeping."

"Oh boy, that's the most I've heard you talk ever."

"I'm going back to sleep."

Alfonso begins to put down his phone when he hears the desperate cries from his supervisor. He brings the phone back up to his ear. "What was that?"

Welch takes a deep breath over the phone. "Red Fist has started playing the game again. We've had an important development, and we need you here by five o'clock sharp. We have a meeting."

"I'm not coming in if it hasn't got anything to do with what's in my job description."

"We need genius minds like yours, Alfonso. Red Fist is winning this game right now. Do you really want to lose the greatest game of your life?"

"How am I losing?" Alfonso's hands grow a bit clammy, the kind of clamminess a gamer gets when things in the game are getting intense.

"I can't discuss details over the phone, but very soon we may have an opportunity to gain a win. Will you come in?"

Alfonso yawns. "What choice do I really have? I signed a contract to help you guys."

Sluggishly, Alfonso finally steps out of his apartment door and waddles to his beat-up 2008 Honda Civic. He mutters complaints as he plops into the driver's seat, the sun not even awake from its own slumber. He cranks the car, and it starts with a pathetic sound. Alfonso groans. He hates this little car. It is a hand-me-down from his two older siblings, and he decided to keep it because it was the cheapest option. With the money he's making now, he can go buy an upgrade, a car that doesn't make him feel like a sardine inside a can.

He pulls out onto the road and begins his drive to the FBI facility, muttering and groaning and yawning his way into the hazy morning. He motivates himself as much as he can on his journey to work because, all in all, the only thing he wants is to win the game. He does not want to lose. He *can't* lose.

If people found out that Alfonso, aka HecticSaber94, one of the world's top gamers across three platforms, in many different games, lost in this type of situation, it would ruin his online reputation. Alfonso worries more about his own mental health. If he doesn't beat Red Fist, the defeat will stick to him for the rest of his life. He won't be able to live it down.

So the chubby man smiles, actually a bit pumped for today's meeting.

He takes his time getting inside the building. In the lobby area, he walks up to the receptionists' desks and grabs a handful of fruity hard candies. None of the receptionists are here yet. He unwraps a couple of the candies as he heads into the elevator, alone, and pops them into his mouth, the sweet crunch satisfying. The hacker hums to himself as the elevator takes him up to floor seventeen, where the meeting is scheduled to take place.

His phone buzzes in the brown pockets of his shorts. Again, it's Welch. *Where r u?*

Alfonso slams the phone back into his pocket and sighs. What an annoying man. He wonders how someone like Welch even made it into an executive position. Alfonso hasn't once thought Welch was funny, charming, smart, or wise since he's been working here.

Another thing the hacker can't stand about Welch is that he always seems to be in a positive mood. He's always smiling, always hyper and optimistic. And the man has no sense of personal space. He breaks anyone's bubble, his breath either smelling fresh and minty as if he brushed his teeth twelve times a day or laden with the stench of coffee.

Alfonso pays attention to things. He's observant by nature. After all, to be a winner in all the games where he's crushed his peers, a vigilant eye is needed. He knows that his people skills aren't exactly on par, but he doesn't care. He likes himself the way he is, and it doesn't bother him that he's different.

He finishes the candies in his pocket just as he opens the door to room 1706; six pairs of eyes ruin his peaceful composure. He gets a bit red in the face and feels prickles on his skin as he begins to perspire.

Welch is standing at the end of a long, glossy wooden table, in front of a white projector screen. He clears his throat. "Please sit, Mr. Gordon, so we can begin."

Alfonso takes the only chair that's left and sits to Welch's right at the head of the table.

"Simon, play Red Fist 026," Welch commands loudly to some invisible AI.

A robot-like voice comes down from the ceiling: "Playing Red Fist 026."

The lights in the room grow dim, and Welch moves off into the corner. The video reel begins with the camera shaking all around, and then it focuses. A man is standing to the left on the screen, leaning all of his weight on a crutch. He's smirking at the camera, and his left hand is resting on top of the head of a dark-haired individual who is seated and seems to be unconscious.

The standing man begins to talk. "Hey guys," he says with a smile. "Red Fist here. If you guys are wondering why I don't have my voice altered, it's because the Feds know who I am. No point in hiding." He takes a handgun from the holster on his right side and transfers it to his left hand, standing a little more upright.

Alfonso remembers that the man's first name is Ali, and he knows the man's mother's first name as well, but the two do not share the same last name. After his own personal searches, Alfonso doesn't think Ali has a last name that sticks.

Ali points the gun at the seated man's head. "FBI, CIA, whoever. I'm going to keep this short and simple. I want my little brother back, or this guy dies. We'll make a trade. Tonight. If you fail to comply, things will get ugly." He taps the guy on the head with the butt of the pistol and the man raises his head, showing his face to everyone.

Alfonso recognizes him. It's one of the agents that stayed glued to Welch. Alfonso erupts internally. *Damn Red Fist made their moves fast.*

Ali continues. "I want to remind you all of the last time you failed to negotiate with us. I believe you're still missing a senator. The details are in this man's apartment, on his cell phone. You have eight hours from the time this is posted on the Internet to respond. Stay strong, guys, we're working hard for you all. Red Fist out."

The video blacks out and the lights in the room glow once again with their former brightness.

Welch takes a sip from his glass of water and shakes his head. "That was Agent Jung. They've taken my guy." Alfonso sees that for the first time, Welch is frustrated, maybe even angry.

"We need a plan," Welch says. "Suggestions. I've asked all you here because you're the leaders behind the task force tackling these terrorists. This can be an opportunity for us to make a move on them."

Across from and to the right of Alfonso, an older white lady, who has one of those pinched faces that always seems irritated, raises her hand to gain everyone's attention. She looks like a witch to Alfonso because of the hooked nose clawing down her face, and her graying blonde hair. He doesn't know this lady's position, but according to Welch, she is essential. Alfonso doesn't care what any of them have to say. He already has a plan.

"Sir," the woman says, "I know you care greatly for the people under you, but this may be an opportunity to erase them all."

"Helen, are you insane? Wage a small war? They'd send another group to antagonize us the very next day. We need negotiation. We don't even know the location of where we'll be meeting them."

A bald, young-looking white man on Alfonso's side of the table speaks up. "But we also need an asset. We need the one on the screen. Or at least another member of Red Fist that knows more about their organization than the boy." The man's hands are clasped together. His lips are pressed into a tight smile on his face, and his frosty blue eyes are peculiarly striking.

"I don't think they would agree to that, Richard," says the man in between Alfonso and Richard. He has sand-colored hair and the same hefty build as Alfonso, although he dresses more professionally. He even has his mustache and goatee trimmed. Alfonso thinks his glasses are too small for his fat face and look as if they're trying to jump off; the man holds them at bay every so often by pushing them back up his nose. Alfonso immediately dismisses the man's presence and decides he'll ignore him for the rest of the meeting.

Welch speaks up once again. "Here's what we have. We have Levi Conoway. Son to the police officer, Alice Rodriguez, and apparently son to one of the leaders of Red Fist, according to the CIA."

"And?" It's Helen.

"The CIA had an investigation of their own going on, and the information between them and us is limited. Our partnership on the matter is insignificant, but according to the CIA, Levi's father is an ex-soldier, Special Forces. Apparently, he went MIA eight years ago. He was presumed dead, but the CIA has him down as one of the leaders of this organization. If that's the case, then he's not going to let his son stay in our custody for long." Heads nod all around the table. "I believe they will negotiate with us."

"Why don't we just keep him and work with the CIA to get to the big dog," Richard suggests. "We take him down, everything crumbles."

"You had better know, like all of us, that Red Fist has more than one leader."

Helen curses under her breath. "We need more information from the CIA. How did they even confirm the relationship between the two? How do we know this is true?"

"They have a mole."

Helen shakes her head. "It's amazing the talent the CIA finds."

Welch looks to Alfonso. "So, Mr. Gordon, I assume I know why you've been so quiet."

Everyone looks at Alfonso, and his skin flares up again with that uncomfortable itch he gets when unwanted attention rolls over him.

Welch smiles. "Okay, then, we're all ears. Let's hear it. How can we catch Red Fist off guard and get what we want?"

Alfonso cheers for himself on the inside, even though he'd rather die than be in the spotlight. This entire ordeal with Red Fist wanting their chess piece back is great because now he can take the game more seriously, and get into it for real. He can deliver a blow that could possibly be crippling.

Alfonso picks himself up out of the chair and stands next to Welch, who is eyeing him curiously. He takes a deep breath, and on the exhale says with a shrug, "Well...we don't." And the rest of his brilliant idea flows from his lips.

Red Fist is undoubtedly in for a surprise.

24.

Union Station, Washington, D.C.
2:25 A.M. Saturday

Welch is followed by Dragon, Frankie, the one-eyed CIA agent, and two other CIA agents. They're holding a blindfolded Levi as they go through the unlocked door and enter the upper level of Union Station. The lights are off, but they spark to life when Welch and his group come in. Their steps echo on the glossy floors, the sound rising up and bouncing off the surrounding white archways with gold lining. Majestic-pillars loom over them, holding up the ceiling.

Standing still, toward the back of the room, is a shadow by the closed gates that lead to the lower levels and metro trains of the station: Red Fist.

Welch had not expected to see them so soon. He stops suddenly, and so does everyone else behind him. It's been a long time since he's been in the field. He feels an unusual sensation in his chest; it explodes, branching out all over his body. Excitement? Anticipation? Welch can't pinpoint how he feels; he just knows he needs this operation to go smoothly. The last thing he needs is for things to get heated and for blood to be spilled. This should be a simple transaction. Smooth and easy.

He takes a step forward, scanning the six people ahead of him. He spots Jung, also blindfolded, his mouth taped shut. He seems okay for the most part, but Welch can tell that the Red Fist members have done some beating on him: his skin is bruised and blue where it should be tan, and his lip is busted.

They begin to move forward, and all Welch can hear is the cadence of their footsteps. He unclenches his fists as they get closer and closer to Red Fist. He reminds himself that he must stay calm. He knows what they want, and he knows what he wants. Finally, after what seems like hours to Welch, the two groups meet in the middle. They stop about ten feet away from each other. The leader of the terrorist group and Welch burn holes into each other as their eyes meet.

Ali points to Levi. "Take his blindfold off."

Welch can see that Red Fist is already working on Jung. After motioning for his men to do as the man requested, he grabs Levi by the arm and brings him forward, along with Dragon. "As you can see," he says to Ali, "he's unharmed."

Ali squints. "Looks like you beat the shit out of my baby brother. Why is there a bandage on his hand?"

Welch shrugs. "That's not the main concern. Let's get this over with."

"Of course." Ali pushes Jung forward, letting him walk on his own, and Welch does the same with Levi.

The two hostages pass each other in silence, and that's when it happens. Everything and everybody stops. The air in the station grows stale, lifeless. Welch can hear his blood raging a war through his veins.

"What the fuck are you doing, Welch?" Ali roars.

Dragon steps forward and aims his gun at Levi's head, motioning for Jung to keep walking. Levi pauses, and Dragon takes hold of him. Frankie and his two agents have their guns pointed at Red Fist before any of the members can react, and they're frozen as the three men skirt around them, making sure they don't try to pull out their weapons.

As soon as Jung has passed by him, Welch answers Ali. "We just want you or the big guy to come with us."

Ali pulls out his own gun, despite Frankie's warnings. "You're not gonna kill us. Give Levi back and leave."

The other members of Red Fist draw their weapons. It's a standoff. Welch doesn't want blood on his hands. They could win the gunfight from their positioning alone, but they'd still lose two, maybe three men before the bullets stopped flying.

Welch stands firm. "Just comply with our demands, there doesn't have to be any unnecessary bloodshed."

Ali looks like he's about to spontaneously combust. "You started this, Welch. I swear I'll kill *you* at least."

Welch sighs, playing his part. "Back off!"

Dragon pushes Levi forward, and Frankie and his men back up slowly, forming a huddle around Welch and Jung. When Levi reaches Ali, and his hands are free, he turns around to give Welch the finger. Welch's heart burns with rage,

Ali frowns at Welch, repulsed by him. "Get out of here."

Welch doesn't know what to say. He is conflicted. How can a group like that show compassion? How can they have so much power to do as they please? Why do they show no fear? Welch cannot answer his own questions.

He wraps his arm around Jung, and as his group heads for the door, he smiles. At least Red Fist will believe that the FBI did not get all that they wanted. All Welch wants now is for Levi to get back home safe and sound.

***

Jung looks up at Welch, who seems merry. He wonders why the man is in such a good mood. Jung feels something he hasn't felt in a long time. Something archaic. Something dense that grinds into his gut. Shame. He fortifies himself once again and grins, remembering who welcomed him with open arms when the world was trying to toss him aside, remembering who is giving him the chance to break everything the way he wishes.

PART TWO

The Difference in Skins

25

Four Days Later

The fluorescent lights shine too brightly as I walk into the room and sit up on the bed, waiting for Dr. Murano, our own personal doctor. I told Ali and the others everything that happened to me. I told them how I fought three CIA agents and got my ass beat. I told them about that one-eyed fuck, and Welch, and that basically, all the Feds wanted was more information. They can't catch us.

We had all laughed after my story and celebrated my return. I know that Red Fist can't be beaten by the government, with its competitive, frail system of bureaucratic bullshit and mind control. I begin to laugh to myself as Dr. Murano walks in with a clipboard in her hand, eyeing me questionably.

"Feeling better today, Levi?"

I nod with a slight smile as Dr. Murano places her clipboard down. She begins rummaging through cabinets. It's still so amazing to me how Red Fist has managed to have this entire apartment building converted into their base of operations, with specialized rooms for training, living quarters, and even medical examinations and procedures. I belong here.

Dr. Murano steps up to me, looking into my eyes. Her reddish-brown hair is up in a messy bun, and her warm hazelnut-colored eyes ease their way inside my mind.

"Close your eyes," she says. "All right," I hear her say, feeling the soft touch of her hand on my hand, and then my nose, which she put back in place. It was a bloody mess. "I need you to remain very still and very calm."

Uneasiness drips down into my gut, and I shift uncomfortably.

"Everything's fine," Dr. Murano reassures me.

I don't even feel the needle prick. Fear rampages through me, and I try to resist the cold that's creeping up my veins towards my brain. My body, from bottom to top, goes numb fast. I breathe out; there's a monkey in my throat, squeezing my windpipes. When I do manage to release a full breath, I see a cold mist leave my mouth. Terror racks my soul as a familiar darkness grabs hold of my heart.

Dr. Murano's distant voice fades into nothingness. I'm like a rock, sinking into the ocean, motionless and stiff, pregnant with doubt, and regressing downward into my mind, back to that place where the other me is.

A cobra-like arm coils around my neck, constricting tightly. It's the original Levi, strangling me from inside his cage. I claw at his arm, trying to get it from around me. I dig into the opaque darkness, my feet feeling wet, and I push forward, hearing his face bang up against the bars. I do this repeatedly until his grip weakens and I break free. I take a couple of deep breaths, silencing the anxiety in my heart.

I turn around to see the shadow of the person I used to be. Weak, scrawny, brittle, nothing but bones. I smile. **"You really thought you could beat me?"**

The pathetic Levi is vain, but he still manages to drag himself up. Even through the darkness, I can tell his eyes are slicing daggers through me.

"You wanna fight, punk? I guess it's time I got rid of you for good. You've been holding me back."

He laughs. *"What? Holding you back? You're afraid of me."*

"You're delusional. Without me out here, you'd be dead by now. You'd be hopeless, a nobody. I got us into Red Fist. I'm the one putting in the work, trying hard so we can see Dad. So we can help the world."

The caged and defeated Levi turns his back to me, resting on the bars.

I rush forward and grab his shoulders. **"Turn around when I'm talking to you."**

"I can always hear you anyway."

"Turn around!"

He flips on me, grabbing me by my soggy shirt. He puts his face to the bars, his teeth bared, his eyes—my eyes—seething with…strength? Anger? What is that in his eyes? It's radiating off of him in waves. He's *stealing* from me.

"Look at you," he hisses, *"so afraid of being weak. So afraid of yourself and your decisions that you're losing yourself."*

I pull away from him, but his grip on my shirt grows stronger. **"Get off me. I don't need you."**

He rumbles again with laughter. He's all of everything it takes to be nothing. Grotesque. Antique. And yet he finds me funny?

"It's not that you don't need me. We need each other."

"You're weak. You can't do the hard things when they need to be done."

"I'm not weak. It's just that you're stronger than me because you lack something human."

155

I curl my fingers around the bars and press my head into them; our noses smash together.

"What?"

"True empathy. You're ruthless."

"Rather be ruthless than dead."

"My mom—"

"*Our* mom."

The other Levi looks down and drops his hand from my shirt. *"If you hurt her, I swear I'll kill you."*

"When you say that, look me in the face."

He pushes his face up against the bars even harder, and our eyes mesh once again. *"I'll kill you. I swear it. If you hurt my mom, I'll be sure to end everything."*

I smile and turn around, walking away, looking up at the cracks of light breaking through this insanity.

He screams at me. *"Did you fucking hear me?"*

I put my hand up, waving goodbye, the light now reaching down to cup me in its palm. As I float up, I stare down at the old Levi, the one who's looking up at me with pure disgust and hatred. The feeling of animosity I get from him gives me a high, it makes me feel alive. I wave at him again before I disappear from that fragile part of my mind that I intend to corrupt to the fullest extent of my power.

26

Ali downs the rest of his whiskey before he sits down in between Ghost and Bear on his couch. Sugar is standing in the kitchen area. Dr. Murano is sitting in the recliner chair and appears to be looking at the TV although there's nothing on it.

"Levi's asleep," Ali tells the group, nodding at Dr. Murano. "So, final results?"

The woman clears her throat. "I didn't see any major signs of this when I originally examined him during his processing into our organization. I assumed it was hormones, so I thought nothing of it and just made notes. I will say before I get to the unexpected part of this discussion that he's in the clear. I didn't find any traces of bugs, or any signs of major damage done to his body. He's golden on that front."

Ali smiles, happy his little brother is safe and sound, back with his family. He never really thought he'd grow so attached to the guy.

157

Dr. Murano looks Ali in the eye, catching the drift of his mind. "Perhaps we should let your father know as well."

Ali becomes annoyed. "What is it?"

She sighs, shaking her head. "It seems Levi has dissociation identity disorder."

Ali looks at Ghost, who shrugs.

Dr. Murano smiles tightly at their lack of comprehension. "Multiple personality disorder. Split personality disorder, better known today as dissociation identity disorder."

Ali throws his head back. "So he's a nutcase? Those fucking Feds did something to him."

Dr. Murano stands, pushing out her hands for Ali to calm down. "No, no, this seems to have always been a problem for him, it just wasn't so severe until recently."

"What do you mean?"

"The other personality has taken over for the time being. It hasn't been in control for too long, but long enough to suppress the real Levi."

"What's this other personality like?" Ali asks. "We can't have Levi on ops with us if he's unstable."

"Well, as far as I've confirmed, the other personality is harsher, stronger, and more violent than the real Levi. Most likely, it manifested as a response to Levi's feelings of weakness; it's a defense mechanism, in other words. His protector, so to speak."

"How long has the true Levi been gone?" Ghost asks.

Dr. Murano sucks in a quick breath. "It's hard to tell. Did any of you notice a change in his behavior? This new Levi is cruel. He lacks empathy. He's irritable, moody, somewhat more disrespectful."

Heads shake all around, and Dr. Murano lapses into deep thought.

Bear clears his throat to get the doctor's attention. "Is there a cure, anything we can do? Is there anything else we should be aware of?"

The doctor looks around the room with a dour expression. "There's the possibility that the new Levi has ulterior motives, so you guys should keep tabs on him. There's currently no cure, but there are methods and measures we can take to control the mental imbalance within Levi. Medication. Antidepressants. Talking. Therapy. But be warned, as far as I know, this new Levi seems to be following the old Levi's plan and is very keen, very observant, and he will almost certainly notice a change in your attitude towards him."

Ali balls his fists. "So, what should we do?"

"Just treat him like normal for now. I'll give him some medication that will help keep his emotions in check. And I'll also call him in periodically for therapy."

"And what happens if this new Levi goes off the deep end? What if he doesn't want the medicine?" Sugar questions from the kitchen.

"It's different with every person." Dr. Murano and Ali lock eyes briefly, and Ali can see that she's thinking of her bleak future. She's afraid. She knows what could happen to her if the operations they're running are ruined because of her initial failure to analyze Levi correctly.

Ali moves in on her, intimidating her with her presence. Dr. Murano can't tell why, but something about Ali truly frightens her.

"When he goes batshit crazy on an op, what do I do?" he asks.

The doctor recoils, steeling herself, unsure if she should even say what she's thinking. She is a doctor for Red Fist. She is an agent, but she has never killed. She has never been on an operation. She is a non-combatant, and to say these words is a surprise even to her.

"Do what you have to do for a mission to be a success," she tells him, her hazelnut-colored eyes becoming red, like her hair, embers from a flame, touching the world that is to be set on fire with chaos.

27

Alice rushes up behind a lumbering Alfonso, tapping his shoulder. "Sir?" He ignores her, continuing to walk as if she isn't there.

Alice is not about to quit. She has been tossed aside by the FBI, her father has given up on Levi, and what she has been doing ever since is stalking Alfonso. She needs information. She has been surveilling outside of where he lives for the past week or so. If the FBI has been watching her, then they have been watching him as well. He's crucial to their plans.

Alice had finally come up with the idea of dressing like a beggar.

"Sir?" she repeats.

"I don't have drugs, lady, and I don't want your services. Get out of here." Alfonso shoos her away with a hand.

"Mr. Alfonso Gordon."

Alfonso stops and turns around, his exhaustion-plagued eyes lighting up when he notices who is standing before him. He pulls out his cell phone and clicks a few buttons. "My bad, Alice. I'm running a loop now. I hope you haven't been seen by any of the cameras coming here. They're always trying to watch everyone, you know."

"There are probably agents holed up somewhere around here watching you, too." She smiles.

Alfonso stiffens, but Alice rests a hand on his shoulder.

The two go inside the apartment, and Alfonso goes straight to the fridge. "I'm getting a glass of milk," he says, "do you want something to drink?"

Alice declines, still floating around in his doorway. Alfonso's apartment looks like one would expect from a single, technology junky. Junk is strewn everywhere. Old computer monitors are arranged around his living room in their respective spots, some split open, with their guts pouring out.

The light in the living room is dim. Every now and then, it flickers. There is one couch, with a white crocheted mini quilt draped over it. It's a green couch, and Alice thinks it's ugly.

A small coffee table is littered with gadgets and documents, and in front of that, where a TV should be, is a rusty bicycle. The chain is slack, hanging loose, and the back tire is deflated.

Alice watches Alfonso search around in the fridge. He pushes around some things on his counter to make room for his milk. He grunts to gain Alice's attention, and she moves towards him.

"You can put that box on the floor, so you can sit down," he says, sipping his milk. "Oh, yeah, sorry about the mess." But he doesn't sound sorry.

Alice takes the unopened box and puts it on the floor carefully. She slides onto the stool, looking at the gadgets, papers, screws and junk spread across the countertop.

Alfonso does not like people in his home. He doesn't really understand why he even invited her in. Maybe he's becoming soft.

Perhaps he actually likes this woman. But he barely knows her. He shakes his head. What is he thinking?

"So, you want information?" he asks.

"Smart man."

He sips some more of his milk. "Hmm, maybe. I don't want to compromise my game—I mean job."

Alice giggles. "I need this, Alfonso. You're the only one I can turn to at this point." She expected to have to grovel more than this. She knows she has him.

Alfonso stares at her for a moment, taking her in. Despite himself, he blushes when they exchange brief glances. "Fine. I'll give you some information. I want to help you for some reason."

He places the empty glass onto the countertop and heads down the hallway, moving unusually fast. Alice sees that his kitchen is actually relatively clean. The light above the countertop has a loud and ominous hum. As she waits, her eyes move to the walls of the living room, and she notices that the man has nothing to show of family or achievements. He doesn't seem like the decorative type.

Alfonso returns with a folder, handing it across the counter to Alice. "In there are pictures of all the known members of Red Fist in this particular cell and the address of their base of operations. There's also a file on your son. You're going to want to check it."

Alice nods. "I heard you guys had returned Levi to them."

"Ah, yeah. I'm not the only friend you have." He laughs, which Alice finds strange. In as long as she has worked for the FBI, she has never seen him smile once.

"I thank you so much for this, Alfonso. You're so sweet, and I promise I will never forget this." Alice stands, extending her hand across the countertop.

The two shake and Alice feels the clamminess of the man's palm. Alfonso is mesmerized by how beautiful, and put-together Alice is after experiencing so much trauma.

She stands up and backs away a little. "I can let myself out. I really do appreciate this. You truly are an amazing person. A friend." She heads for the door and twists the doorknob.

"Wait!" Alfonso screams.

She turns from the door and gives him her full attention. Anything he has regarding her son, she wants.

"Listen. I'm not exactly sure when...but at that address...something big is happening in a few days."

***

FBI Headquarters
05:00

Welch stands in front of a crowd of agents, all shifting around anxiously. The front row consists of all his supervisors and the people he meets with daily to control his department within the FBI. Alfonso sits on the end of that row, staring off aimlessly.

Seeing the room before him filled with agents, Welch is suddenly overcome by nostalgia. He thinks of his past self, in their shoes, awaiting orders, awaiting possible glory and promotion for excellence. He knows how hard it was to climb to what he considers the top, but he also misses the exhilarating thrill of going on missions.

He watches his audience. This operation he's planning to set forth will not fail, he believes that in his heart. This time, for sure, they will capture someone valuable, someone with more information, someone who could bring them a step closer to knocking Red Fist off their pedestal. Welch wants the big dogs because once you get the big dogs, he believes, the puppies are yours for the taking. He grunts, his cue that he's ready to begin.

The tide of voices dulls into a curious silence, and all eyes rest on Welch, who has a white screen at his back. "Ladies and gentlemen, in a few hours, we will finally have won a round against Red Fist. I need you all to listen very carefully to every detail of this operation..."

28

10:00

Stumbling out of my room, stretching and yawning, scraping the clinging exhaustion off my body, my healing nose gets introduced to the smell of eggs. I swear it feels as if I've slept forever, but I still feel unrested. I pad into the kitchen area to see Ali standing at the stove.

"What's up, baby bro?" he says, giving me his usual sly grin. "I know you're hungry."

I look over his shoulder at the eggs frying in the pan. My stomach growls as the sizzling intensifies. He adds a dash of salt and pepper.

"You're cooking," I state, not having seen Ali in my minds-eye as someone who cooks anything at all.

Ali moves back a little and pulls the oven door open. The nose seduction that takes place in that instant makes my mouth water.

"Bacon, too. Wow, what's the occasion?" I ask, hopping up on the stool.

He shrugs and closes the oven door, turning around to face me, his eyes a bit inquisitive. "I don't know. Just felt like doing something different. I haven't cooked in a long time. And you're here, so I figured I'd do something nice. Wanna help?"

I look around and smile. I have to play nice. I can relax finally. Light is filtering in through the windows, brightening up everything, making this place feel so much like home. Being interrogated for a week was not fun.

Ali is still staring at me, waiting for my answer.

"Sure," I tell him, sliding off the stool. "What can I do, chef?"

He punches me in the shoulder, and I laugh, a little too hard. "Your taste buds will be begging for more, bitch."

Ali watches me a moment longer than he should. He's acting odd. He knows.

I reach for the bread on top of the refrigerator to make toast. I need to play it cool. It's difficult for me to act like the other Levi. "If I get food poisoning, I'll sue you."

"Fuck off." Ali turns the heat off under the eggs and gives me a harsh look, breaking into my bliss. I begin laughing immediately. He joins in, wrapping his arm around me as I'm trying to put the bread into the toaster. His arm tightens around me. Ali is trying to assert dominance over me; he's trying to tell me he's the boss.

"Stop it, motherfucker, I'm trying to make toast."

"You're the phony," Ali whispers in my ear. "I know it!"

I want to push him off, but I want him to trust me. An odd feeling flows up my spine. There's something foul about Ali. He reeks. He's depraved.

As I struggle to get out of his grasp, a new voice stops both of us in our tracks.

"Aw, this is too cute."

The white flash of a photo being taken blinds both of us. Ghost is standing outside the kitchen area, smiling at us. "You two are too fucking cute. Brotherly love melts my cold heart."

Ali pushes me away and turns back towards the stove, grinning. "You're annoying," he says to her.

Ghost shrugs and hops up onto the stool where I was sitting, "I hope you guys made enough for three."

Ali pops open the oven door again. "You can go fuck yourself. I didn't hear a knock. I didn't get a text."

He pulls the cookie sheet with the bacon on it out of the oven and lets it rest on the stove. The toaster dings, telling me the toast is ready. I place two of pieces on one plate and two on the other, nudging Ali in the shoulder. He takes the plates and loads them both with eggs and bacon.

My stomach growls again, and I see Ghost eyeing the food desirously. She stands, crossing her arms, giving Ali daggers, but he doesn't notice. He heads out of the kitchen and into the living room, where the news is playing on the TV.

I smile at Ghost awkwardly.

She follows Ali with her eyes and then looks at me. Those green gems plow too deep. I realize they all know. She focuses back on Ali. The guy would be dead if she had laser vision.

"I texted him," Ghost says to nobody in particular.

I move past her and into the living room, deciding that the best thing to do is to say nothing. She follows, plopping down into the recliner with an attitude. I watch the corners of Ali's mouth curve upwards and shake my head. Whatever's going on between these two is beyond me.

I tune into the news; the reporter is talking about the weather, predicting a slightly overcast day with a sixty-seven-percent chance of rain. I look out the window and see sunlight, doubting that it will rain today.

"…Thank you, Mark," I hear from the TV. "Now over to Cindy Caberolli for *This Just In!* Okay, Cindy, over to you."

The screen cuts to an average-looking woman with layers of makeup caked onto her face. She's standing outside, and wherever she's at I can see that it's definitely not sunny.

"Again, we want to remind all citizens living in the small neighborhood of Anglia that they should stay inside today because a gas pipe that could cause a massive explosion has been discovered to be damaged and protruding from its rightful place. Citizens are urged to stay out of the way of any law enforcement and to stay out of cordoned-off areas. Please stay safe out there, DC. Back to you, Adam."

Ghost and Ali are looking at each other intensely. Something is off. What is it?

Ali gets up suddenly. He moves to the window beside the TV and peers out. Ghost checks another window, her phone up to her ear.

Ali twists my way, waving at me to get up. "Time to prove your worth, phony. It's time for us to get out of here."

"What?"

"Fucking Christ, Levi. Do what I say. The fucking Feds have found us."

29

I jump up, immediately hearing the sounds of glass breaking in front of us. I watch the shards fall to the floor, then I'm airborne. Everything's in slow motion as I'm blown over the couch by a force so strong that my entire body flips, and I land on my shoulder near the kitchen counter. I hear more glass shattering, and then another boom, the blasts have my ears ringing.

Ali is screaming something at me, trying to haul me up. I push myself up, but he pushes me back down behind the couch. He's still yelling, but I can't hear a word he's saying. I try to tell him that I can't hear, but he's peeking over the couch.

Ghost crawls over to us. I look at her and point at my ears, shaking my head. She nods and then throws down her phone in frustration. I guess the Feds have cut our signal.

Ali makes a gun sign with his hand, looking at Ghost. She nods, looking worried. Ali is talking again, I think he's saying *door*. He and

Ghost move around me. When they crawl into the kitchen, I follow. Ali digs into a drawer and pulls out a gun, handing it to Ghost. We all start crawling towards Ali's room.

I peek back momentarily and see the shadow of a line outside one of the windows. Are the Feds coming? Are they really attacking? How did they find us?

While Ghost stays in the hallway, pulling security, Ali pushes open the bedroom door with his head, motioning for me to follow him. Inside the room, Ali places his palms against my ears with as much pressure as he can and then releases. His words finally start making sense to me as his voice barges into my ears. "Can you hear? Can you hear me?"

I tell him that I can.

He gets up and rushes to his closet, pulling out some kind of AR and putting on a thin bulletproof vest that's already stocked with magazines. He tosses me a vest and takes another to Ghost. He goes to a drawer and pulls out another gun, shoving it down into the waistband of his jeans. He then gets on all fours once again and pulls a case out from under his bed. In the case is a submachine gun, already loaded. He slides the weapon to me.

Just as I'm bending down to get it, I catch sight of a dark figure outside the window in my peripheral vision. "Ali, get down!"

Glass explodes as a person in full body armor and a helmet lands inside, pointing a shotgun around the room.

Ali and I are both lying on the opposite of the bed. The Fed doesn't have a clear sight on us yet. The submachine gun is beside me. I go for it slowly as the man moves around Ali's bed to get a better view of us. Just as my fingers are curling around the grip, I see Ali roll over onto his back, his AR aimed at the man. The guy hesitates, about to say something, but Ali doesn't, and drops him immediately, jumping up to double-tap him.

Ghost peeks inside from the hall. "Guys, we have to go."

Ali takes the dead Fed's earpiece and pushes me out of the room. In the hallway, I take a moment to breathe. This is my time to prove myself wrong. This is my time to show the other Levi that he needs me to survive. I smile. I'll show Ali my worth.

Ali pushes past me, opening the front door, his face a mask of rage. He checks both ways and signals that we'll turn right, away from the emergency exits. I take one last look at the apartment I shared with Ali, and my eyes catch a shadow under my bedroom door. Ali and Ghost have already slipped out. There's a Fed in my bedroom, probably coming in at the same time as the first one, but we didn't hear it.

I aim at the door and move towards it. I'm going kill whoever is in there. Whoever it is that decided crashing into our home was a good idea. I place a sweaty palm on the door handle and listen intently. The person inside isn't making any noise. I shouldn't just burst into the room because whoever's in there may be expecting me.

I step back and pull the trigger, unloading an entire magazine into the door. It slowly swings open, revealing nothing but bullet holes in the walls and in my dresser. My ears pick up on the sound of something like a marble rolling, and instinctively my eyes cut downward. Fuck. White noise. My ears are still resonating from the concussion blast earlier. My head is thumping, and now I can't see.

The Fed barrels into me, knocking me to the floor, and my gun flies away. I try to fight off the Fed, but being unable to see or hear is putting me at a disadvantage. I feel the person stomp on the hand that had held the submachine gun. They grab my left arm and yank it upwards. I feel as though my arm is being pulled out of its socket.

"Sir, I have one," the person says. "It's Levi—"

A gunshot cuts off the female's voice. Ghost is standing in the doorway. "Hurry up. Stay with us."

We're hiding in a service closet, all three of us cramped together. Ali keeps mumbling curses. Ghost is silent. And me? Well, I'm pissed I got bested earlier. I was so slow; so unprepared. I feel like a turtle right now.

Ghost sighs. "So, what are we gonna do, Ali? And Levi, don't worry about earlier, you're probably still sluggish after Dr. Murano's treatment."

That's right. That's why I feel slow.

Thought you were the strong one? You stole my body and can't even use it right. You're useless.

I'll be okay without you, weakling. I'm slow because of Dr. Murano.

Ali slides past me. "We gotta move. Everyone should know to meet at one of the safe houses." He opens the door and shoots out to the right. We're two floors up now, on the seventh. Instead of going down, we've been going up. "Take up the rear," he tells me. "Shoot anybody that looks like a Fed."

I fall in line as we enter another apartment. This one's empty, and there's nothing inside but dusty wooden floors and white walls. All our communications are still jammed. We can't check up on anybody else. We can't strategize. We're pinned down.

The windows here are all covered with blinds. I stay away from them, cautious about what might come through them.

Ali listens on the earpiece he jacked from the Fed he killed. "It seems like they're moving up from the first floor. They sent teams of four to six rappelling up to certain floors."

"So how come we haven't seen any more of them yet?" Ghost asks.

Ali shrugs, pointing at me and then at the front door. I lock it down. "They got Myla, and she's the only one who could have found a way to set off the bomb. None of our phones can send a signal to it."

"Who else?"

Ali ignores her question. "We need to get out of here. If we go to the roof, we'll be trapped. If we go down, we'll be captured." He runs his fingers through his dark hair, thinking out loud. "There are two stairwells on each side of every floor and one elevator. They're probably all occupied with Feds. Taking an emergency exit from the side of the building, or from some of the apartments, is also risky because we don't know what to expect."

"I'll be a decoy," Ghost says. "We can go straight down. At least we know what's there."

Ali rejects that idea with a shake of his head.

This can't be happening. The Feds can't win. My fun can't end. My mission isn't over. Not like this, not like a cornered rat. I want to fight. I glance at Ali. He's pacing anxiously, trying to figure out what to do. Ghost is leaning against a wall with her eyes closed. I wonder what Bear is doing. There's no way that mountain will let anybody catch him. I'm sure Sugar got away with everyone else, too. I've seen them all in action, and I can't imagine them being bested. But look at us; if we're in this situation, their predicament is probably the same.

"We need to group up with the others," I say.

"We don't know where they are," Ali almost screams, his voice coming out strained and edgy.

I smile. The badass, Ali, is losing his shit.

He regains himself. "We need a hostage," he says.

A little hope blossoms in my heart, but it doesn't last long. The door to the apartment is plowed down and a team of Feds storm in. The three of us turn around, our weapons aimed. The first one to enter the living room has a bulletproof shield, with the rest of them behind him. Ghost pops off some rounds at it anyway, but no effect is made. I keep my weapon aimed as we all back up against the wall, watching as the squad of five spreads out, locking us down with barrels pointed our way.

"Lower your weapons!" one of them commands.

Ali grins. "You forget," he says, banging his chest proudly, "we're Red Fist! We don't have to play by the same rules as you do. Shoot us!"

Nobody moves. I wonder if anyone else can hear my heart, it's so loud. Violence. All I can think about is violence. This time, I won't hesitate. I won't be weak. I won't be like the other Levi.

It gets so quiet in the room that I can hear when one of the Feds standing before us shifts uncomfortably. Three versus five isn't ideal, but if this is the place where we take a stand, then so be it.

The Fed in the middle of the group takes off his helmet. He looks like a proud man. He has sweaty black hair. His face is too spread out, and his eyes are big, his pupils a rich black. He's smiling at us, his lips pink and slim. He drops his helmet to the floor. He walks up to Ali and gets right in his face.

"You can't put us all in the same category. I just want you assholes dead."

Ali puffs up his body even more, his gun now at his side. If he shoots, there's a chance we could all end up dead.

The two men are facing each other. I feel a thickness in the room that's serpent-like, and it coils around me. I can't move. Not yet.

The Fed moves fast and unexpectedly. He head-butts Ali and wraps his arms around him, bear-hugging him.

I keep my aim at the other Feds, and so does Ghost.

"Get the fuck off him!" I yell as the Fed throws Ali to the ground. The Fed is six foot something and way bulkier than Ali. I look at Ghost, who sees me twitching. Her eyes tell me not to move.

The Fed is on top of Ali, smashing into his face with his fist. His massive fists rain down blows, and Ali is barely blocking them. The Fed finally grabs Ali's head and smashes it into the floor repeatedly until he doesn't move. The Fed jumps up, wiping the blood from his lips. "Fucker got me."

I look at Ali and tears well in my eyes. I wish he would move. He doesn't. Why do I care? *He's my brother!*

He looks dead. He's just lying there. Motionlessness. He's not dead. That's impossible. The Fed is staring at Ghost. She has her gun aimed at his head. I transfer my aim to the Fed as well.

"You look mad, little guy," he says, looking at me.

Why is this piece of shit so cocky? I can fucking blow his brains out.

"Lower that, kid," he says to me.

Ali, come on, move!

Shut up. I need to concentrate.

Ali still doesn't give any indication that he's alive. I can't even tell if he's breathing. "No," I say. "I'm gonna kill you."

The Fed motions to his team, and they move forward. I put my aim on one of the men, forcing him to stop. In my peripheral vision, I see hands making a grab for me. Ghost shoots and the guy trying to apprehend me falls to one knee. Before the others can get hold of me, I turn and dome him. The shield rips me off my feet, and a boot is shoved deep in my gut. I feel a sharp burn starting in my lower back, and then it's like I get struck by lightning as a jolt of electricity shoots through me. It rages through my body, humming in my ears.

When the current stops, my body deflates. I'm lying on the ground, shaking. I can't even move my fingers. I see that Ghost is getting the same treatment. Something pricks me in the neck.

From my position on the floor, I see Ghost looking my way, and I hear her scream as the same agony streaks through her. Her face is contorted with anguish as she rides the lightning and bucks involuntary. I can almost see the streaks of electricity running rampant through her. I watch gloved black hands inject her with something. I watch her green eyes flutter shut.

We lost. We—Red Fist—lost. Ali might be dead. I'm useless. I'm supposed to better than this. I'm fucking weak. I can't stand this. I can't fucking stand this. I batter myself with insults as I return to that familiar place where the other me lives; the me that is supposed to be weak.

This time I surface, floating in the black water right in front of his cage. He's sneering down at me.

"About time you let me get my body back."

"Fuck off!"

"Look what just happened."

"Same shit or worse if you were there."

The cage opens by itself. I stand up fast, slipping backward. He steps out, looking sickly compared to me.

"I think we both need to be out there," he holds out his hand.

I watch it float there in the darkness. Is taking that hand a good idea? Do I need this version of myself? He's the opposite of me. Does that create a balance? Or does it create an imbalance?

He's in my face. I see me through me. I see what I used to be and what I don't want to be. I see what I need and what I lost.

Balance or imbalance?

I don't know anything. I can't even think here. I need to get back. I need to make things right.

We lock hands, merging into one.

30

A hand is shaking me. I feel it move over my body. I hear a familiar voice. I feel like if I open my eyes, the light from the outside world will sear them out of their sockets. My head is throbbing. I feel like I'm the one who got his face beat in.

"Wake up, dammit." Ali is kneeling over me. Gauze is wrapped around his head, and he's smiling down at me.

Ghost is sitting against the wall, holding her stomach, her skin so pale she looks as if she's dying. I guess I look the same.

"I'm back," I tell Ali.

He nods, grasping my hand, his grip like iron. He pulls me up with him. I hold out my hand to Ghost. She takes it, and I lift her to her feet.

I see that everyone is here except for Myla and Jefferson. To the right of me, tied up against the wall, are the four remaining Feds that attacked us. One of them looks half dead; the other three just keep their heads down. The Fed I shot in the head is still lying where he fell. For a moment I want to kick him in the face. The urge to do that is so overwhelmingly strong that I bite my bottom lip.

Stop that. He's already dead.

One kick.

Listen, we need to be able to work together.

Whatever, Beta.

"Did we get all their shit off them?" Ali asks.

Bear points at the pile of weapons and gear nearer to Ghost.

"Cool," Ali says, kneeling next to the gear and inspecting it. "We were trying to figure out a way to get out of here. You guys got any suggestions?"

"We have the hostages," Ash says. "We need to contact their leaders and let them know that all their lives are in their hands."

Ali looks back at her. "You think Welch will let us go?"

She shrugs. "They're growing desperate. But it's worth a shot."

Ali picks up a grenade. Ghost stoops next to him, picking up the shield that took me off my feet.

Ali stands and turns towards everyone. "Do you guys know if any of them are above us? We need their current locations. We can't just walk around here with hostages. I don't want another standoff."

Everyone is deep in thought, trying to come up with a plan that will get us out of here as we are, without losing anybody else. My eyes slide over to the Feds' gear, their masks, vests, armor, helmets, and weapons. I think back to when they ambushed us in here the second time. I don't remember seeing any of their faces.

I spit out what I'm thinking. "Guys, we can become them. We can use their shit and get down."

Everyone looks at me and then at the Feds' gear.

"That's only five of us. What about the other two?" Asha says, crossing her arms.

"They can be our hostages," I say.

Ali begins to nod slowly. "It could work." He cranks his head towards the Feds, a sinister grin forming on his face. "We're gonna need more information from them first, though."

31

Alice doesn't waste any time when she hears the news about the gas pipe. She knows it's a ruse. She moves fast. She hops in her vehicle, sets down her coffee and speeds off onto the street.

Today is the day she gets to see her son again. She can save him. This time she can talk some sense into him.

She takes her fake FBI badge and ID from the glove compartment. She paid a lot of money for her identification so she can pass as the real deal. The FBI required that she released her government ID and badge when they kicked her to the curb. She knows that what she's getting ready to do is strictly against the law, but doesn't care. Levi is her son. *She* is responsible for him, not the government. Not the FBI. Not Red Fist. And not her father.

The police have been obligated to help the FBI with their search for Red Fist and apprehending them if that situation occurs. Alice couldn't get any information from anybody working the cases with the FBI because she didn't know who was. Her father forbade her from prying into the department's sensitive business, or the FBI's. He kept her in the dark intentionally and made sure none of Alice's colleagues were working on Red Fist.

Alice knows that her father just wants to protect her, but she wants to protect her own child in the very same way. She just wants Levi back. She knows deep down that he can be saved.

Red Fist is manipulating Levi, holding over his head the fantasy that his father is out there. But it can't be true. Her ex-husband has to be dead. Alice knows Alan would have come home if he were alive. He would have been there for Levi all those years when he needed a father. He wouldn't run off, go missing, or desert his country and become a leader of a terrorist organization

She shakes her head, clearing her thoughts. She pulls in near the curb about a block away from the yellow tape. She grabs her gun in case something goes astray, and starts a slow jog down the sidewalk. She slips under the yellow tape and is noticed instantly.

An agent snaps his head in her direction. Wearing body armor and a helmet, the full nine, he runs up to her, positioning his shotgun at the low ready. "Ma'am, you aren't allowed to cross through here. Please go back. It's very unsafe."

Alice pulls out her ID and shoves it in the guy's face.

He takes a step back. "Excuse me," he says, "the director didn't inform—"

"Listen, I'll have you suspended without pay for two weeks. I rushed over here as fast as I could. Now please let me through."

The agent shakes his head.

Alice gives a brief smile. Welch has an iron grip of loyalty within his agents. She needs to get past this man. She pulls out her phone, tapping her foot impatiently on the pavement. As the agent waits, she acts as if she's calling Welch but instead calls Levi's old number that no longer works.

"Dammit, Welch, answer the phone." She drops the hand holding the phone from her ear and begins to move past the agent. When he tries to stop her, she yanks away from him. "Get your hands off me. You can call Welch and tell him I'm heading his way."

Alice knows she doesn't have much time. Before she turns the corner, she can already see the agent talking on his earpiece. There are agents patrolling, looking out for anybody who could be Red Fist. She knows she's still about three blocks away from Red Fist's building and hurries down the street.

She pulls one of the female agents aside, asking her for an update. The woman looks a bit confused, looking Alice up and down. Alice shows the woman her ID, and luckily, the woman does not question Alice's position.

"Thank you," Alice says when the agent complies.

She flicks through the mental images of the Red Fist members in her head. Two have already been captured: a girl and the police station traitor, Jefferson. The others are still inside the building somewhere. She still has time to save her son. If she can just get to him and take him away from the others, everything will be fine. She doesn't care about the repercussions.

Alice has read her son's file. She now knows he has dissociation identity disorder. She never knew; the doctors she'd taken him to in the past just said he had a mild case of anger issues and ADHD. Alice grimaces as she hustles down the street, her boy is mentally unstable, none of this is his fault. The young man who did all those terrible things wasn't her son.

She needs to get into Red Fist's base. She shakes her head when she realizes it will be practically impossible. She feels like an ugly duckling right now. Almost everyone except for those sitting in the armored vehicles is wearing armor. If she goes near an entrance or the front of the building, she will get called out immediately. She's not sure if anyone she used to know while serving with the FBI will notice her, and she'd rather not take any chances.

Alice stumbles to the edge of an alleyway, sure she's on the path to the back of the building. What is Red Fist doing right now? She needs information more than anything. She needs to know where Red Fist is, and what the FBI is doing currently to capture them. With all these agents around, even if Red Fist did manage to make it out of the building, they would not get far.

She watches the men and women move back and forth, their heads seemingly on a swivel, a couple eyeing her meticulously. Generally, the agents all look the same, and for that reason, Alice makes an assumption. She can only think of one scenario where the members of Red Fist make it out uncuffed and still breathing.

She breaks away from the shadows of the alley and moves towards the front of the building. She needs to find where the prisoners are currently being held. She needs to find Welch.

***

Inside the armored vehicle, Welch shakes his head. So far, there are twelve agents confirmed dead on this raid, and another squad of five unaccounted for. He needs this whole operation to be wrapped up quickly. If not, the casualties will just keep stacking up. He can't help but admire the might of Red Fist in this situation. Anybody else other than them would have been snagged at this point. Deep in thought, it takes loud banging on the window to gain his attention. He opens the door.

Words begin to spill out of Dragon's mouth. "We have an update, sir. Two more members of Red Fist have been apprehended."

Welch perks up, jumping out of the vehicle. "Have we confirmed the identities?"

"From our records, it shows that one of them is the ringleader of this cell, the one called Ali, and the other is…gigantic. We've yet to confirm his real identity, but judging by his size, it's been speculated that he's been in several Red Fist videos."

"Good, which squad got them?"

The pair begins to move towards the area where they're keeping Myla, or "the Red Fist hacker girl," as Alfonso likes to call her, and the traitor, Jefferson.

"Reaper Squad just radioed it in, sir," Dragon says.

Welch stops and grabs him. "They went dark on us after they radioed in about possibly finding Red Fist members thirty minutes ago. We heard a few gunshots. And no casualties were reported?"

"They just reported in, sir. Said one was wounded pretty badly."

"I know that. Get them on the line now. I need to know now why they haven't been responding to us. Something isn't right."

Dragon moves away, and Welch glares at the apartment building that his agents are swarming. The building has seen better years. The sky around it is gray, and more clouds are ganging up over the location. Welch gets an uneasy feeling in his stomach. He is sure that something unexpected is coming, something that isn't good for him, or this operation.

32

Clouds are above us, threatening a storm, as we push into the open, out of our hectic home to an audience of Feds, all looking our way, speculating, calculating; some are even smiling. But most are emitting hostility. Their eyes are filled with venom as they stare at our "prisoners". We head towards the vehicle where Jefferson and Myla are supposedly being held.

"Go, Reaper Squad!" someone yells out.

We're surrounded on all sides. An aisle straight to the prisoners' truck is formed, and we are the center of attention.

I hold my head high as I tighten my grip on Ali. He resists, and I push him back in the direction I want him to go, shocking him with a handheld Taser for effect. The Feds have to believe we're the real deal, or this plan of ours will go sideways. We're surrounded, and we're outnumbered. If we try to fight all of them, we will die, and if we don't get mowed down with bullets, we'll be captured.

Sugar is leading us, with Bear as his prisoner, and I'm right behind him with Ghost, Ash, and Asha following in a little huddle. From my perspective, everyone around us looks like us, which means they can't see what we really look like. I was worried because four out of the five real Reaper Squad members had lighter skin than four of us, and only one of them was female.

The downside to this act is if the wrong person sees us or tries to speak to us. Our cover will be blown. We'll have to resort to plan B.

The FBI has a long black truck with big yellow words written on the side: *Federal Bureau of Investigation*. Most of the Feds continue going about their activities as we pass them by, and I'm relieved.

Suddenly Ghost moves up beside me, whispering, "Three o'clock."

Thunder rumbles overhead, and I turn my head causally to see a woman charging right at us, almost in a sprint. Heads are turning her way. My heart begins to race because it's not just any woman. It's my mom. She's about thirty meters away from us, and the only one not wearing protection of some sort. She sticks out, drawing attention, and she's heading straight for us.

Sugar looks back and sighs. "Welch and his lackey are by the truck, waiting. They're beginning to move our way. We can't go there."

I hear him, but my eyes are on my mom. Her eyes go from us to the prisoners' truck, and she changes direction, going towards Welch.

Ali starts to cough, and he falls to his knees. I let him go and kneel next to him, motioning for Ghost to point a weapon at him. "What are you doing?" I ask.

"Making a scene. It looks like your mom knows who we are. Listen, Welch must know something's up. We're gonna go with plan B."

I nod and check Ali as if I missed a wound.

Welch is speaking into his earpiece, and around us, I begin to see Feds close in on us.

My mom jumps in front of Welch, surprising him. He steps back and holds up his hands. She lays into him. She's distracting him for us?

This was a shit plan.

"Do it now," Ali says. "We'll have to leave Myla and Jefferson for now."

I'm drenched in sweat. Three smoke grenades aren't going to be enough. There are too many Feds here. I'm already shaking my head as the sky roars, and we burst into a plume of purplish smoke.

33

Pure rage stiffens Welch as he pushes Alice aside and screams into his mic, "Everyone that's not Reaper Squad—I repeat, that's *not* Reaper Squad—it's Red Fist. Capture them. Shoot to kill if necessary. Don't let them get away."

Dragon begins to run into the smoke, but Welch tells him to stop. Alice is grabbed by Welch. "What the hell are you doing here?" he says through clenched teeth.

Chaos breaks out around the agents as they scurry around trying to figure exactly where Red Fist is. Everyone looks alike, and the smoke screen doesn't help, either.

Welch doesn't hear Alice's answer over the gunfire, but he doesn't care. He just knows that he has terrorists to catch and that she got in his way at the precise moment he was about to act on the suspicion that the Reaper Squad that walked out those front doors wasn't his Reaper Squad.

He takes the handcuffs from his belt, tightens his grip on Alice's wrist and handcuffs her to him.

"You're staying with me. You can't be trusted," he snaps, his anger ever growing. He knows he needs to calm down or everything will get out from under him even more. "Lead out," he says to Dragon. "I have an idea. I can't keep playing by the rules."

Dragon slips into the smoke that has spread far and wide, the density of it beginning to dissipate as it mixes with the firm, steel-colored clouds. Welch has a hand on Dragon's shoulder and drags Alice with him. Gunshots are still being fired, and information on Red Fist is coming over the radio in waves. Everyone is confused, but one piece of information sticks out. Welch is going to have to cut his losses. It seems that Red Fist has split up, and the two that were not in uniform have made it two blocks away.

They clear the smoke and Welch taps Dragon on the shoulder. They duck behind an FBI vehicle. Welch is sick and tired of Red Fist having their way. They have been winning. His reputation will be shot if he loses them, especially with the casualties he's taken. The Red Fist members in uniform will likely get away, that's a given. With the pandemonium around, they'll slink away smoothly, but Welch can't let the other two just mosey on out of his box.

He gets on the mic. "Everyone, capture the two Red Fist members *not* in disguise. Shoot to kill if they resist. Do not waste any effort on the ones in disguise. Do not hesitate."

Dragon looks back at Welch, his eyes questioning his superior's orders.

Welch swallows. "I know, Dragon, but we need to show them that they can lose, too. That this soil isn't their playground."

***

I'm sitting with Asha and Ghost in the dark recesses of an alleyway behind a restaurant, our confirmed meeting spot. When I hear Welch's command over the radio, I let out a sharp breath. Sugar and Ash haven't shown up yet.

"We have to go back," I say, standing.

Ghost takes hold of my hand, staring at me with her emerald-green eyes and shaking her head.

"They'll kill them," I almost scream.

Asha stands as I pull away from Ghost and jumps in front of me, her stinging palm fiery hot, stopping me in my tracks. "This isn't a game. Everyone knows the risks in what we do. We can't go back."

"That's my brother…"

Asha scrunches her nose up, her dark eyes a mixture of dejection and indignation. "They're my family, too, but we cannot go back."

Switch, Beta. They aren't gonna let you go.

I need Ali.

I know. Switch.

I push past Asha, and she twists my arm behind my back, but I twist with it, getting behind her and using my momentum to shove her against the cold brick wall, jerking her arm upwards. She squeaks out in pain. I'm stronger. I put fear in her. "I'll break it."

"Levi!"

It's Sugar. He and Ash are walking up silently.

"Let her go, man," Sugar warns, aiming at me with his gun.

I release Asha, and she whirls on me. "We're *family*. We don't fight."

I begin to smile because she looks like a hurt puppy. The hurt in her eyes is real, and I can't distinguish if it's because I really did try to break her arm, or because she really is down about our "family" situation right now. I don't care. I want to save the one guy who isn't afraid of anything. I want to save him because he actually has balls.

"And family doesn't leave family to die in the streets like dogs," I retort.

Sugar and Ash are blocking my exit. Ghost and Asha are behind me. I can't get out. They'll overpower me. I want to fight them. I want to break their bones. I want them to move.

"Please. Move," I say to Sugar.

Sugar shakes his head. "We're safe here. We'll wait a little longer then go to the safe house. We need to figure out how the Feds found us."

Before I can argue, gunfire rattles my brain. My mic is open. I don't close it. I hear a voice: "Targets in our sight, one injured—" The transmission is cut.

Another. "Closing in, we got them this time—"

"See, Bear and Ali are perfectly capable of handling their own." Sugar rests a hand on my shoulder. "They'll make it back to us. We don't have time, you're jeopardizing everyone and the mission of Red Fist as a whole right now by acting like a child."

My whole body is hot. The FBI getup I'm wearing is sticky, restricting. I need to punch something. I need to release this aggression on someone. My fists have their own heartbeat, and I see that Sugar is watching me intently. He thinks he can stop me. I'll show him. I'll show him. I'm about to, but Beta calms me. He mixes in with me, sharing the mind.

"Whatever," I say. "Sounds like they're being executed."

Ghost wraps her arms around my waist and whispers in my ear, "Ali will be okay. He's the strongest out of all of us, and you have to be strong for him, too. They'll make it back to us."

I turn to Ghost and see that her green diamonds are shattered, broken shards that are contaminated. She's lying. She doesn't believe her own words. They see everything around us, taking in the situation, and they don't look sure of what she just said.

I punch the brick wall next to me instead of someone's face.

The softer side of me takes Ghost's hand as the sounds of gunfire hang in the sky like a phantom, waiting to plunge down on us and tell us that Ali and Bear are dead.

191

34

Two Days Later

Ghost sits up in the darkness from her slouched position in the tiny, cramped one-bedroom apartment. The walls are the kind of ugly white that comes when a place is roach infested and cheap, a place with blotches of an even uglier white with holes behind them that the owners tried to fill in halfheartedly. The safe house is a dump. Red Fist upgraded the security around the shithole and placed a code lock on the door when they first came to the city.

Ghost wishes they'd made more of an effort to furnish the interior. Occupying the only chair there, she faces the door. Her back is aching. She stretches out her legs, her shoes grunting over the coarse carpet, and she sighs loudly. This is the fifth safe house they've jumped to in two days. She can't stop seeing Ali and Bear dead in the streets, with

FBI agents pouring around them, looking at them with blood-lusted eyes, merciless, full of pride.

She can't stop thinking about how she doesn't believe she will ever see Ali again. She can't stop herself from crying. She is up alone at three in the morning, being the lookout in case the Feds come, or Bear, or Ali, or the doc. She cries quietly, only wiping her tears when she hears the beeps as the security code is punched in. Somebody is trying to get out. She looks up.

"Levi? What are you doing?"

"You're crying. Let's go save him. I know you didn't believe what you said."

She slides out of the chair and steps towards him cautiously. If she's honest with herself, the guy kind of frightens her. His mental disorder makes him so unpredictable. She has to stay wary after what she saw him do to Asha.

"Go back to bed."

Levi ignores her and Ghost moans, striking like a cat with the handheld Taser, bringing him to his knees. Sugar comes out of the back room at the sound of Levi's cry, and Ghost glances at him. "We need the doc. He's getting worse. We can't keep shocking him."

"I know."

"Sugar, how much longer are we going to wait?"

"Another twenty-four hours. If nobody shows, we leave the country for a while."

Ghost drops her head, struck by a sword in her gut. She staggers to the side. She can't believe this. If Ali, Bear, and the doc haven't shown up yet, then they most likely will not. Myla and Jefferson were captured, and no one but Myla has the skills to track them down. She's losing everything again.

Sugar comforts her. "They will show."

Before Ghost can deny Sugar's false hope, three back-to-back knocks ring in her ears, and then three more, separated by a two-second pause. Sugar springs forward, punching the code into the door and swinging it open. Ghost is flooded with joy. She squeals out so loudly that Asha and Ash come out from the back with their pistols ready to rock.

Bear and Dr. Murano push through the door. Bear is leaning on the doctor, struggling to hold himself up. She sits him in the chair that Ghost had jumped out of and kneels next to him.

Someone flips on the lights. Sugar closes the door, and Ghost's joy is shot down by a missile. Ali will not be joining them. Her heart explodes.

Sweat is all over the giant's face, and his skin is ashen. His breathing is labored, but he smiles at the group, weakly saying "family" in his native language.

Dr. Murano digs in her bag, searching for something. She sticks a needle in Bear's arm and pushes some fluid into his veins. "This should help the pain subside again."

"Where's he hurt, Doc?" Ash crouches next to her, rubbing Bear's knee.

"He took five bullets protecting Ali, two in his right shoulder, one in the back of his left thigh. I'm not going to get technical on you guys, but the bullet in his thigh is what's doing the most damage. The other two were through and through in his midsection, fortunately missing major organs. His right shoulder will be okay, but he won't be able to use it properly for the rest of his life. I don't know if he'll be walking unassisted again if I can't do proper surgery soon."

"We have to leave." Ash stands, staring at Sugar.

Sugar nods. "Everyone, start packing your things. Doc, do you know where Ali is?"

Dr. Murano sighs. "I only escaped because the Feds weren't worried about me. They were after Ali and Bear. When Bear shielded Ali the first time, he went down. When the Feds came, Ali killed five of them and helped Bear up. The second time, they were almost out of the cordoned-off area when they got shot at again. Somehow Bear shielded Ali again. Bear passed out. I watched Ali drag him into an alley and then run off towards the Feds, shouting. I had on a uniform from one of the dead men in our building, so I just ran up and gave Bear an adrenaline shot, and we escaped. I honestly don't know where Ali is."

Bear stirs. "Ali is alive," he says. "He told me to keep his little brother safe until he gets back."

Ghost looks away, not wanting anyone to see her cry.

Levi is staring angrily at Bear. He's about to say something but then snaps his mouth shut and walks away, stopping in the doorway that leads to the back room. He looks back at everyone with a grim, severe expression on his face. "Stop protecting me like I'm some useless kitten. I don't want or need your help," he tells them and then disappears into the back room.

"What are we going to do about Myla and Jefferson?" Ash says. "Ali, too, assuming they decided to capture him. And before everyone forgets, we don't know how the Feds found us. Me and Sugar were thinking they bugged Levi somehow."

Dr. Murano nods. "Yes, I've been thinking about that. With the current technology out, the only reasonable thing they could have done is bugged his digestion system for me to not have found it. He had to have eaten something while in their hands. That's the only thing that wouldn't have shown up when I checked him. I didn't even consider it."

"He should've used the bathroom by now." Ash looks towards the bathroom.

The doctor nods and gets up. "If he hasn't, then he needs to."

Bear calls for Levi. He comes out of the back room, leaning against the wall, and the doctor goes up to him and whispers in his ear. He nods, closing his eyes, no doubt blaming himself for everything. He lashes out at the wall.

Bear is quick to dig into him. "Stop acting like a child. Things happen. Man up. Your brother would hate to see you like this."

Levi's eyes grow dark, and he starts towards Bear. Everyone inches closer together, guarding Bear.

Levi stops. "What?"

Ghost holds up her hands. "You need to calm down, little bro."

"Why are you guys acting like you're afraid of me or something?"

"You know why, Levi. You're fucking mental." Ghost says.

Sugar's hand stops Levi from rushing at Ghost, but Levi smacks it off, half turning away from everyone.

"Yeah, well," Levi says, "it sucks that you guys are stuck with somebody who doesn't even know who he is."

Ghost sees him. Levi. The guy crying out for help. The guy lost in his own mind. He is a prisoner in his own body. This is how he has always felt about himself. The room is silent. Levi breaks away, running into the bathroom, slamming the door shut.

Ghost looks at Dr. Murano, whose face is creased with worry. "We need to leave so I can help him and Bear."

"Everyone," Sugar raises his voice, "get ready to move out."

Ghost already has her bag sitting against the wall by the door. She goes to it and crumbles in on herself. She's losing again. She's losing everything. Her family is breaking apart again, just like her old one did, and there's not much she can do to stop it. She stares up at the buzzing light that's attached to the spinning ceiling fan. The girl who is so good at vanishing into thin air and receding from existence itself wants to disperse into nothing right now. She wants to erase herself from everything, so these messed-up feelings and this depression she's experiencing will go away.

Ghost brings her knees to her face, so her arms have a place to rest when she buries her face into them and cries, wishing she didn't have feelings for Ali. She wishes she didn't care so much about him, or anyone, for that matter. She thought she was strong all this time, but she was dead wrong. She knows that opening her heart to people and actually caring for them always winds up with her own heart feeling the most abuse. She feels so useless and pathetic.

Why is she with Red Fist if she can't even help her new family? She can't help Ali. She can't do anything for the tormented Levi.

Ghost stares up at the ceiling fan, tired of feeling sorry for herself, and wipes away her tears. Damn. If it is this hard for her to deal with *one* person's emotions and bullshit, she can't imagine how Levi is feeling.

35

He shuts off the engine to his vehicle and sits back in his seat, exhaustion hitting him like a train. Paperwork really is a bitch. Mentally, he is absolutely flattened and defeated, beat down by the painful reminder that he got twenty-seven agents killed in the raid of the Red Fist base three weeks ago. He had written many condolence letters to the families. He had written such letters before, but this time it really stung. Their deaths were his fault. They died because of him and his failure to see ahead of the game.

Welch despises himself, and today he has just learned that his entire operation dealing with Red Fist is to be forfeited immediately.

The POTUS called him on the phone while he was laboring over the last condolence letter, white-knuckled, eyes half shut from not wanting to see the words on the screen.

"Welch, it has been agreed that your work regarding Red Fist has been extremely valuable to the United States," the president said, "but it has been decided that the FBI will no longer be handling the threat of Red Fist alone. You and your men are off the case. Someone will come in a few days to do a debriefing, and to gather all the intel and prisoners you have collected thus far."

Welch had almost swiped the keyboard off his desk, but he had controlled his inner fury and spoken calmly. It was the president, after all.

"Mr. President, may I ask why it's you calling me? And for what reason are we being stripped of our efforts to put down Red Fist?"

The president lamented softly over the phone, no doubt wanting the conversation to end. "Welch, well, the FBI has other businesses to attend to, for one. And for two, all of NATO has agreed to make a joint task force to take on Red Fist collectively. Of course, our own agencies will still be working hard to root out and get rid of these terrorists, but we want to work with a more focused group of people. This task force will have a singular purpose."

Welch shook his head, reading some of the words in his condolence letter. He bit his tongue, in fear of what he might've spat through the phone. "What about the others?"

"Others?"

"Russia? China? Australia? Japan? Countries like those?"

"Ah. You certainly are curious," the president said, laughing dryly. "Well, those countries have been dealing with the same problems we have, so they've agreed to be a part of this task force as well, even though they aren't apart of the NATO alliance."

Welch still couldn't believe his hard work was just being upended like that. "Thank you for the phone call, Mr. President."

"Welch, I want to thank you personally for your services. If there's anything I can do for you, do let me know. I will be sure to reward you for your efforts. Have a great night."

The phone call ended, and Welch continued to feel cheated as he gritted his teeth and fought to finish the letter he would then send to the grieving family of a woman he got killed in the line of duty.

Welch finally finds the strength to exit his vehicle. As he unlocks the front door to the home that he shares with his two Great Danes, Molly and Flint, he thinks back on the last sentence that the president spoke to him. He steps through the doorway, dropping his suitcase by the door as it shuts and locks automatically. His dogs pad up to him and greet him, rubbing against him, and he pets both of them. Flint tries to jump up on him. Welch manages to push the giant creature back down on all fours. The goofball still hasn't learned yet how big of a dog he is. Welch smiles, heading up the glossy wooden stairs to his bedroom, the word *reward*, as spoken in the president's voice, playing in his mind over and over again. It pisses him off.

Welch doesn't care about some medal that he'll get in the mail. He cares about credit. All the work he's done; all those late nights and early mornings will be ripped away from him. But that's not the sole reason why Welch is vexed. He is not a selfish man. Shouldn't all the men and women who died be recognized, too? Shouldn't they also get a medal from the president? Welch knows he's the one that will have to put in the orders for a special plaque to be made for their families and for the very best tombstone to be prepared for their burials. Nobody else will, because nobody else cares.

Welch feels all the muscles in his body relax as he takes off his clothes and shoes, and he falls onto his plush king-sized bed. The springs sing softly as he stares up at the dim ceiling light above him. No one above him cares about the men and women under his command that gave their lives. They don't care about the hard work his department has done, and he knows the government will act as though he and his team have done nothing for the cause. Welch knows with all his heart that this is what will happen.

If history plays out the way it usually does, Welch knows that the wrong person will get credit for something his men and women have accomplished. And they just won't claim part of it; they will claim all of it. Welch can't accept that. He has put far too many long hours, days and nights, sweat and blood into this country for somebody else to take his work away, his pride.

If Welch is brutally honest with himself, one of the main reasons he can't come to terms with any decisions made without consideration for his feelings on the subject is the bone-riddling realization that the twenty-seven lives lost in the raid were utterly meaningless. His prisoners were going to be taken, all the evidence and his entire department's effort gone.

He lifts himself off his bed and drags himself into the bathroom, slamming the door shut.

He emerges from the bedroom, fresh out of a steaming shower. The slippers feel cozy and warm on his damp feet as he slowly descends the stairs and walks down the hall towards the kitchen. The kitchen is clean, just the way he left it.

He goes into the pantry and drags out the dog food, rustling it loudly. Not even three seconds later, his two massive dogs are slipping across the tiled floor, excited. He pours the dry dog chow into the silver bowls with their names engraved on them and steps back. Both dogs plunge into it, their long heads deep in their bowls.

He laughs a little and moves over to the fridge, wondering what he will eat himself. His stomach is not really in the mood for much. After the day he's had, he just wants a few whiskeys, so he can go to sleep and forget everything for the night. After a few minutes of looking through the fridge, he decides to have a turkey and cheese sandwich with a tumbler of whiskey.

He leaves the kitchen and his noisy, seemingly starving dogs, and goes into his office. He needs to unwind, and whiskey isn't going to be enough. He powers up his laptop, taking a bite out of his sandwich. He's about to open the internet browser when he notices he has notifications on his personal email, which is odd to him because he hasn't used his private account in months, opting to use his work email for everything.

Welch taps on the screen and opens his personal email account. He has three unread messages all from the same sender. He almost spits out his whiskey when he reads the sender's address: RED FIST007@ gmail.com.

He sits up from his slouched position in the chair, setting down his drink. He opens the top drawer and takes out his gun, peering behind him. What if someone is watching him right now? What if Red Fist is in his house at this moment? They could be here wanting to kill him for taking three of their people prisoner. What they did to that poor family is still ripe in Welch's mind. He listens intently, with nothing but the rattling of dog food reaching his ears.

He calms down for a moment. He has top-of-the-line security and two Great Danes. Then he immediately dismisses his lax attitude. This is Red Fist. He must check his entire house.

He whistles for the dogs, and they come to him with their tails wagging.

"Attention," he whispers.

The dogs' entire bodies perk up as they listen and sniff the air. Molly looks back at Welch first, whining and nudging him with her head. Flint goes to the front door and begins to bark, and Welch's blood stills. He quiets Flint and creeps towards his door silently. He puts his hand on the golden doorknob and peeps through the peephole.

36

Nothing. It's clear. The paranoid FBI executive director lets out a breath. He drops the gun to his side and goes back into his office, leaving the door open in case his dogs pick up on something. He eyes the computer screen for a long time, wondering what exactly Red Fist wants him to see. He finally works up the nerve to click on the first email. The message is brief.

Hello there, Mr. Welch. This is Alan Conoway, Levi and Ali's father. I know you may be confused as to why I'm contacting you, but there are some things I want you to see. I want you to know that you are on the wrong side and that my son's detainment is a mistake that will cost many their lives when we find out where he's being held. This and all of the following messages will be deleted after opening. Any attempt to copy or move these messages will end with your computer being shut down. Open the next one.

Welch isn't breathing as he clicks on the next email, not believing what he has just read. How did they get his personal email address? He opens the next one. It contains multiple documents and PDFs with attached pictures. The message is short.

It's going to take you a while to sift through all of this. I promise you it's all legitimate evidence. We have more. I'll be up tonight waiting for your response.

Welch spends hours reading and looking at pictures of men and women doing shady business. He finds a video recording of tradeoffs, and evidence of weapons deals. There are photographs of important men and women within the US dressed in drab clothes doing exchanges. If these pictures got leaked to the public, it would ruin them.

He reads a document signed by the still missing, presumed dead Senator Griffin on illegal merchandise sales, with the type of merchandise not stated, only the weight. The distributor isn't even a real. It's a contracting company that goes overseas. There is a picture attached to this document, which shows this company selling weapons to the now almost nonexistent radical group, ISIS.

Welch reads article after article. He clicks on picture after picture. He zooms in, and he zooms out because there's a strong possibility that Red Fist created this proof. He knows that they are just trying to make it seem like taking lives whenever they please is justifiable because of the corrupt government system. Welch has always known the government has been corrupt, but without some form of order, there is only chaos.

He finally makes it to the last file. It's a file on him. On his past, to be exact, when he was serving with the FBI's SWAT team. Technically, the team he was a part of did not exist, but somehow Red Fist has managed to dig up his secrets. Why would they bring this to his attention? He already knows what he did. His particular SWAT team was always tasked with finding certain drug dealers, carrying out raids, and making sure that the missions ended with the dealers and their counterparts dead. No lockups. Just lead screaming through flesh and a lot of drugs to haul off afterward.

Welch scrolls down, finding a name that looks familiar. Tony Ramirez Davidson; deceased at forty-two years of age. Welch remembers the guy running for the window and getting gunned down before he could jump out of it. Welch remembers his younger, crueler self smiling at the way the man's body flopped to the ground.

Welch messages Alan.

Why show me this?

Because that entire killing spree you guys went on was only because that man had information on the US that, if leaked to the general public, would cause major distrust. They even sent the DEA and CIA to Mexico to find and eliminate anybody else they suspected of working with him. Look at the picture. We found a survivor, a niece who managed to escape and change her name and appearance.

Welch scrolls a bit farther down, checking out the picture of a beautiful woman who is smiling and holding a small child in her arms.

The woman looks strangely familiar, like someone he's seen before. Under her picture is a letter written to the woman from the dead Tony, telling her everything he knew about the US government's drug smuggling operations, and the assassinations in Mexico. Welch laughs to himself. It all makes some sense to him, but he's still skeptical about the whole thing.

He closes the email and opens the last one from Alan.

This may not have been enough to change your loyalties, but you should know the truth. We are not the only bad guys here. Everyone. All of them are worse. We just want one unified world, without all the secrets. America is deliberately keeping the poor from rising. It is keeping the addicts addicted. All for power. All for control.

Welch messages Alan again. What happened to the girl?

They killed her. They caught up with her. Luckily, they didn't know she had a ten-year-old daughter at the time.

Where's the daughter?

You guys have her. We want her back.

Impossible. I'm not working for terrorists. If you emailed me to try and get me to become a traitor, you failed.

Not my intention, Mr. Welch. Knowledge is power. I just want you to understand that the beast you're slaving for is precisely that, a beast. A tyrant that rules with secrets.

Welch reads Alan's reply and waits a moment. He thinks. He breathes. He sips the last of his whiskey and types.

You and your organization are wrong. What you guys are doing is wrong. I want YOU to understand that. It is disgusting.

We all have sins we must live with.

What kind of father are you?

Welch waits. Alan does not reply instantly. In the corner of Welch's computer screen, the time shows eleven-thirty. He knows he will regret this conversation he's having with a terrorist tomorrow morning when his dogs wake him.

Alan finally responds. A father who wants to protect his sons. A father who wants his sons' children to grow up in a better world.

What do you want from me, father of the year?

I only want you to learn. To know. To see. I want Ali back.

Then I think we're pretty much done here. Ali is none of your concern.

Wake up well, Welch, before it's too late. Tell me where Ali is.

Welch shuts down his computer and gets up, his knees cracking. He will not speak with a damned terrorist!

When he reaches the kitchen, he drops his empty glass on the floor and Flint barks at the sudden sound. Welch curses and starts to clean up the broken glass. Why didn't he try to capture the conversation? Why didn't he contact Alfonso? Alfonso could have gotten all the information from the emails off his computer without Red Fist knowing.

But then Welch questions himself about why he wants the emails. It's not like he's going to take them to the director and show him he's been in contact with the leader of the terrorist group that's been wreaking havoc all over the world. He won't tell anyone about tonight.

He tosses the broken glass into the trashcan and leaves the kitchen, deciding that it's clean enough for tonight. He's tired and has many things to think about. He hates to admit it to himself, but it seems that Red Fist, or Alan, has been successful in one thing tonight: Alan has managed to plant a seed in Welch's mind that will blossom into something more overnight.

The next morning, around eight, the sun's fingers are reaching though Welch's window, slithering onto his bed. He wakes, and the seed that was planted last night is now a sprout, almost ready to burst into an idea. He sits up with a loud yawn, and his dogs bound into his room, jumping onto his bed, trampling all over him.

"Down! Get down!" he yells at them.

After a bit more horseplay and a few more bounces on the bed, the two dogs hop down and prance around the room.

It's not until later that morning after Welch has had a bagel and eggs, with a fresh cup of coffee, that the idea is fully developed in his mind.

He ponders on the idea, the lightbulb hanging brightly behind his eyes, which are filled with doubt and insecurity. That light shines intensely in his mind as he watches the dogs run around his enormous backyard.

The illumination inside his head is so strong that he says it. He says the idea, the thought that has grown since last night into something worth being said, something with wavy branches and freedom. He can't take this back, and he doesn't think he will. He believes he will go through with it.

He sees the sunlight shining through the leaves of the giant oak tree in the yard and feels the tickle of the breeze on his face. He loves the burn of the whiskey as it takes a trip down his throat. This bliss, this peace he feels is so rich. He hasn't felt so unencumbered for so long that the feeling of absolute serenity is alien to him.

He knows he could have this every day, for the rest of his life. He's done more than enough for a country that doesn't give a shit about the hard work he's done, and the lives he's sent to other side for its sake. Welch loves the United States and everything it has offered him, but he realizes now that he has to love himself more than his job, and that he must resign, he must quit.

Welch says the words aloud, with a smile, and full of conviction: "I will quit!"

Welch wants no more worries. He doesn't want the blood of others on his hands anymore. He doesn't want to write any more condolence letters. He doesn't want to deal with the FBI's bullshit. He just wants to not care, because not caring is possibly the best thing he can do for his mental health at this point.

He can't control the outcome of what's happening at the moment. He can't beat Red Fist. He can't face more men and women and tell them to die for people who don't care about them, at the hands of people who care about them even less. Welch wants none of it. He wants to live his life on his own terms. He wants to live freely with his two dogs, doing what he's doing right now, on this surreal Saturday morning, basking in sunlight mixed with shade, watching his two Great Danes stretch their long legs to their heart's content.

On Monday morning, Welch submits his resignation paperwork and makes sure all of the agents who died get plaques sent to their families and the best tombstones the FBI can afford. He goes through his debriefing and starts to say his goodbyes. It'll be another week before he can officially leave his workplace and never come back. He has someone lined up to replace him as the executive assistant director of counterintelligence/counterterrorism, and the president has confirmed that this person will be a great fit.

Before Welch leaves work, he decides that he will even go easy on Alice Rodriguez. She isn't his problem anymore. He makes one phone call and orders for her to be released.

Welch smiles to himself as he starts his car at the end of the day, unprepared for the release of flames and smoldering heat that instantly turns him to ash, to nothing but dust.

37

Alice slurps down another margarita, the music humming over her. While Strong flirts with the bartender, Alice and Grant sit quietly together. Both women are in a stupor; Alice because of Levi, and Grant because of Red Fist's savage murder of her boss a few days ago.

"Girls, let's go dance!" Strong says, trying to liven up the mood. She drags both of them onto the empty dance floor. For a Friday night, the bar is surprisingly dead. Strong gets excited as the music changes. "This is my jam!"

Strong shows them her moves, and Alice is shocked by how beautiful her friend is. Strong opens her eyes momentarily and sees Alice and Grant standing like statues. She grabs both their hands and beams at them. "Dance with me," she says and moves their arms up and down. They can't help but join in.

"Shake it out, baby," Strong tells them.

Alice moves her hips from side to side and sways. Grant does the little two-step that everybody does when they don't know how to dance to a song.

Alice begins to feel herself; her body reacts to each beat, and she lets the music control her. She keeps going until another song begins to play, something more to her taste. A Puerto Rican song, one she knows she can swing her hips to.

Before Alice's mother passed away, she made sure her daughter knew how to dance. She always told Alice, "Nothing is worse than a woman who doesn't know how to use her body. I will not leave this earth until you are a decent dancer. I will not worry in the heavens about your heavy foot."

Alice can feel the smile creep onto her lips as the memory of her and her mother twisting and stepping around the old living room plays in her mind. A hand glides onto her shoulder, and she stops dancing. She spins around. A man is before her, a handsome being of darkness. Her friends have slinked back towards the bar.

"Can we share this dance?" the man says. "You look so beautiful. I can't pass this up."

Alice looks at Strong and Grant, and the two women giggle and nod. Alice and the mysterious stranger's eyes meet. Something in her tells her that she knows this man. His voice and his presence are all too familiar.

They began to dance, and Alice finds it insanely wild how effortlessly the man is leading her. She tries to get a closer look at his face, but she's a mini tornado, spinning and spinning. The bar is cast into shadows except for the strobe lights over the dance floor, but even those are multicolored rainbow streaks of flashing lights that make Alice dizzy. She feels so calm, so warm and safe with this stranger as they spin and cling to one another. So much so that she becomes afraid.

The man presses his body close to Alice's, so close and so intensely that it's as if he's trying to mesh with her by force. He nuzzles his face against hers, and Alice gets a waft of a familiar smell she thought she had forgotten long ago. But how could she know this man? She pulls away from him, her instincts telling her that something is not right, that she should get away.

The man pulls her back in, his lips brushing against her ear. "Alice, don't be afraid. Follow me after this dance."

Alice's body freezes. Everything underneath her skin becomes a typhoon, chaos. Who is this stranger? *That voice...*

The song ends, and the man takes hold of Alice's hand. "Will you come with me? If not, I'll just find you later."

Alice doesn't recognize him. He doesn't bear any resemblance to the man she knew in the past. His eyes are darker, and his hair is a different color, a dirty blond. Rage swells underneath her skin, but the fire soon becomes smoke as it's replaced by facts. All facts that make Alice's skin crawl. Just being this close to him makes her feel nauseous. He has poisoned her bubble. He has tainted her soul. He has taken her life. Alice almost passes out. The blood in her body is boiling as it swooshes through her veins.

Her first reaction is to slap him, but she controls the outrageously hard to manage impulse. She briefly makes eye contact with her friends, who are both watching them intensely.

Alice wants to vomit. He smiles, just like he always used to when he got his way. Just like Levi.

"Lead the way, Alan," she says, animosity dripping from her heart.

38

Alan picks a booth in the darkest corner of the bar and slides in. Alice stands, her fist clenched. He looks up at her. "Sit."

Alice can't speak. She's afraid she might go berserk.

"Alice—"

"Don't. Say. My. Name." Alice is barely able to contain her seething rage.

Alan looks down and then moves out of the booth. "I'll get some drinks. You sit down and calm yourself. When I get back we need to talk."

Alice knows she needs to concentrate, but Alan is here. Her ex-husband. Her presumed-dead husband from her past life. Her son's father. He's here. For what? How? And where's Levi?

Alice takes a deep breath and tries to loosen up. She has questions, and she desperately needs answers. She sits in the booth on the rough but comfortable leather padding. Alan pushes a tray of drinks onto the table less than a minute later; she sees two glasses of water, two large shots of dark liquor, and one regular shot of white liquor.

Alice peers over at her friends, who are still watching them. She smiles at them. She is confident that they can see everything that's going on.

Alan takes one of the shot glasses and knocks it back, slamming the glass onto the table, his dark eyes preying on Alice. "Stop being scared, Alice. I didn't mess with the drinks. I'm not here to hurt you."

Alice doesn't know how to react to this man she once loved. How can he just appear in her face and act as if everything is okay? "Why are you here? Where's my son?"

Alan doesn't answer; he just smiles.

Alice loses it. "Where is he, you son of a bitch?"

Alan throws up his hands apologetically, "Whoa. He's our son, Alice. I have every right to be in his life—"

"He's a fucking terrorist because of you!"

"You believe that?"

"You think this is a joke?" Alice says, digging her nails into the table. "I'll arrest you. Answer my questions."

Alan shakes his head, and that persistent cocky grin on his face wriggles under Alice's skin like a worm through wet dirt.

Alan grabs one of the glasses of water off the tray and sips. "I don't appreciate you calling my organization a terrorist group. We're revolutionaries."

"Save me the story. I don't care. I want Levi back home."

"Of course, you do." Alan fingers the shot of clear liquid on the tray, finally cupping three fingers around it and downing it before returning it to the tray, "But that's his choice. He's a grown man now."

"You've brainwashed him. He doesn't want to come back now because of you. Do you even know anything about him? He's messed up, Alan, and it's your fault because he wasn't like that before."

For a moment, Alan's face twists into something other than a smile. He coughs. "His disorder is a genetic thing. It can be managed. I didn't come here to talk about Levi coming back, because the fact is, he's not, at least not to you."

Alice stands and looks down at Levi's father with so much disgust that her stomach roils on the inside. She grabs it in fear that something sinister might corkscrew out of it. "You disgust me. I hate you!"

She moves out of the booth, but before she can get far, Alan grabs her wrist. This is what she did not want to happen. A scene. She whirls on him and barrels a fist into his jaw.

Alan quickly recovers, rubbing his jaw. "Guess I deserved that."

"Why are you here?" Alice can feel the tears coming. She can feel her strength being zapped.

Alan steps closer to her, grabs both of her hands, and looks down at her. Those dark eyes of his catch hers, and in that moment, she feels as though she's looking into a starry night sky. Old feelings flood her sense of self. Her body is hot, and her skin tingles as he rubs his thumbs against the sides of her wrists.

Alan looks down at her, getting as close as he can get without kissing her. He loves this feeling; a part of him still has insanely powerful feelings for Alice. They are both caught up in memories of past love. Past kisses and past touches. Laughs and hot morning breath.

The net over them is ripped off by Strong and Grant, who have stepped up to them. "Everything all right here, Alice?" Strong asks.

Alice blinks and then tells her friend that everything is fine. Strong shrugs and turns away.

Alan looks away. Grant is staring at him. She stays a moment longer, her gaze lingering on Alan, who keeps his face turned away. A pit grows in Alice's stomach; she feels like she's being sucked up inside of herself. After another moment, Grant moves away. Alice also takes a step away from Alan.

Alan turns back to Alice. "I just wanted to tell you, Alice, that I'm sorry for everything. Really. And that everything's going to be okay. I promise you that I'll keep Levi safe."

Alice feels the ball of revulsion growing again and walks away from him. "Alice?"

She flips on him. "Alan, do everyone a favor and never come back. I don't want to ever see you again. Ever. If I do, I'll shoot you. And that's a promise. I will bring Levi back, no matter what, so whatever you plan on doing with him, can it. You're not his father. He doesn't have one as far as I'm concerned."

Alice returns to her friends, leaving Alan to blend in with the darkness of the bar; disappearing with his feelings of guilt. He just wanted to try to make things better, but he knows all too well that in order to gain something, sometimes it's necessary to first lose everything.

Alice keeps her head turned towards the bartender for as long as possible. She doesn't want to see Alan's face. Her insides are a tsunami, and she feels sick. How dare he? How could he? Who is he? Why did he? All these questions are zipping frantically through Alice's mind and smashing into a brick wall. There are no answers in sight.

Strong is chatting with the bartender, and Grant sits beside Alice, poking at her cup of liquor. She finally looks at Alice, who doesn't seem to really be there.

"Who was that?" Grant asks.

Alice keeps her eyes focused straight ahead. "My past."

Grant scoots closer, putting herself in Alice's line of sight. "Alice, he's gone. I didn't see him leave, but he's gone. Relax."

Alice gets up, looking at Grant. "I'm going to go home and rest. I feel sick."

Strong comes back and rejoins her friends. "Alice? Who was that?"

Alice can't talk anymore. Her heart hurts. She is wilted and dying, a flower unable to eat sunlight. She shakes her head and walks away.

Strong asks Grant, "Who was that? What's wrong with Alice?"

Grant guesses correctly. "I honestly think it was Levi's father. He matches the description and photos. I'm going to make some phone calls after this."

Strong rushes after Alice, who has already begun walking down the street, and Grant follows. Alice hears them calling to her, but she doesn't care. She just wants to stop all this pain that's flowing through her.

Her friends catch up to her, and Strong grabs her shoulder tightly, forcing her to stop. "Girl, you gonna make me slap you."

"Alice, you need to stop doing this to yourself," Grant tells her in exasperation. She knows that her friend isn't her usual self. "You need to get it together. Yeah, you might feel guilty as a mother. Yeah, you may hate Alan. Yeah, you want to get Levi back. But you still have a lot of life left, and you can't spend it being mad and in pain because of things in the past and being…like this because of things you can't control. They made their own choices."

"Levi is my son. Why can't anyone understand that?" Alice pulls away from Strong, "You all just want me to forget that. I thought you guys were my friends."

Strong doesn't say anything, but Grant keeps going. "We *are* your friends. You're not alone in this, Alice. Why can't you see that? And I think it is incredibly selfish of you to only be trying to save Levi when he's—"

Alice's eyes halt Grant's words immediately. "You don't have kids. You wouldn't understand. You're just like my father." She turns to Strong. "Do you think that, too? That I should just give up on Levi?"

Strong averts her face from Alice's gaze.

Alice shakes her head and backs away from the other two women.

Strong lets her walk away, even though she knows it's wrong to let her friend be alone at a time like this. She allows Alice to walk away because she needs to find herself again, and Strong knows this. She remembers how Alice used to be. She was motivated and outgoing, and she was a damn good police officer. All of those things flew out of the window when this Levi thing came down on her. That boy ruined her. Strong watches her lost friend continue down the street alone, hugging herself as if the world around her is made of ice.

PART THREE

Too Many Fucking Skins

39

"We'll be landing at Ronald Regan Washington National Airport in five minutes. Get ready for landing and keep your seatbelts fastened until we're completely stopped," the flight attendant's cheery voice informs us over the intercom.

Next to me are a mother and her child. I watch the mother put her hand on her sleeping child's thigh and take a deep breath. She's scared, but she knows she must be a pillar for her kid. I quickly look away. I don't want to think about her yet.

I'm returning to the United States; Red Fist has a mission we must carry out that we did not get to finish because of the raid six months ago. I told my father that after the last operation that I wanted to leave the area for good. Go somewhere different and start over. There are ghosts here to haunt me.

I will never forgive myself for what happened to Devin. Ever. His blood is on my hands. Everything that happened to him is my fault because I couldn't leave him in the dark. I can't forgive myself, and I can't forgive my brothers and sisters either, although I understand why they did what they did.

I only learned about Devin's death through my sessions with Dr. Murano in Cairo, Egypt. She helped me with Dark Levi. She helped us co-exist better. She offered medication to suppress him, but I couldn't just lock him down in that cramped cage. And what if the medication didn't work? Of our many sessions, the one I remember most is when she mentioned Devin's death.

I pushed open the door to Dr. Murano's office, and the cool air flowed into my face. I celebrated because some of the rooms in the building were not air-conditioned. There was a problem with the ventilation system, and my dad swore up and down he was going kill the HVAC guys if they didn't fix the problem soon. Dr. Murano's office was clean and neat. She had no decorations on the wall or any flowers. The only thing in the room was a plush gray chair for me to sit in. On her desk was one photo, which stood in the corner facing her. Other than that, all she had was her laptop computer.

She looked up at me momentarily, giving a brief smile, and her fingers continued tapping on the keyboard. She made a couple of dramatic clicks and then shut the laptop. "There we go. And Mr. Conoway, how are you doing today?"

I sat down in the chair, closing my eyes to take in the AC. "Great. Still not used to the heat here."

She shook her head and craned her neck to look at the wall behind her, which was made of glass and showed the glimmering city of Cairo as the unforgiving sun rose. "Oh, I know. Why do you think I stay inside?"

"You're a non-combatant mostly, so you don't have to train. Bear's training regimen is brutal."

Dr. Murano took off her glasses. "He should still be taking it easy, but I knew he wouldn't. Anyway, enough about everything else, our time spent here is dedicated to helping you out with the other you."

"I know. So, what's on the agenda today?"

"Well, today I just want to talk."

"Cool. So, what do you want to talk about?"

I really didn't have a problem with Dr. Murano's sessions. I learned something new about myself each time, and I was conquering my "disorder" without medication.

Dr. Murano stretched back in her chair, and then came forward again, clasping her palms together. "You need to be able to control yourself. You can't lose control of who you really are. I know that sometimes you need strength and that's okay, but in the past you've sometimes let him out to do the dirty work when you're angry or frustrated."

I shrugged. "Okay. He wants to. That's his job. We agreed to that."

She sighed. "Say you want a girl, and you've been talking to her for quite some time, but before you can ask her out, another guy does, and she stops talking to you as much, so you get mad. You don't like this other guy, and you repeatedly see these two together and happy. This makes you upset. What do you do?"

"I dunno. I tell her how I feel."

"Okay, so you tell her, and she informs you that she doesn't feel the same. What's next?"

"I tell her she's a piece of shit because she knew I liked her first."

"Okay, so you're angry while talking to her at this point?"

"I mean, yeah, like, why would she talk to me at all if she was going to pick somebody else?"

"She's exploring her options. This girl notices that you're angry and tells you she has to go, but you grab her hand, and she turns around and slaps you. What now?"

"I push her away from me."

"All right." Dr. Murano's eyes pulled me in. She kept firing questions at me, fast. "Her boyfriend sees this, runs over and spears you to the ground and punches you in the face once. He's bigger than you. Do you fight back?"

"Of course."

"You get the upper hand, you're over him, punching him in the face. The girl you like is screaming for you to stop, but do you? Can you?"

"I don't think he deserves it. He touched me first, so I won't stop until I break him."

"Ahh." The doc sat back. "You've switched. Good. Even little things like that get you going."

I grinned. "I feed off the negative, I guess."

"Now we're going to switch gears. How do you feel about Devin?" Dr. Murano straightened herself, shimmying around in her chair.

I had my hands in my lap, but hearing Devin's name made me ball both of them into fists. I shook my head.

"What's wrong, Mr. Conoway?"

"I don't want to talk about this."

Dr. Murano cocked her head to the side. "Which are you now?"

"The one everyone's afraid of."

"I'm not afraid of you. But I do want to know why you don't want to talk about your best friend."

"Because if the other Levi loses focus… You want us to be stable, right? You bring up Devin…that's bad memories." I glanced down at my balled fists.

Dr. Murano raised her eyebrows. "Interesting. Do you know? Did they tell you?"

I squinted my eyes up at her. "Tell me what?"

"That Devin is dead."

The words didn't register in my brain for the longest time. I just sat there in that plush chair and let them marinate into my being. They echoed deep down inside of me. So profound, I felt my bones ache with an indescribable pain. I felt my heart constrict as if it were being strangled. I didn't know what to do with my face. Devin was Beta's best friend, but he was also *my* best friend.

Everything was so quiet. I looked at Dr. Murano's face. She was studying me, waiting for my reaction.

Finally, I asked, "What did you say?"

She let out a breath. "Devin's dead. Red Fist killed him and his family. They were liabilities."

40

shot out of my chair and pounded on her desk. "You're lying! This is a fucked-up test. I'm outta here." I turned to leave the room.

"Ask them," Dr. Murano said. "This test is about control. Control your emotions. Control yourselves. You don't want to become unstable. I know you want to protect yourselves, but this is what you need."

I rushed through the door, slammed it shut, and leaned against it.

I have to find out.

Beta, she was lying.

Switch back.

Okay, but if things get outta hand, it's your fault.

I rushed down to the first floor of the building, where the lobby and cafeteria was. Red Fist owned some businesses that made apps, built websites, and found and resold certain items that people around the world wanted for a better price. I was told the company was called

Traftor Industries, named after one of the other founders of Red Fist. A lot of our money came from Traftor.

I got a lot of new gadgets and electronics from that building before I left Egypt. My dad had called it a jack-of-all-trades company when I asked him about it.

I rammed open the doors to the cafeteria and saw Bear sitting at a table in the corner by himself, eating boiled eggs and fried spam. He popped an entire boiled egg into his mouth as I sat down across from him and watched him chew.

He wiped his mouth and focused on me, raising his eyebrows. "I thought you said you weren't hungry yet."

"Breakfast really ain't my cup of tea. Bear..." I took a deep breath. I didn't want to come off as prematurely pissed off. "Bear, I need to know about Devin."

Bear blinked at me a couple of times, his face a blank canvas. He muttered something in his native language under his breath, and then in English said, "What's that woman up there doing to you?"

I pummeled the table with a fist. "Bear!"

He reached for my balled fist, but I moved it away and stood. "Just tell me, man. Please."

"He's dead, Levi."

"Did you guys do it? Or was it the drug?"

"You always find a way to blame yourself, that's why I didn't want to tell you."

I shook my head. My body was steaming. Fortunately, the cafeteria's AC hadn't been janky. "Who was it, Bear? Why did you guys kill him? His mom? His dad?"

"Sit down."

I felt a flaring and prickling sensation all over my body like my skin was rising with my anger. I glared at Bear in disgust and contempt.

"Yes, Levi. We did. We had to because Devin was a liability to us. To you. The CIA used him without his parents' knowledge to capture you, and the FBI knew about it and let it slide. We had to do something because we knew how close you two were."

"Who killed Devin?"

"Levi, please calm down."

Other Red Fist agents and civilian workers inside the cafeteria were starting to raise their heads from their quiet meals.

"Who?" I repeated.

"We broke in. We killed his mom outside, in the backyard, and his dad in the living room. Devin came downstairs and we...killed him there."

"Who pulled the trigger?"

Bear stood. "Enough!"

"Who pulled the trigger?"

"Levi..."

Beta...

This is my fight. I don't need you this time. Stay out of this!

I ignored my other self and held firm in my position with Bear in our intense stare-down. At some point Ghost and Ash walked in and stood behind Bear, who still hadn't answered me.

"Guys, what are you two doing? You're making a scene," said Ghost.

"Who killed Devin?" I asked Ghost, my hands shaking at my sides.

Her eyes couldn't hide the alarm she felt when she heard my question, so she averted them and rubbed her arm. After another moment or so of nobody telling me anything, I shouldered past all three of them. I knew who it was. Why they didn't want to tell me was a different story.

How could I trust people who went behind my back and killed my innocent best friend? So what if he was the reason I got captured? *I'm* the one who made his mind jelly. *I'm* the one who beat his face in. I deserved to get caught. I deserved all the punches I got back then. I deserved all the pain and torture. Devin didn't deserve to be murdered. He was a great friend. He was my *only* friend. Devin was my star. I looked up to him. I wanted to be like him, but I never made it to that point of understanding myself, and without him, I probably never would.

Devin had dreams. He always knew what he wanted. But he never got to realize his dreams of becoming a nanoscientist because Red Fist—no, Ali—decided he had to die.

I felt eyes follow me out of the cafeteria, and I was thankful when the doors closed behind me. I checked to see if anybody was in the lobby. There was no one there except the receptionist, who was busy with a phone call. My heart had never stopped being a victim to pain, and the knot in my chest pulsed with sadness. The pain was unbearable. Unshakable. I couldn't breathe. Tears flowed freely from my eyes. I hadn't cried in a long time, but the news that my only friend had been snatched from existence was too much for me to handle, too much for me carry.

Beta, switch out. You're being weak.

He was your friend, too.

I know...

I ran for the elevator, and as the doors slid shut I battered the wall and crumpled to the ground, covering my face, squeezing my eyes, trying to stop the tears, the warm regret, the liquid torment. Devin was murdered because of me. I knew why Ali had done it. He thought Devin was a part of me that I could never get rid of, so he killed him. Ali was the one who shot Devin. I knew it.

"Devin, I'm so sorry. I'm so sorry. I'm so sorry. I'm so sorry. I'm so sorry."

I just kept repeating myself, each time the words weighing more and more, meaning less and less, because Devin was gone, and I was there in that elevator, wishing with everything I had that he could hear me, that he could come back. How had Devin felt? His last view must have been horrific; his last view had been Ali.

I opened the door to my room, which was on the fifteenth floor. I had all the blinds and curtains shut. I fell on my bed and just laid there, thinking about Devin and his smile. We had had a lot of miraculous times together.

I had hoped that after all was said and done, and my mission was finished, I could go back to the States and make amends with him, explain everything, so he didn't despise me forever. I realized that I could never do that because Ali had taken him from me. I wanted to hate Ali, but no matter how hard I tried, I couldn't do it because the rational part of me understood why he had made that choice.

I closed my eyes and went back in time. I wanted to see Devin for everything he was. He was magnificent, a true relic of greatness. He had always been something more. Devin shouldn't have chosen me to be his best friend. That was his one fatal mistake. Picking me. He could have gone to any university in the United States if I hadn't convinced him to stay and go to community college with me, so we'd be closer for a couple more years. I was always holding him back. I was always the one shitting on Devin for being a nerd.

A robust truth carves itself into my being. I admitted it to myself right there on my bed in the darkness: "I, Levi Conoway, killed my best friend, Devin. Everything is my fault. I just want to say, Devin, that I am truly sorry, and I pray and wish with all my fucked up-heart that I pay for what I did."

I stopped and brought the covers to my face to rub away the wetness. "Devin, I know you hate to hear me say sorry so much, but what else can I do? You're *gone*. After everything I've done, I'm still lost. I still haven't found out who I really am, and I don't think I ever will because you were a big part of that."

There in the darkness, for the rest of the day, I continued to speak to somebody who couldn't hear me and probably wouldn't want to even if they could. I talked and talked and talked and talked and talked until my body shut down, and my eyes sealed themselves shut. My mind drifted off into the rapids of harsh nightmares, revelations and cruel visions of black snakes tightening themselves around my mom, somebody I knew that, sooner or later, I would get killed, too.

41

grab my backpack from the storage area and shuffle down the aisle of the plane with everyone else. At least by now Bear and Asha should be at the safe house.

A couple of flight attendants are waving and saying, "Have a happy Valentine's Day!" to every passenger that squeezes by them up ahead. I pay them no mind as I exit the plane into the terminal.

I see green restroom signs about twenty to thirty meters on my left and head there. I pull out my cell phone and turn it on. I grab one of the stalls and lock it, texting Bear to let him know I've arrived. I tilt my head up. We're back. Red Fist is back. I smile.

I wanted Dad to come with us. I asked him again before I left Cairo, and he refused. I spent a lot of time with him while I was there. He explained everything to me, and now I fully understand our purpose. My dad is a great man, a man with vision and ambition. As soon as we arrived in Cairo, he wasted no time getting to me. He scheduled a time for us to hang out the next day, so we could catch up, and I could learn the truth.

The Nile River was sparkling in the sunlight as the heat pressed down on us. My dad threw a rock into the river, and I watched it sink until I could see it no more. We were protected from the water by a smooth stone barrier.

My dad turned from the river and leaned up against the wall, staring at me. He hadn't changed as much as I thought he would have. His hair was dyed a dirty blond, but his dark beard was graying. His eyes, which were still light brown, were glimmering in the light. Like me, I felt he had things he wanted to say but didn't know how to. I rested my arms on the wall and sighed.

"Been a while, yeah?" he said.

"Too long, I guess."

"My fault, for sure."

I was peering down into the water. I couldn't look up at him. When I didn't say anything, he continued.

"I have some things to make up for. I just want you to know that everything will be all right. I promise."

I laughed. "Right."

He nudged me in the shoulder. "What's funny?"

"All of this, Dad." I finally looked at him. "I can't believe any of it. I just can't. I don't understand any of it."

"What are you so confused about?"

"This organization. Why you never came back. Ali."

My dad blew air out his nose, stifling a laugh. "I do have some explaining to do. I never came back because I had to disappear. The other Red Fist founders were growing anxious about me still working with my Special Forces unit while I was working with them. We had to build Red Fist from the ground up. I couldn't just…come back home. I deserted. I would've been thrown in prison."

"How'd you meet these people, the other founders? Why are we called Red Fist?"

"They approached me. A long time ago. Some years before you were born. I refused them repeatedly, but finally, I had to accept. I couldn't just stand by and watch this world keep going in the direction it was going."

My dad showed me his right palm. The letter *R* was there, just like mine.

"We're the Fingers, Levi. To the Fist." My dad's palm clenched into a fist. "Red because of the blood that's been shed recklessly, and all the blood that will be spilled to gain something righteous. The Fist stands for togetherness, power, and persistence. We are that. With you, one who is part of the Fist, we can attain all that we hope to."

Passion burned in my dad's eyes. It radiated off him.

And still, I wondered why. What made my father so special?

"Why you? Why'd they come to you?"

My dad looked out onto the Nile.

"A good friend of mine died while we were on an op. He was Russian, and I was distraught. Angry. My friend's uncle approached me at the funeral and said, 'You can keep crying. Or you can do something about it.' I didn't know what he met then, but when he came again, he properly introduced himself and told me the goal of Red Fist, and that he wanted me to join the cause because he sensed I could rally individuals that he couldn't. He wanted someone who could break America. He gave me the tools, and I built an empire far greater than they imagined. They were so delighted by my success that they made me a Finger."

"I don't get it. Who is this guy?"

"One of the other Fingers. He's a dangerous man, Levi. Unfortunately, we've had a falling out because our views seem to differ," my dad said, looking at me, eyebrows raised, waiting for my next question.

"What are we trying to attain, exactly? Ali told me world domination."

"Precisely. To a degree." My dad straightened up and walked away. I had to follow. "We're revolutionaries, not terrorists. We don't seek only Western destruction; we don't seek destruction at all. We seek ultimate peace. Look at all the conflict the world is in. Look at America. Look at Russia, China, the UK. Look at Syria, Ukraine, and Africa. We want to help, but before we can help the way we want to, we have to get rid of the powers at play—the governments and systems so engraved into these societies. We have to annihilate them all and start new and become as unified as possible."

I nodded, and my dad stopped. He placed a hand on my shoulder. "Do you understand now? We want to reshape the world. Get rid of the secrets and lies. End poverty. End hunger. End racial injustice. We will change everything."

"I get it. It all makes sense. I just wasn't sure if I was doing the right thing all this time. Dad, I hurt people. Grandpa. My mom. Devin..."

"Son, if you want to walk away from all of this, if it's tiring your soul, then you're free to do so, but remember the consequences. I can help you get a new identity and a new life somewhere else, but if you get sniffed out somehow, I don't know if I'll be able to help."

"I get it. I'm not leaving. I don't want to." I slid out of his grasp and went back to the wall to look at the Nile. It was still early in the morning. A few people were out enjoying the breeze coming off the river.

"So, explain Ali," I said to my dad when he joined me. "How come I have an older brother? Did you cheat on Mom while you were away?"

My dad turned away, but he still answered my question. "We were on a very long mission to find some of the ringleaders in Al-Qaeda and the Taliban. Refugees and freedom fighters were supporting us. My unit did things...differently. Ali's mom was a refugee and a freedom fighter, and she helped us a great deal on our operations. Quick learner. Deadly. But yes, I did. Am I ashamed? No. Things happen, and I cannot go back and change what I did, nor do I wish to. Ali is a blessing to me. He is amazing."

"You would say that. I guess you don't understand how much Mom was struggling without you." He was starting to piss me off. "And Ali can be an asshole," I added.

"I love your mother, Levi. I always will. She is my one and only true love, but let me tell you something. If you ever went through what I did... I saw hell. All the blood and sweat and isolation, and poor, scrawny, orphaned children. All the explosions and body parts... I couldn't stop it back then. I needed somebody to quell that pit of heat; that dread inside of me. And letters and care packages just didn't do the trick. I needed a distraction, and Syrena was it."

My dad was an asshole. At least he was an honest asshole. "Wow. You're a piece of shit."

We both laughed.

"I did care for Syrena, and I'm thankful she took care of my child before she sacrificed herself for us. She will forever hold a special place in my heart."

I nodded. "Dad?"

He gestured for me to go ahead. "We need to get Ali back. Everything went sideways because of me. I owe him."

My father's eyes twinkled, and he wrapped his arm around me, bringing me in close so he could kiss me on top of my head. He held me, and I let him, even though it felt weird. Even though I was a grown man.

"We will. Ali is strong. Whatever they do to him, do not worry. It's not your fault, son. I love you so much, and I don't want you to blame yourself for anything." My dad squeezed me tight. "You must remember, my son. Sometimes...things just happen."

42

Bear is not happy with me right now. He wants me to follow the plan, but I just can't. I have to go and see Devin's grave. I have to apologize again even though it won't change anything.

My Uber driver is a cute girl, with a round face and sparkling blue eyes. She has a splash of freckles across her nose, beneath bright red glasses that look too big for her face. She types the address I gave her into her phone and gives me a smile.

"Hmm, that's an odd place to go once you get off a plane," she says, as we start moving.

"Yeah. I've been studying abroad. Something terrible happened to my best friend, so he's the first one I want to see," I tell her.

"Ah." Her eyes hint at sorrow as she glances at me. "Sorry for your loss. What are you studying?"

"Thanks. World history. I want to become an archeologist."

"Cool. Same."

I raise my eyebrows. How could it be that this random thing I plucked from my mind is the exact thing this girl wants to do, too? I grow suspicious. There's a chance that the Feds are already moving now, and there's also a chance that they already have me in their claws.

The girl sees my expression and turns red in the face. "Oh. I meant I'm in college, too." She laughs. "Sorry about that. My name is Cassie, by the way."

My suspicion falters. "I'm…" I'm trying not to take too long to come up with a fake name, but I never thought of one. "You can call me…Levi."

"You sure?"

"Positive."

Cassie giggles and finally we're away from the airport. She focuses on the interstate highway. There's a modest amount of traffic, and the sky is a weird hue of bluish-gray.

I glance at the girl, studying her. She seems pretty nerdy. Her brown hair is kind of messy looking, but it suits her just fine.

She notices me watching her and smiles. "So, you from here?"

"Something like that," I answer.

"Same. I don't like it, though. Too busy. I wanna move to the country. Maybe down south."

"Cool. So, what do you do?"

I still can't deem this girl safe. In all honesty, it's not like it really matters. I already told her my real name. She knows where I'm going. If she's a Fed, she can have me ambushed any minute. I know all this, and yet I said the things I did because most people, I've learned, display natural twitches or ticks when they're hiding something. I've been looking for signs of nervousness this entire time. Cassie has shown none.

"I drive for Uber three days out of the week for extra money, so I can just barely scrape by, and I also work at a library."

"Maybe I can borrow a book sometime?"

She stares at me. Her nose scrunches up. "How old are you?"

"Nineteen now." Why all these questions?

"Okay...so do you do anything else besides school?"

"I'm a professional revolutionary." I do my best to have the most genuine smile I can manage on my face.

Cassie grins and peers through her mirror briefly. "Who are you rebelling against?"

"The world."

"Legit. I wish I could do that." Cassie speeds past a few cars.

"The world's really messed up, don't you think?"

"For sure, Levi. Super. I hate it. It's disgusting. All the injustice and mass shootings and murders and bigotry and selfishness."

Cassie jumps onto an exit, and we head into my old hometown. I pull the hood over my head. She asks me if I'm cold. She has the heat on. I tell her I'm fine. I don't want anybody to see me. Cassie doesn't say anything more.

I peer out the window at the white grass, sparkling in the sun that's beginning to set as we pass my high school.

"Ah, so you went there, yeah?" Cassie points out the window.

I pull my hood tighter over my head.

"You all right?" she asks, slowing down as children run across the street.

"Yeah. Just really nervous about seeing my friend."

"Everything will be all right," Cassie says.

I look at her. Why would a stranger try to comfort me? "Thank you. You're really nice."

We pull up to the church. From all the information I gathered back in Cairo, I know that this is where Devin and his parents got buried.

Cassie gives me a reserved grin. "You're cute. Actually, you look kind of familiar." She cocks her head ever so slightly, examining me.

I blush, and I open the door. I have to get away from this girl. Cold air blasts me in the face. "Thank you, Cassie. Have a great day. I'll give you five stars."

I grab my bag and shut the door to the blue Honda Civic. I begin across the grass, each step a crisp crunch of the frozen grass that is standing at attention. The sound is soothing. There wasn't any crunchy grass in Cairo. Behind me, I hear frozen grass breaking under pressure and whirl around, ready for a fight.

43

My fight instincts fall by the wayside when I see Cassie. She's bundled up in a gray coat with a gray scarf covering half her face. A gray beanie hugs her head. She steps up to me, her eyes watery from the biting cold.

"We never shook hands," she kind of yells because the wind is whipping by us.

I smile at her.

She has her hand in her pocket, and when she pulls it out, she moves fast. She grabs my hand, and I instinctively jerk away, thinking she's about to try something, but she doesn't. She unwraps the scarf from around her face, and she's wearing a smile; her cheeks are a rosy red. In this cold, I grow warm.

She lets go of my hand and swings away from me, lifting a hand up in the air in farewell. "See you around, Mr. Revolutionary. Might wanna get some gloves."

I watch her until she jumps back in her car and pulls away. It isn't until I'm nearing Maurice's grave that I realize I have a piece of folded paper in my gloveless hand. I unfold it. Ten digits are scribbled down on it. She even wrote me a note: *You're interesting. Mysterious. I like it. HMU sometime please, Levi.*

I feel my lips curving into a smile.

Don't go falling in love, Beta.

I won't. Shut up. I'm not stupid.

She was pretty cute, though.

I keep smiling until I reach Devin's dad's grave. My dad was never around, so whenever I was over at Devin's place or went somewhere with his family, Maurice treated me as his own son. He was generous and always had great things to say about everything. I look up at the sky, half of it shrouded in gray, the other half lit by the orange sun that is too far away. I wish it could warm me now because the cold gripping my heart is severe.

"I'm so sorry, Maurice, so sorry. This is all my fault. Everything is. I don't know if I'll ever be able to forgive myself and I don't expect you to. I just wanted to 'fess up. To apologize."

I shift over once to the left, to Darla's grave. That woman made the best pineapple upside down cake I had ever had. I always bugged her to make more for me, and she always would, for each of my birthdays. For every great report card, I'd get a slice of Darla's cake.

I cry, the hole in my chest aching. I feel like my heart is in my stomach. "Darla, you're the best ever. You made the best cakes. I'm sorry I took your son away from you. I love you and Maurice and… I just wanted to apologize."

I move over to Devin's grave and immediately look away. I don't want to read the words or date on the tombstone. I don't want to acknowledge the fact that he had a very short life because of me. I collapse to my knees and press my head against the freezing stone, everything in me flushing out.

"Devin, I can't ever make up for this. You're literally the best thing that ever happened to me. You're the best there is in every way, and I took everything away from you. I took you for granted. I know sorry ain't enough. It never will be, but what else can say? Huh? Devin?"

I bang my head against the stone. I'm so fucking pissed off. Why'd my life have to be like this? Why did Devin have to get the shitty end of the stick?

I finally look at the writing on his tombstone. The wind smacks me brutally. It's so frigid I feel like it's cutting my face, but when I reach up to check for blood, I can't feel anything. My fingers are numb, and my ears are stinging, but I don't care. I jam my hands into my coat pockets and talk. I tell Devin my story. I tell him everything. Every detail. I want him to understand me. I want him to know that my heart is shattered. It takes me thirty minutes to get through it all.

When I'm done, I let out a white breath. "Bye, buddy. I'll be back. I promise."

I look up at the receding sun as it begins to cower behind the tall trees, the relentless chill and darkness overpowering it. I slowly walk away from Devin's grave, every inch of me feeling chilled. I dig my fingernails deep into the palm of my left hand after I rub my hands together to make sure I'm here, that I actually exist. Crunch after crunch, each step like a meteorite, no doubt, to the grass that can't keep warm.

I step onto the sidewalk, finally out of the cemetery. I kind of feel more at ease now. Talking to Devin always made me feel better, and it obviously still works, even when he's not physically here. I let out another cold breath just as a finger taps my shoulder. I tense up and then spin around. The cold air that I draw in burns my throat going down.

I take a step back. "Darla?"

How can Devin's mother be here right now, in front of me? Why is she standing here in front of me with her arm outstretched, her hand out? She's come to take me to Devin. There's a warm smile on her brown face. She sports a large black pea coat and scarf. She extends her hand closer to me now, still smiling. I have to go. Devin is owed my company at least.

I realize that whoever this woman is, she can't possibly be Darla.

I take her hand, and we shake. She tells me her name is Dhasia and that she's Devin's aunt, Darla's little sister. I look down. I can't look this woman in the eye.

"I believe I heard about you the last time I saw Devin," she says. "He couldn't stop talking about you. You guys were best friends, right?"

I snap my head back up towards her, focusing on her lips. Devin talked about me? I tell the woman sorry.

"For what? Levi, is it?"

I step back again. This woman recognized me instantly. Even without my long hair.

"Everything. And I took a lot of time over there. I'm really sorry," I say to her and turn away.

"Wait!"

I stop, knowing I shouldn't.

"I've been thinking about it, about Devin and his mental decline. Darla and Maurice tried to keep everything secret, but she never was any good at lying to me. She mentioned your name. You can't even look me in the eye, Levi. You look guilty, unsettled, and I want to know why."

The words bite me. I squeeze my eyes shut. I have to accept responsibility for what I did over and over again. It's something I will never be able to forget. I can't go back in time and change anything. I turn back towards Dhasia. When I don't say anything, she marches forward.

"Look at me!"

I look at the pain ripping across the woman's face and instantly break down. "I just miss him so much. I wish I'd been a better friend. I always got him into trouble. I feel like it's my fault."

It *is* my fault, but I can't tell this woman the exact details. Not now. I know she deserves to know why her sister, nephew, and brother-in-law are now gone forever, but she can't know, not yet.

"We all feel that way, Levi. We all feel like there's something more we could've done, or that we should've been there. But it isn't your fault or mine. The men that broke into their home and murdered them will pay one day, I believe that. They'll atone for their atrocities."

"How?"

In Dhasia's eyes, I see Devin's, so vibrant and brown, like warm caramel, but at the same time, there's something dark there, something like burnt wood, something that has smoldered for so long that I can almost smell it.

"I believe there's a place for people who murder in cold blood," she says, "a place for people who commit heinous crimes. I believe when they finish living their pathetic lives, they burn. They burn deep, they burn slow, and they burn forever."

Dhasia's words excite me. I smile at her, looking forward to the time when I can feel that wave of heat lick me with whips filled with distant and past cries of men and women who can never escape from purgatory, from hell.

44

The yard is how I remember it. The house is still the same shade of pale dirty blue. It's around six-thirty in the morning, and the sun is still yawning in the sky, not even fully awake. I don't know why I'm here. I know he hates me. How could he not? If I were in his place, I don't think I would forgive me. So, what? I have to do this. This is part of being a man. Dad told me I should try to make amends. He said I should at least try to make them understand. He said I needed to apologize to my grandpa. He said I just needed to say it, that's all.

I hope my dad understood what he was telling me to do because I'm sure my grandpa can't stand my very existence. What if he shoots me dead? What if he gets one over on me and captures me? I'll end up just like Ali. I smack my face with both gloved hands. I can't be thinking these thoughts. Ali is strong. Formidable. Unbreakable. I need to be like him.

I am like him.

Of course, you are.

I have nothing to worry about here. I can talk to my grandpa.

I walk up the sidewalk with balled fists. I get to the door and raise my fist to knock, but freeze in a moment of hesitation and doubt. The door swings open anyway, and I jump backward, surprised.

My grandpa is standing in the doorway, motionless. His round face is creased with exhaustion. His beady eyes flicker through so many different things that I can't tell what he's thinking. One hand is around his case, full of work, and the other is already up at his side, grasping his gun.

I take a small step forward. "Grand—"

The first thing I see is his case falling to the ground. He's on me, pulling me close. He gets in my face, his eyes straining wide with restlessness and bitterness. His mouth is snagged into a tight grimace. He doesn't say anything. His eyes bore into me. He looks confused like he doesn't really believe I'm here.

His grip on my coat collar relaxes, and my feet rest on the ground again. He pushes me away from him; he doesn't want to see my face. "What are *you* doing here?"

I open my mouth, and cold air rushes inside. I still don't know exactly what I came here to do

"You've already done enough damage." He bends down to pick up his case. "Go away. You're a nightmare."

The words bite me. They sink deep into my flesh until I feel rotten. I am spoiled goods.

He shoulders pass me. I can't just let him go. "Grandpa."

His speed is incredible. Before I can move or do anything else at all, he has a gun pressed to my forehead. "I told you that the next time I saw you, I wouldn't be so nice."

I twitch. Dark Levi takes control for a moment. "You gonna shoot your only grandson? Go ahead and do it," I grab the gun barrel. "Shoot me! Shoot me! I deserve it."

The expression on my grandpa's face is conflicted as he battles with his different feelings towards me. He looks off in disappointment, dropping his gun back into its holster. "Why are you back?"

"I want to apologize. For hurting you. I know it doesn't mean much, but I just want you to know that I'm doing my best."

"Doing your best at what? Being a murderer?"

"Grandpa, please. I want you to understand."

He turns away from me again. "I'll never understand, Levi. Never. You should leave. Keep your mother out of this."

I want to reach out and grab him as he walks towards his truck. "This is my duty, Grandpa. I can't stop."

He freezes by the passenger door. "Your duty, huh?" He shakes his head, "Those loonies have really gotten into your head." He opens the door, throws his case inside and turns to face me, "Well, let me tell you this. Whatever it is your terrorist buddies are planning to do to my people, I won't let it happen. I won't let you escape this time. I can't kill you, but somebody else can. I'm telling you this now, Levi—*leave*." With those words, he goes around to the other side of the truck and jumps in.

I run towards it and bang on the window. He lets it down but doesn't face me. "Grandpa, I love you."

Why are you being pathetic?

Can it.

His face wrinkles with outrage, but then it softens. "I love you, too, Levi, but that doesn't change what I have to do. It doesn't change what you did. It doesn't change that you're messed up in the head and need help."

"So, what does it do then?"

"Love?"

"Yeah."

"It just makes everything more painful," he tells me, putting the window back up and driving off, the truck's windows still frosted from the cold.

45

Hot breath. The entire room is a tank of hot breath. Alice can barely breathe, and the sweat on her brow is growing more intense. She gets up, throwing on her clothes as fast as she can.

The guy she just finished having sex with for the third time that night stirs. "What's going on?"

"Nothing." She finds her heels. "I have to go."

He sits up, and Alice bites her bottom lip. His hairy chest is appealing. She wants to jump back in bed.

"Why?" he asks.

"I have to get to work tomorrow. If I stay here, I'll be late."

The man, whose name Alice can't remember, drops his head back onto the pillow. "Well, it was certainly fun."

"Yes. Indeed."

She opens the motel door and a gust of cold air toys with her. She's half tempted to close the door and jump back in the bed with the man she met at the bar. She steps outside, and the strong wind blows her dark hair back. She shakes her head as she calls for an Uber, and stands near the motel lobby, where a half-asleep receptionist is visible through the window.

She doesn't know why she had this random hook-up. She still can't remember the man's name. Then she realizes that she just wanted to feel something other than what she had been feeling since the night Alan showed up. But the emptiness inside her is coming back, and already she feels the way she did when she came out of the house that evening looking for something to take her mind off everything that pained her.

The Uber, a blue Honda Civic, pulls up.

Alice is thankful for the heat blasting inside the vehicle. "Thank you for getting here so fast," she says.

"No problem, ma'am." The Uber driver is a young woman with bright red glasses.

Alice looks out at the barren streets, thinking about silly things to keep her mind off of what's really bothering her. It's been an entire six months since Alan had come, and she can't forget his face. She can't forget his words. She can't forget the way he smelled. She can't forget the way he made her feel. That giant messy mixture of emotions, frothing and churning around inside of her until her body can't handle them anymore.

Alice turns to the young woman. She needs to talk to someone. "Busy night?"

"Not really. I was actually surprised to get a notification. The winter nights are usually really lame."

Alice fiddles with her fingers in her lap. "Gives you a lot of time to think though, I bet."

"Yeah, sometimes," the girl replies, smiling.

"Who has got you glowing like that?"

"I don't really know why, but I've been thinking about him all day since I picked him up at the airport. How'd you know?"

Alice turns towards the girl, intrigued. "I used to be a young girl, too."

The girl giggles. "Nah. I'm just super-curious about him. He's cool. Mysterious. Makes me think. I like that."

"Well, I certainly hope you found a way to let him know you were interested."

"I gave him my number. What's your name, ma'am?"

"Alice. And yours?" Alice offers her hand.

"Cassie." They shake hands. "What about you?"

Alice furrows her brow, and then she sees the mischievous smile dancing on Cassie's face. Alice touches her cheek, feeling the heat rising off it.

"Just a fling, I guess," she finally answers.

Alice decides she doesn't care. She's single. She has nothing to hide. She looks for any kind of reaction from the girl, but Cassie just nods, keeping her thoughts to herself.

Alice takes the conversation further, deciding she must. As Cassie turns onto Alice's street, Alice says, "You ever had one?"

"An affair?" Cassie jerks away from Alice, her eyes stricken with alarm at such a question.

"No, not an affair. I'm single. I mean a random hook-up."

"Oh, no," Cassie says. "I've only ever had one boyfriend." She pulls up in front of the house, stopping the car. "Here you are, Alice."

Alice feels the need to explain herself to this girl. "Sometimes, people just need to forget. I needed a break, and that was the best way."

"A break from what?" Cassie asks, knowing it really isn't her business, but the woman in her car obviously has a lot going on and nobody to talk to.

Alice plays with her keys. "From myself. My thoughts."

"Life can be like that sometimes. You've just gotta push through." Cassie smiles as sincerely as she can.

"Not when your son is a radical off with a bunch of lunatics. You can't just push through that."

Cassie's eyes sparkle with excitement. "Are you talking about Red Fist? Is your son the one on the wanted posters? You're that cop? I thought you looked familiar."

Alice dips her head, beginning to feel as if a black hole is swallowing everything in her.

"O-M-G!" Cassie says a bit too loudly.

Alice cuts her eyes at the young woman in disgust. "Are you a fan of theirs?"

Alice moves her hand towards the unlock button of the car in the darkness. If this girl is a supporter of Red Fist, she wants to get away.

"I'm not," Cassie says. "So, your son, his name is Levi, right?"

"Yes."

Cassie looks away for a moment. She checks her phone. "That's crazy. Levi is Mr. Mysterious."

"What?"

Cassie shows Alice the picture on her phone with excitement. "My dashcam takes a picture of every passenger I have. I do it for safety reasons. Just in case something happens. Perfectly legal, since it's announced when people schedule me. I can't believe this."

Alice tunes Cassie out while she stares at the phone in shock.

Her son has returned.

46

Silence. Alice doesn't know what to say. Everyone is waiting for her to say something. She called this meeting. She feels she needs to make things right. Her father, Strong, Alfonso, and Grant sit quietly in her living room. Grant still hasn't met Alice's eyes. Her father looks drained of all life.

Alice clears her throat. She needs all of them. "I called you all here today to apologize. I was brooding for months and distant. I said some hurtful things, and I just want you all to know that I need each of you in my life. You're all I have to lean on." She pauses, glancing at Grant, "Second, I have some news."

Grant finally looks towards Alice.

"Levi is back."

Alfonso jumps up, and Grant pulls out her phone.

"Wait. *Wait*, guys." Alice holds out her hands. "I need you all. I want you all to help me." She looks at her father, but there's nothing showing on his face. The news doesn't surprise him. He looks guilty. "Father?"

A single tear is coming from the man's eye. The man who is the epitome of steel is leaking. Alice crouches down next to him. "What's wrong?"

They gaze into each other's eyes. Alice can see the exhaustion tumbling out of his. He hasn't been sleeping.

"Levi…" he mumbles. "I saw him yesterday. He came to my house, Alice. After everything, he came to me. The boy needs help. I can't hate him anymore, Alice. I want to save him."

Alice hugs her father, and they hold each other together. They both know that they are the only ones who can keep stitching each other back whole.

Strong claps, causing the two to break apart. "So, what's the plan, boss?"

Alice turns away from her father and is overcome with joy. All of her friends are standing with smiles on their faces, awaiting her plan.

47

I'm a block of ice. I'm not really here in the flesh. A couple of days have passed since I saw my grandpa and I've been thinking about what he said to me before he drove off. I've also been staring at the number that Cassie girl gave me, wondering if I should call her. I throw the note to the floor. Relationships and this life that I've decided to live don't mix well. I don't want to hurt anybody else.

"Levi?"

A hand touches mine. Ghost, Bear, Sugar, Asha, and Ash are all looking at me with concern. We're sitting in the living room of our three-bedroom apartment.

"Dude. You good?" Ghost asks.

"Yeah, just zoned out. My bad."

Bear throws a magazine at my face. "Wake up, sleepyhead. You need to pay attention. We're going to be running this op in a few weeks."

257

I slam the magazine to the floor and sit up, giving Bear my unyielding attention.

"All right, as I was saying," he continues, "we need to start scouting out the different Smithsonian museums tomorrow. I also want to have a list of sculptures and exhibits that will be destroyed. I really would like to keep civilian casualties down to a minimum, so I need you guys to be aware of which exhibits are likely to have a lot of people near them."

Ghost raises her hand like she's in a classroom and not planning a terrorist attack. Bear looks at her. "We're not ruining *all* of the museums, are we?"

"Only three," he answers. "The Museum of National American History, the National Air and Space Museum, and the National Museum of Natural History."

Ghost nods.

From our door comes the sound of three loud knocks and two soft ones. At first, I tense up, but then my body relaxes because only Red Fist operatives know the knock sequence of the day. It must be Jung. Bear mentioned earlier Jung was coming by to go over some details with us. He's officially part of our team now. We need him because we're down three members.

Ash walks over to the door and peers through the peephole. We all watch as she opens the door. None of the alarms we set up had gone off, so that meant nobody with weapons had come up to our floor. We each have a single handgun, not much if something wild happens.

Jung steps inside, waving at us with a cheeky grin, his yellow skin pale from the temperature outside. The lanky Asian is just as I remember him, except that this time he's wearing a leather jacket with fur around the collar, and jeans.

"Hello, guys, long time no see."

He and Sugar shake hands, and Jung sits on the one couch in the room, to the right behind me. The rest of us are all sitting at the table we set up. I don't know a lot about Jung except for the fact that he was a double agent for Red Fist; he was our mole here in DC with the FBI.

"Any news?" Bear asks Jung, who is inspecting his nails.

"Ah, yes." Jung stands and steps in close behind me. I grow agitated. I don't know what it is about Mr. Double Agent, but something about him seems off to me. "Well, this just happened today, but I did just like the Fingers wanted. I got accepted into the JNT."

Ghost and I exchange lost glances.

"I'm sure you all already know," Jung says, "but the FBI ain't the guys you should be keeping tabs on anymore. It's the Joint Nations Taskforce."

No one says anything, so Jung continues. "They have all of the previous evidence on you guys and the prisoners."

I turn around and say to Jung, "Do you know where?"

He laughs off my question. He keeps right on talking and doesn't even try to answer it. "Listen, these guys are the best of the best. We need to be careful, I know they're watching, waiting."

What an asshole. I pick up the note I dropped earlier. "Bear, I'm gonna get some fresh air."

"Before you go, on the operation you're going to be partnered with Jung and Ghost in the Natural History Museum."

I give him a thumbs-up and try to hide my dissatisfaction with being grouped with Jung, who's smiling at me as I open the door and slip out. Who does he think he is? If he turns out to be a traitor, at least I'll be able to snap his neck.

Calm down.

Shut up. Don't tell me what to do.

Well, we're out here now, so what are we gonna do?

I head down the stairs and stand in the entryway, looking out into the parking lot. I don't need to sit around these boring meetings and listen to them go on about the same things. Just tell me what to do, and

I'll do it. I especially don't need to be there when Jung is there, acting like a smartass. Anxiety pulses within me. The cold bites me, and I shiver. All I'm wearing is a black hoodie and jeans. I turn my palms up and inspect them. They're sort of pinkish, already suffering from the disrespectful breeze.

No gloves. Cassie would probably have something to say about that. Why do I think about her? I don't even know the girl. I need to forget about her. I burrow my hands in my pockets, and my right hand encounters the scrap paper. Cassie's number. I fish it out and stare at it, holding it up to the dull sun.

What should we do?

Switch. We can't get close to her, no matter what.

Then why call her?

Nothing else to do.

Good point, Beta.

I pull my phone out of my hoodie pocket. Dark Levi isn't too good with others. He's socially awkward.

I just don't take bullshit like you.

Whatever.

I dial the number and bring the phone to my ear. A smile is already creeping over my face, there's this giddiness in my stomach. I tell myself that I'm feeling this sensation because the other Levi and I are on great terms and have been working together well for the past few months. I try to convince myself of this, but Cassie answers.

"Hello?"

And the simple words I should say in reply get caught in my throat. It's like my own hello is trapped behind a hatch.

Say something, dipshit!

"Hello? Hello?" I finally breathe out, fake coughing, "Sorry, I was choking. I couldn't breathe for a minute."

Cassie giggles. "I was just thinking about you, actually, Mr. Revolutionary."

"Yeah?" I smile. I don't know what this is or what it's supposed to be. I've never had a girlfriend before. I just know Cassie turns me on.

"I want to see you. Can you come over? My roommate's out of town, her grandpa just died. I'm lonely."

Holy. Shit.

I don't even know if I should answer the question. My head is spinning.

Cassie asks me again if I can come over. She says she's cold and needs my warm body.

I haven't been too interested in girls lately because my life has been way too hectic, but Cassie is different. Something in me knows I just can't say no to her. I have to go. I *need* to go, if only for a little while. This is what guys my age should be doing. I just want to feel normal again. In this cold, I'm stiff and freezing. All the blood that is supposed to be circulating around my body and keeping my extremities warm is focused on only one of them.

Finally, I answer, hiding the excitement in my voice. "Sure. Text me the address, and I'll be right over."

Cassie rolls off me, letting out the breath she had been holding in. My heart is beating triumphantly. My entire body is paralyzed, and yet I feel a tingling sensation, like the softest hands in the world are ever so delicately skiing over my skin.

Cassie smacks me in the chest with the back of her hand. "For a virgin, you handled round two like a champ."

I don't know what to say to that. "Thanks…"

"Round three?"

I shake my head on the pillow. The scratch marks Cassie's nails left on my chest sting a bit. I feel like I ran a marathon.

She laughs. "It's okay, you're still a baby."

"Fuck off," I tell her.

"I'm going to sleep. Please don't go."

"I won't," I tell her, even though I know everything will be better if I just leave.

Cassie shifts around and presses her butt against my thigh. I stare up into the darkness, not believing what just happened. Eventually, even though I tell myself to get up and go, I turn and wrap myself around her, pulling her close.

The next morning, I wake up and immediately check my phone. I have seven missed calls. "Oh, shit."

Cassie comes running out of the bathroom. "What's wrong?"

"I gotta go, I'm late for something. Where are my pants?" I frantically search the room with my eyes.

Cassie walks past me and bends down on the other side of the bed. She comes back up with my jeans and throws them at me.

"I was gonna make you breakfast," she says, falling onto the bed and looking at me from an upside-down position. "What are you late for?"

"Revolutionary shit." I'm already jamming my feet into my shoes when I hear Cassie say a name. My blood stills. "What did you say?"

Cassie smiles at me sardonically. "I said I know you're with Red Fist. Your mom's that cop, right? Alice?"

What have I done? I have to get out of here. Cassie's been playing me this whole time.

She runs for the door and slides in front of it.

"Move," I warn.

She smiles. "I like bad boys, Levi. I promise I won't tell anybody." She grabs my crotch and then caresses my face. "I want to help you, Levi. Be by your side. I want to help the world. I promise I do."

48

Cassie smiles wryly, her heart screaming in her chest. She's ruined everything. She didn't think this would happen.

"I didn't think we would meet again, Alice," she says.

"Can I come in?" Alice tilts her head, and Cassie steps back. Seeing the woman in uniform makes her seem more intimidating somehow.

Alice strolls inside, followed by Strong and Grant. Alice peers around Cassie's living room.

Cassie is still by the door, speechless. She's excited but afraid. Do they know she's with Red Fist now?

"We wanted to ask you some questions," Alice gestures towards the couches, "mind if we sit?"

"Sure, would you like coffee or water?"

All three women refuse. Cassie goes to the kitchen anyway and pours them some water. She can't stop laughing on the inside.

Alice says from the living room, "We want you to help us."

Cassie puts on her best smile as she hands the women their glasses of water. "With what?"

"My son."

Cassie dismisses that with a wave. "Oh, Alice, he never contacted me."

Alice sets her glass down, standing up to threaten the girl. "Do you want to go to jail?"

Cassie bottoms out. Her knees feel weak.

"We've had your phone tapped for the past few days. You will help us, or your life as you know it is over. You think you're in? He would never tell his buddies about you. He's lying to you, Cassie."

"I-I-I don't know what you're talking about."

"Of course, you don't." Alice pulls out her handcuffs.

Cassie stumbles back. "You can't just come in here and accuse me of aiding terrorists. Get out! You have no proof. I have too much to lose."

"We have both of you on recording, sweetie," Strong tells her, and sips from her glass.

"I said get out," Cassie points to her door.

Grant shakes her head. Alice twirls the cuffs in her hand. "You sure you don't want to help us? We can do this the easy way or the hard way. Either will work. We're giving you a chance to redeem yourself."

Cassie cannot believe she's been caught already.

Alice smiles. The girl has two choices, and only one will guarantee her freedom. "What do you say, Cassie?" she says, extending her hand.

Cassie glares at her. "I want immunity. Guarantee my safety from the law and Red Fist."

Alice motions for the girl to grab her hand. The two shake.

Alice grins. "You have a deal."

49

Three Weeks Later

Jung swishes the water around his mouth, tightens the ball cap on his head, and pulls the bill down lower. He's wearing dark blue jeans, boots, and a white T-shirt under his jacket. He has a camera dangling from his neck that he's using to take pictures. The way he's dressed right now, he looks like a poor college student doing research. He checks his watch. They were going to meet outside at noon.

He aims his camera lens at a group of children on a field trip and watches them, something odd grabbing hold of his heart. Some of the children are grinning and not paying attention to their guide's information, and others look uninterested in the entire ordeal.

Jung drops his camera and lets it dangle near his stomach. Is he really the good guy here?

He has lied, cheated, and stolen all his life, maneuvering his way into the worse of places that had the best benefits for him. He grew up on the streets with his older brother, who got them into a gang of well-off drug dealers back in Shanghai. That's where Jung learned the harsh truths of this world. Jung became a man far too early, and he has never trusted anyone, not even his own brother. The bastard had tried to swindle money from him.

Jung doesn't ever remember an instance where he genuinely did something nice for anyone. He has never loved anyone or told anyone about his past. He let his past define who he is today. He let his worthless addict father, and weak-hearted, stupid mother determine that he was to be nothing more than a street rat.

China was a cesspool. Jung became sick of the streets, and the selfishness. He became exhausted from stealing and manipulating others and grew out of the childish idea of *me, me, me*. He started to want his life to mean something; he wanted to help the world.

Now Jung is here, with Red Fist, where all his skills match what they need. He has been with Red Fist for seven years and has learned that everything is far from black and white. He *was* okay with Red Fist's idea of world domination because of the way they approached it.

Red Fist wants to end nearly all the problems in the world by making it one. There cannot be war with another if everyone is under the same umbrella, ruled by one just government. There cannot be secrets. There cannot be rich and poor. There cannot be those with healthcare and those without. There cannot be countries living with disgusting amounts of money and resources, while others are on the brink of extinction.

Red Fist is shooting for a better world. Jung keeps telling himself that, but after being deep undercover with the FBI for a few years and serving under Welch, he feels differently. To want what Red Fist wants—world domination, world peace and wellness for all is an admirable ambition, but at the same time, the entire notion is inherently impossible. Jung believes this now, because of Welch.

At the thought of Welch, Jung's heart cries out in sorrow. He can't stop the pain there. Jung has never had guilt cling to him like this before. He misses the man who had acted like his father; who had treated him like a son. No one has ever been there for Jung so much. No one has ever tried to understand him like Welch did. He's never had a family, as far as he's concerned. He has always been alone. Until Welch. And now, Jung is alone again, because he betrayed the only person who wanted to understand him.

One afternoon last summer, when he and Welch were sitting on Welch's back porch drinking and talking, Welch had said, "No matter how much we try to fix this world, rebuild the people, sweep up all the dirt and ugliness, there will always be people out there who just want to watch the world burn."

As the orange glow of the setting sun reached over the backyard, Jung had asked, "So why do you do what you do if you don't think there's an ultimate reason?"

Welch had downed the last of his beer and said, "I do my job because if I can do my part, just a little bit, and help someone, just a little, then at least I know I have helped that person feel safe. At least I have changed something."

Jung nodded and looked out at the trees dancing to the windy music. A part of him understood what Welch was getting at, and the other part of him didn't care.

Now, Jung looks around, grinning. He can't wait to hear the cries of the people running out of this place in a few days. He is just another one of those lost victims in a world full of irreparable souls. He is only in it for fun now. He stopped caring long ago when he learned that everything was pointless. Every time he stole, lied, cheated or killed, a small piece of goodness within him got chipped away, like wood shavings in a grinder.

Jung is grinning into the briskness of the day because he finds it hilariously ironic that he has become one of the people Welch had described; the people who just want to watch the world burn. His grin does not fade, because he wants to watch everything that makes this world whole implode, to crumble and break and wither into oblivion. At least then he will be able to feel camaraderie with something. All the people will cry until they dry up and become nothing but ashes. Jung will still be smiling, even as he is turning to dust himself because at least he will have changed something.

50

I watch Jung come out of the museum laughing to himself and wonder what's so funny. He slides past us. "Come on, we're finished here."

Walking and texting Cassie at the same time proves difficult, so I shove my phone in my pocket after I bump into Ghost, who turns around and pushes me. "Stop texting her!"

"You jealous?"

Ghost rolls her eyes. "You wish. I'm telling you to stop."

"Yeah, well, I don't take orders from you."

"I'm your senior. What you're doing is putting us all in danger."

I tear away from her. "I didn't see you saying that with Ali."

Anger erupts in her green eyes. "That's not the same, and you know it. He's one of us."

I shrug and catch up to Jung, who is still smiling. He's so deep in thought he doesn't recognize that I'm beside him. "Yo," I say.

He stirs from his own mind and looks at me, blinking stupidly.

Ghost pushes in between us and jerks her thumb at me. "Tell dingus over here that talking to that girl is stupid."

Jung looks down at me, frowning. "She's right. You could get us all burned."

"Whatever," I mumble.

"Think about Devin," Ghost adds.

I stop dead in my tracks. I tilt my head back and take a deep breath, letting the cold air cool the fire within me. I scowl at Ghost. She steps back.

Jung wraps his arm around me as the wind bashes us in the face. All I think about, on the way to the car, is choking Ghost out until she looks like one.

When we get back to our temporary hideout, Jung asks Bear if I can crash at his crib until the operation. Bear agrees. Surprise must be stamped on my face because Jung grins at me. He walks over to me. "Grab your things so we can go."

"You serious?"

"Why wouldn't I be?" He cocks his head slightly to one side.

"Dunno, but thanks."

Jung opens the door to his apartment. When he flicks on the light switch, the glossy, wooden floors shine. The living room is furnished with two black couches and a recliner grouped around a black coffee table in a perfect bracket shape. The main sofa faces the wall where a mounted TV watches over the room. The greatest appeal for me is the room's fourth wall, made entirely of glass, showing me Washington DC's hazy skyline.

Jung sees me staring out the large window. "It's tinted on the outside. Nobody can see in."

He hangs up his jacket, takes off his shoes, and places them by the door. He waits for me to do the same and then walks off, waiting for me by one of two small stairways that lead to the kitchen area to our right. He skips up the stairs, and I follow, bumping into him when he stops.

"As you can see, this is the kitchen," he says.

The kitchen is cramped, and I figure there's just enough room for me to spread out my arms. There's a newer model refrigerator, next to that the dishwasher, and then the sink and stove. When I turn around, I can see the living room through the mini-bar area. A couple of stools are tucked underneath the overlap of the bar, and I accidentally kick one on my way around.

"I do it all the time." Jung gives me a friendly smile.

Why has he invited me to stay with him? What's his deal? I accepted his offer so fast because I was tired of being in that apartment with everyone else. They were always staring, always watching and side-eying me, treating me like a child. And Ghost, she'd been pissing me off about Cassie for the last three weeks. Ghost thinks she's my mom, at least, that what she acts like. I just need a break from all of them.

He leads me back into the living room. He picks up the TV remote and turns it on, then tosses it onto the couch and goes to the window.

I come up next to him and ask, "What's your deal?"

I need to know if I can trust this man or not. Something about him just doesn't sit well in my stomach.

"Well, you're on my team," he answers, "and I figured you want to get away from Ghost. She's been on your back, yeah?"

I nod and look out across the city. "She doesn't have Ali to annoy anymore."

"It seems like she can be…a bitch." I laugh, and he pats me on the back. "Come on, I'll show you your room now."

He leads me down a hallway that's adjacent to the front door. The hall is very short. He points to the door at the end of it.

"That's the bathroom. It's clean, and the shower's good, but it's cramped." He taps open the door to his left with his foot. "This is my room."

271

I can see the plush, king-sized bed in the room, snoozing in the comfortable darkness.

Jung grabs the knob of the door across from his and swings it open. "And this one's yours. It's supposed to be a child's bedroom if you're wondering why it's so much smaller than mine."

I walk into the room and drop my bag on the bed, which is snug against the wall to my right and very low to the floor. There's nothing else in the room except a closet, and its mouth is wide open as though asking for the nourishment of clothes. There's a window at the far end of the room, with a small dead plant on its windowsill.

Jung moves past me and grabs the plant. "Sorry about the dead plant," he says, "I forgot I put it in here." He turns back towards me before he leaves, "You're free to use anything, man. I'm not cooking tonight or anything, but I'm going to order in pizza. What kind do you like?"

"Doesn't matter. Thanks."

"Great." Jung closes the door behind him and leaves me alone. I stare around the tight room. Why do I feel like I've fallen into a trap?

51

Jung opens the door for the pizza delivery boy, who has a flat expression on his pimply face. Jung gives the guy his flashiest grin anyway and hands him a two-dollar tip.

The kid hands over the two boxes and dips his head with a frown.

"Thank you," he says, but the dissatisfaction is clear in his voice.

Jung closes the door in the kid's face without saying anything further, mirroring the kid's attitude. Jung puts the pies on the coffee table and picks up the remote, flipping through the channels until he finds something decent.

"Ehhh, Levi, the food's here," he calls out, plopping down onto the couch facing the TV, thinking about how he can turn Levi into his own personal bomb of insanity. He knows the kid has daddy issues. He knows the kid is mentally unstable, plagued with DID. Jung runs his fingers through his hair as Levi comes out of his room and into the living room.

Levi sits on the couch with Jung so they both can reach the pizza. "Smells good," he says.

Jung is staring at the TV with the remote in his hand. He puts it down and opens the top box. Inside is a steaming-hot, fluffy, golden-crust, gooey-cheese pizza. His stomach growls, and he realizes he hasn't eaten since morning.

"Help yourself," Jung gets up to grab napkins, "Little prick didn't even bring any napkins," he mumbles.

Levi tries to chew a piece of burning pizza, opening his mouth to take in cool air. Jung hands him a napkin, and he quickly spits it out.

The two sit in silence, with a slice of pizza cooling off on each of their plates, as they watch some humorless sit-com. Jung finally bites into his pizza and looks at Levi, who is nibbling on his piece, afraid it might burn him again. Jung laughs, and Levi shakes his head.

"Sorry I don't have any game systems or anything. You're gonna get bored here," Jung says.

"Nah, it's fine, man. I appreciate you doing this for me. Sometimes I feel like I might explode with all of them nagging me."

"Why do you feel like that?"

"It doesn't matter."

Jung puts his pizza down. "I know you don't exactly know me, but you can talk to me about your problems. You don't want them to pile up and become too much for you to handle. We're a team." Jung knows that Levi is skating on thin ice within himself and that he must become someone Levi can trust. "You can trust me, man. I'm just here for this mission, then I'm on my own again. We can be friends. You can say whatever you want to me." He can see that Levi is trying to figure him out by the look on his face.

"I don't need any friends. Why do you even care?"

"Because I know how you feel. This work that we're doing is rough, a real strain on the mind, and let me tell you, you can't beat it on your own."

"And I can't beat it with everybody else, either." Levi takes a giant bite out of his slice of pizza.

Jung waits for him to swallow, sensing he has more to say.

"You and everybody else think you can figure me out. You guys think you can help me with my problems. But you can't. None of you has another you in your head. You didn't get captured. You weren't the reason for the raid on our base. You didn't get your best friend killed. So how could any of you understand?" He grabs a second slice of cheese pizza, keeping his eyes away from Jung.

"But you've come this far. Once this operation's over you can take a break. Figure everything out and be by yourself for a bit."

"My entire life has changed. And I can never go back to how it was. You know, I think actually I want to be an archeologist. I want to explore the world and dig up bones, but that will never happen now."

"It can when Red Fist wins," Jung says this with much confidence, even though he's sure that the war Red Fist is waging against the world will be a long one, one of the longest in history.

Levi cracks up. "Yeah, well, I don't think I'll last that long."

"Why?"

"There's another me inside my head. The doc told me that if I don't stay stable, there's a chance another me could barge in, and I don't want that. I can't live normally with two of me, let alone three."

Jung now feels for the guy; the sympathy comes unwillingly. How has Levi made it this far with all the stress of another voice in his head? He can't help but admire the kid's strength. Jung is a sadist, and he cannot help his reaction now. Even though the fist of remorse has struck his heart, it subsides into nothing. He wants to see Levi break. He wants this entire operation to go up in flames. He wants to bring everything to its knees so that when he's watching from the shadows, he can feel the pleasure of ruining somebody completely.

52

The Next Day

Jung lets me borrow his car to go see Cassie. He said I should have some fun before we all have to disappear again. Her door is unlocked for me. Inside her apartment, throaty rock music is blasting, and the living room is a mess. I walk through the living room to peek inside her bedroom. She's dancing, shaking and bobbing her head so vigorously I think it might fly off.

I stand there and watch her be so wholly herself, becoming jealous because I can never be myself.

I pick up one of the many shirts she's thrown onto the floor and slam it into the side of her face. She stops dancing, turns towards her bed, and picks up her phone. The music shuts off, and she turns towards me. That's when I notice she's only wearing a baggy navy-blue sweatshirt and panties, her bare legs thin and exposed.

We lock eyes, and she steps forward, kissing me. I don't stop her. She turns me around and pushes me onto the bed. I wonder where this aggression is coming from.

"Cassie!"

She doesn't stop. She's working her way down to my jeans. I scoot out from under her and push her off. She gasps, looking offended.

"I told you we need to talk."

She bites her bottom lip, her eyes glimmering with passion. "Can we please talk later. I want you right now."

She wouldn't think that if she knew the truth.

"Cassie. Later." I grab both her hands and dive into her eyes, which are holding something that astonishes me. Shame.

She looks away from me and gets off the bed to slide on some sweatpants she finds on the floor. "What do you wanna talk about it?" She crosses her arms, and I can see that her whole vibe is off.

I motion for her to come sit beside me. "I need to tell you something." She moves towards the bed. I lied to her about joining Red Fist. "Listen, Cassie—"

She kisses me.

Beta, something feels off.

I push her off. "What's wrong with you?"

Cassie is crying. "I'm so sorry."

Beta, her ear—

Her bedroom door flies open. My mother, grandfather, and some brunette lady are aiming their guns at me.

Cassie has plastered herself against the wall. Dark Levi scrambles out of me so fast I can't take a breath. I start towards her, sneering, "You stupid bitch. What the—"

I look down. The world spins. There is a small dart in my chest. I feel like I'm floating. The floor is coming up to meet me...

53

Later That Morning

"**W**hat the fuck did you do with him?" Ghost has Jung up against the wall, her fingers clenched around his shirt.

Jung is indifferent, as Ash and Asha pry Ghost away from him. "I told you I let him borrow my car and he never came back."

"I knew we couldn't trust you," Ghost says. "Whose side are you really on?"

Jung shrugs. He can literally see the hairs starting to rise on Ghost's head as she puffs up like a cat getting ready to attack.

"Why don't you care? Our entire op is fucked now. Bear, I'm telling you we can't trust him."

The beast of a Tongan man steps up beside Ghost. "We need to think rationally. Go outside, Ghost."

Ghost begins to complain, but Ash and Asha grab her on both sides and drag her out of the apartment. Jung locks eyes with her the entire way, and she sticks her middle finger up at him before the door splits them apart. He shakes his head, snickering on the inside. That's what he likes, that rage.

Bear and Sugar move in close to him.

Sugar, who has had a bad taste in his mouth all day, is sucking vigorously on a peppermint. "Tell us the truth. Where is he?"

"I honestly don't know."

Bear shoves Jung roughly against the wall, knocking the wind out of his lungs, and pins him there with a giant arm across his chest. "Liar!"

Jung raises his hands. "Okay, he went to go see some girl he's been talking to. He didn't want me to tell you guys." Bear and Sugar exchange confused glances, and Jung realizes that they know nothing of Levi's little girlfriend. "Ask Ghost, she knows. I'm surprised she didn't tell you guys."

Sugar pulls out his phone and sends a text. A few minutes later the girls come back in, Ghost, mean-mugging Jung, who is brazenly smirking at her.

"Tell us about this girl, Ghost," Bear demands.

"I told Levi to ditch her. He wouldn't listen to me. I didn't think he was this stupid. Is that where he's at?" Ghost shakes her head.

Bear keeps his composure. He reminds himself that Levi is unstable. These things are not Levi's fault. Bear reminds himself that he promised Ali to keep Levi safe. He takes a deep breath. "All right, Asha, Jung, Sugar and I will go get him."

Ghost objects immediately, and Bear holds up his hand. "I don't need two children to babysit." He moves past her, telling the other three Red Fist operatives to follow him.

***

279

Cassie was supposed to leave hours ago, for three weeks, until everything was cleared up. Alice had given her enough money to go stay in some hotel for that long, but Cassie is packing now, over everything, numb to it all. She needs more time to process everything. She needs time to accept things for what they are. She zips up the duffel bag and turns to leave. She opens her bedroom door and jumps back, almost falling onto the bed.

There are four people in her living room. The one standing right by her door is a tall, dark-skinned man with a shaved head. He's glaring at her with dark eyes, a lollipop stick protruding from between his thick lips. He shakes his finger and speaks.

"Hello, Cassie. We have some questions for you." His African accent froths off the tip of every word.

Cassie cringes. She clutches her bag close to her chest and says, "I'm going to call the police."

Alice's father had informed Cassie that there would be two police officers near her place at all times in case somebody "unwanted" came for her.

"Come out into the living room," the man says. "We don't want to hurt you."

"What do you want?" Cassie is shaken, on the verge of tears. She's messed up. She's sure they're here to kill her.

A dark woman, short and beautiful, her dreads dangling down from her head like vines, pushes the man back, and her golden-brown eyes twinkle when she smiles at Cassie. Asha reaches out for Cassie.

Cassie flinches. "Do not touch me!"

"I want to help you leave. But you need to talk to us."

"You're Red Fist, aren't you?"

Asha nods. "Levi is our family. We just want to find out what happened to him."

Cassie shakes her head; her hair is a mess, bent every which way. She backs into her bedroom. "He said I was one of you. I'll help you guys find him, please..."

Asha steps into the room with Cassie and closes the door behind her.

Jung sits on the couch in the living room with his legs crossed, and his eyes closed; he is deep in thought. Bear does not trust him. He has always been a valued informant, but now he doesn't know how he feels about him.

A few moments later, Asha opens the door, her brow furrowed.

"Where?" Bear asks.

Asha seems to be perplexed, and she makes the statement sound like a question. "He's with his mother and grandfather."

Jung's lips curve into a smile subtly. Everyone is wondering the same thing. How could that possibly have happened?

Everybody is silent, and Asha continues. "The girl said that she picked Levi up from the airport and took him to a gravesite, and that same night, or rather the next morning, she picked up Alice, too. That's how she met both of them."

"Uber!" Sugar spins around shaking his head, "Unlucky."

"She said Alice threatened her. She would have jail time for being our accomplices."

Sugar turns to Bear. "Should we kill her?"

Bear disagrees. He doesn't like killing if he doesn't have to. "No, it seems she was manipulated into doing this." He's looking past them all into the room where the girl has her head on the floor, barely moving.

"Then what?" Sugar is growing impatient with this country. He just wants to leave and catch his much-needed break.

"We find him," Bear says.

"The operation is *tomorrow*. We need to re-plan for it. Levi has dug his grave more times than once. Who knows what he's told that girl, and who knows what he's telling his mother."

Bear faces off with Sugar. "He's family. We can't just leave him."

Sugar snorts. "Ali and Alan have you by the balls, eh?"

"I'm just trying to do what's right. Don't argue with me."

Their eyes are burning into each other. They are both experienced agents within Red Fist, and either one of them has the skill and knowledge to take charge in Ali's absence. Sugar did step down when Bear came back into the picture, though, and now he breaks away from Bear's gaze.

"Very well," Sugar says.

Bear issues the order. "Let's go."

As quickly as they broke into Cassie's apartment and interrogated her, they disperse from it, as though they were never there.

54

oor boy. Vance stretches, finally looking up at Levi, who has been blathering nonsense and threats since they tied him up eight hours ago. It's now seven-thirty in the evening. Vance checks his wristwatch and moves forward, sitting down in the chair that has been placed five feet away from his grandson.

Vance talks over Levi's sputtering. "I'm done in thirty minutes, kid. You gonna talk that whole time, or will you listen?"

If Levi's eyes could kill, Vance would be dead. "No, *you* need to listen. If you don't let me go, you'll die."

Vance says nothing. The trust his grandson has in these people he's been with is frightening. "You're going to stay here until this all blows over. Your friends ain't coming." Vance says this matter-of-factly, but in the back of his mind, he is concerned. If Red Fist comes here for Levi, things will go south.

Vance gets up and goes behind Levi, tightening the handcuffs, and then pulls at the rope near his feet, cinching Levi's ankles against the chair.

"I can't feel them now," Levi complains.

"Great, because I don't trust you. I want you to stay put."

"Grandpa…" Levi's voice is different: softer, weaker, and less sinister.

Vance moves around to the front and stands over his grandson, who is looking up at him, tears in his eyes. "Please, let me go. I'm afraid."

Vance steps away, almost tripping over the chair. When he breathes in, it hurts.

"Grandpa, I'm telling you, they're gonna hurt you. Please. Let me protect you. Let me go."

"I'll be fine."

Levi's face changes, and just like that he's back to his other, wicked self. Vance doesn't know if what he just heard was an act or if it was the other personality coming out of the mess that is now his grandson.

"Your funeral," Levi says.

"I'll be fine," Vance repeats, leaning against the dusty cement wall, the basement light blinking.

"Everyone says that before they die."

Vance reminds himself that the boy in front of him who just said that is not his grandson. "I'll be fine," Vance repeats again. But unsure, he takes out his phone and jabs in a text message to Alice, telling her to check the cameras.

Levi stops talking and hangs his head. The hair that would have hung to his knees in that position has gone now, replaced by a far shorter haircut. Vance is depressed by this sight; his grandson might be gone forever.

***

9:05 P.M.

Alice twiddles her fingers nervously as she sits watching her son, who has not lifted his head for an hour and fifteen minutes. Her father was worried about her being down here alone with Levi because he had been talking a lot. But that's what she wants, to talk to her son.

"Lift your head up, Levi."

He ignores her.

She brings his head up and places her forehead against his. He won't look at her. She wants to cry, because seeing her only child like this, having to go to these lengths to stop him, is crushing her. With their foreheads together, Levi grins widely, and Alice backs away.

"Why don't you hate me?"

"I'll never hate you. You're my son."

Levi cocks his head to one side. "Will you still say that when Grandpa is dead?"

Alice's hand is moving before she can stop it. She brings it across his face. "Give me back my son!"

"I am your son." Levi's eyes are blacker than coal as he burrows into her very being, devouring her strength and devotion. "This is what you get now. This is all me, Mom."

Alice wants to cry, but instead, she takes a deep breath. She knows this is the best time for her to try to quell the demon inside of her son. "I can help you. You need to want to help yourself."

"I'm helping the world."

"By doing what? Causing mass terror? How is that helping anything?"

"A show of dominance. We're going to break these countries down. One by one."

Alice looks away, trembling. That Alan, curse him to hell. He has taken her son. "Whatever your father told you is not true. He's a lost man. Delusional."

"More awake than you ever were."

"Levi, please, come back to me."

"Beg more. I like that. I told you, this is who you get. You don't like it, let me go."

"Let you go?" Alice is more determined now than ever. "Never. I'm getting my son back. I'll do anything."

How had she not seen the turmoil going on inside her boy all these years? What kind of mother doesn't see that her son is sick? Maybe she could have stopped all of this if she had just noticed sooner.

"Don't beat yourself up, Mom," Levi says.

He has Alice's attention. She thinks it's her real son because his voice isn't so edgy, and his demeanor isn't so hateful.

"My problem is mine," Levi says. "It came, and I tamed it."

"I was too focused on other things to pay attention you," Alice admits.

"Too focused on that shit-stain."

Alice stands, the chair sliding backward. Levi's lips are moving rapidly. All hate. All darkness.

"I killed him. I hated him. I hated him so much. That was one of my first missions. I went in there, started the fight, and I killed him. I—"

"*Shut up! Shut up! Shut up!*" Alice screams.

She tries to block out his words, but everything that fires out of his mouth strikes her, shattering her conviction. She moves farther away from him, towards the hatch door. She can still hear him. The words aren't the worst part. It's the fact that she can hear him changing each time, back and forth, back and forth.

He tells her he loves her.

Then he utters harsh words, evil words.

She can feel her son's pain every time he switches positions, alternating with that thing that lives inside of him, feeding off everything negative. She watches him twitch and shake. She needs to stop this. Her son is in agony.

"Let Levi live," she says to the Levi who is not her Levi. "Why do you want to be with the people who killed Devin?"

"Devin is none of your business."

"Who are you?"

"The Chameleon."

Alice bites her tongue. The Chameleon? What's that, a code name? Another personality? This other personality is trying to take over Levi completely. If he succeeds, what happens then? Does her Levi just not exist anymore? Does he forget about her?

She shakes Levi's shoulders. "Levi, listen to me, baby. You get back here. You are strong."

Vance and Grant come down the basement stairs, and Grant immediately pulls Alice away.

"That thing is trying to steal my son!"

Vance is saddened by the pain he sees in his daughter's eyes. If this other Levi is causing her to hate her own son, then things are going to be much more complicated from here on.

"We've got this, Alice. Go upstairs," he tells her.

Before she takes the first step away from him, Levi says something that rocks her heart to its core. She almost falls over. She can't breathe. She only sees that devilish grin on her son's face. Each beat of her heart is a reverberating implosion, threatening her sanity. She runs backs to him, her hands out. She will choke that monster out of him if this is how he's going to play with her, play with her son.

Vance gives Alice a bear hug, but she is distraught. That ugly, pathetic thing living inside her boy, like the worst type of parasite, said, his voice relentlessly scratching the inside of Alice's skull over and over again like a broken record: "Soon you're not even gonna exist to him."

55

12:00 A.M.

I still can't find a way out of these restraints. My body is sore and numb. I can't feel my hands or feet. I'm done talking to these people. They've been trying all day to cast me out. Beta needs me. We need each other. Why can't they understand that? I even let Beta take control a couple of times to tell these idiots that they need to let me go because I'm sure Red Fist is coming for me. And when they come, it won't be pretty. The woman, the one Alice calls Grant, is down here with me, not paying me much mind. I decide to toy with her.

"You write a will yet?"

She snorts. "You have a lot of mouth, don't you?"

"I'm warning you guys, is all. You'll die if you don't release me."

"Don't you think they would have come already, kid? They don't need you."

288

"We'll see." I hang my head. I know they will come for me. I just know it. I have to believe in them.

12:05 A.M.

Vance is making a pot of coffee; he knows he must maintain his vigilance throughout the rest of the morning. He doesn't want any surprises. He checks his watch, wondering where Strong and Alfonso are. He sent them to the store an hour ago. They should have been back by now. He pulls out his phone, already paranoid.

She answers on the fourth ring, "What's up, boss?"

"Where the hell are you guys?"

"Well, it is midnight, so finding a store was hard. We're pulling—what the fuck?"

The phone screams in Vance's ear with static, and then he hears a commotion on the other end of the line. He leaves his pot of brewing coffee and goes to the living room windows, peaking through the blinds, his hand already drawing his gun from the holster. He sees nothing in his front yard. He sees headlights down the road and tries to see what's going on, but can't. He doesn't want to open the door because he already knows they're here.

He's sprinting towards the basement when he hears a shuffling sound coming from upstairs. He stops and aims his gun. Alice steps down the stairs, startled by the direction in which the gun is pointed.

"Get downstairs, Alice." He lowers his gun. "They're here."

The two rush down to the basement and Grant jumps up. She can tell by the look on their faces that something is astray.

"They're here," Vance informs Grant. "I think they might've stopped Strong and Alfonso before they came back. I don't know what happened to them, the call disconnected just now."

"We can't stay here," Grant says, pulling out her own weapon.

"If we go outside without knowing where they're at, we lose Levi," Alice says. She stands behind Levi, her gun drawn.

"Get away from him, Alice," Vance says.

"He's my son, my responsibility."

Vance grabs her by the arm and pulls her aside. "You need to get a grip. Things are about to get very serious. Everyone coming down those stairs that isn't Strong or Alfonso needs to be shot."

Alice nods, looking away, ashamed of herself. *What was I going to do?*

"Grant, cover the top of the stairs. Alice, get over in the corner and provide support. I'll guard Levi directly," Vance commands.

Levi perks up. "I told you guys."

"Shut up!" Vance places himself behind Levi.

Vance's hands are shaking terribly. He takes a deep breath, not wanting his aim to be messy. All in all, he knows they're not in the best position and are most likely outnumbered. The only advantage they have is the fact that there are only two ways to get into the basement, the main one being the stairs. Vance hasn't used the hatch that leads to his backyard in years. It's been locked for a long time now. The one humming light in the basement flickers and flutters and his heart bottoms out as they're cast into darkness, unable to see.

He hears footsteps above them. He blinks, trying to get his eyes to adjust to the solid sheet of blackness. He hears a moan, then something thumping down the stairs like a large bag of potatoes.

"Grant! Grant!" he whispers but gets no reply.

The light awakens from its slumber, opening its eyes to the view of a dead Grant at the bottom of the stairs with a bullet hole in her head. Blood bubbles and gushes from her cranium, pooling onto the floor.

Alice is about to run over to her but is stopped by a gun barrel tapping against her forehead. The woman holding Alice at gunpoint has autumn-colored hair and high cheekbones. For some reason, she is wearing sunglasses.

She looks to her father, who is also in the same predicament, with his hands up. The man holding him in place is tall and dark, his shiny bald head glistening in the basement light. He's crunching on a piece of candy.

A man comes lumbering down the steps with a shotgun, unlike the other two, who are wielding rifles with silencers. He steps off the bottom step into the basement, and somehow his presence takes up too much space in the room.

Levi is looking at all of them, excitement in his eyes.

Bear taps Sugar on the shoulder twice. The African man tightens his grip on the weapon and says a prayer in his native language. He stares at Vance, who looks back with fearful eyes, his face stricken in terror as he makes a daunting realization.

Sugar pulls the trigger, executing the chief of the DC Metropolitan Police Department right there in his own home. Taking the life of Vance Rodriguez, Alice's father, right in front of everybody. Sugar watches the man drop to the ground, the hot bullet taking all the color and life from his body.

Alice wails. The cry is guttural, like the bellow of a sick animal in the forest. She runs over to her father and cradles his head, crying, tears sprinting down her face.

56

I get covered in the blood of my grandfather. It sprinkles over me. I look down beside me and see him lying there, lifeless. I hear my mother cry out, and for a moment I think she's been shot, too, but no, she's there, cradling my grandpa, muttering indistinguishable things.

I look up at Bear, who has zero emotion on his face. I don't know what to do. They just murdered my grandpa. I don't even know how to feel.

"Levi?" Ash is kneeling down next to me. "Focus on me."

Grandpa is dead. They shot him. He's gone. My mom is wailing. She's dying on the inside. No, she is dead. They killed her.

I can't focus on you, Ash; there are dead bodies down here. There's my dead grandpa right there. His blood is on my face. I feel this sensation under my skin. It's vibrating. Rippling. There are bugs under my skin. I can feel them. I can feel them. "I can't focus, Ash."

It feels as if layers and layers of myself are being peeled back. Some God, some being, some higher force is frustrated, and it grabs its blade to strip me of myself, right then and there. I feel it. I am delaminated, robbed of being either Levi, light, or dark. I am baseless. I'm the Chameleon, and once again, I am changing my skin.

Ash grabs my face, making me focus on her and not the blood erupting from that man's head. Who... is that man? Do I know him?

That is my grandpa! Some voice in me bites at me as if I should know that information.

"I'm okay," I tell her. "Free me."

She nods and begins to cut at my ropes with her knife. I look at the woman who is crying over the dead man; these voices inside my head tell me she is my mother.

She sees me through her tears and reaches for me. "Please don't leave me like this."

Don't leave her like what? What is wrong with her?

Bear wraps his arm around me and turns me away from the bloody scene. "Go up those stairs and wait for us," he says in a low voice.

I do as I'm told, my mother's voice following me, trying to catch my ears all the way up the stairs.

She shrieks, *"Levi!"* It's a name I don't know, but I guess it's mine. At least that's what the voices tell me.

***

Vance doesn't die right away like he always thought he would. He believed he would die righteously, being a hero, saving lives, and death would come to him swiftly. But no, even with a bullet in his head, he is alive. He can't move. He can't close his eyes. He can't feel any pain. He can still see, barely, but his ears do not aid him.

293

Vance is a car with a gas leak. Blood is flowing from his head. It slides down into his mouth, and he acquires a real, deep taste of his life for the few seconds he has left. He sees everything. His entire life is a movie reel; a preview scrolls through his mind, which is rupturing and crumbling and becoming even more of a dark, lightless zone.

He sees his wife, his children's mother, who he cast away because of her dementia. He sees Levi as a small boy, running into his arms. The chief of the DC Metropolitan Police Department watches his daughter, Alice, graduate from the academy. He watches so many things flash and flurry in and out of existence. Vance doesn't know if he's shedding his last tears or if it's just blood. His wife is beaming down at him, all brightness, all light, not angry at him for throwing her away. She's reaching for him, beckoning him towards the light.

57

2:13 P.M.

For some reason, Ghost keeps giving me sideways glances as we walk around the museum together, acting as if we're ordinary people here to enjoy the history of nature. I ignore the constant jabs of worry she aims at me. She thinks I'm some weak little boy who can't handle blood. What happened at that man's house is nothing to me. He doesn't even matter. I can't even remember his name, much less how I even got in that situation.

Searing and vicious, memories claw into the existence of my mind, and I see them: the dead man who is supposedly my grandfather and the woman who is apparently my mother. I shake my head, trying to wipe away these intrusive visions before they distract me too much.

Ghost stops me, looking into my eyes. "Levi?"

Why does she keep calling me that? That can't be my name. More memories flare behind my eyes. "I'm fine. Stop calling me that."

"What?"

Memories, memories of things I don't recall ever happening skyrocket down into my mind's eye and fester in a pile, a landfill of forgotten things. The inside of my skull racks and bellows. A headache. No, a migraine. I rub my temples. Why do I feel sick? Who is this Levi?

"I'm going to go to the bathroom," I tell Ghost.

I break away from her and find the nearest bathroom. Luckily, there's no one inside. A giant mirror stretches from one end of the wall to the other. I see this person in the mirror and almost puke into the sink because there's a weird feeling in my stomach. I take a handful of my hair in between my fingers, trying to calm down. I don't know what's going on with me. My entire body feels like it's breaking into different pieces, and there's nothing I can do to stop it. The guy in the mirror looks detached, unaware, and confused.

This guy is me.

This guy is a dog that is just becoming self-aware.

I bark at myself.

"Who am I?" I ask this question again and again.

I ask it so many times that eventually the guy in the mirror splits into three. I lose the air in my lungs. My legs tremble, I feel weightless. I swing my head to the right and left. There are clones of myself standing beside me. They are reflections in the mirror, and both of them are glaring at me.

The one on the right laughs. **"Pathetic. You don't even know who you are. I think you might die today."**

The other one, the one on the left, is not smiling and sends a hateful stare towards the right clone. *"If he dies, we both die."*

"This guy is a loony," the guy on the right says. **"Maybe it's better if we off ourselves."**

I slam my fist onto the counter, grabbing their attention. "Who are you guys? Who am I?"

The right clone is grinning wickedly at me. I think I must be going insane because reflections aren't supposed to talk back to you. **"We're you, dumbass,"** he says. **"Your name is Levi. You're the Chameleon. I don't get it. How can he show up in our minds and be so confused?"**

"He's what the doc was talking about," the left guy says. *"I guess seeing my grandpa…"*

"He got blasted. Oh, well. See, look what happens when your feelings fuck up everything. Now we have another one to deal with. And he's in control, for the best part."

"Fuck off! It'll be all right. We just need to help him through this, so we can take my body back."

"Whatever you say, Beta." The right guy disappears.

I'm left staring at two reflections of myself, and one of them is frowning at me. I can't tell what he's thinking. Do reflections even think? They must if they can talk to me.

"All right, listen to me," the remaining clone says. *"We're going to help you because you're just an unstable version of me. The doc warned me this would happen. Listen, forget that. You need to stay calm for the rest of the day until we can come back together, all right?"*

I nod at myself. He's a lot nicer than the other one. "I'm sorry," I tell him.

I feel like messed something up. Am I a mistake?

"Yeah, well, right now we're running out of time. Listen to us. Don't do anything unless we tell you. Do everything we say."

I nod again and back away from the mirror, watching my reflection vanish into the light. I leave the bathroom and smile, laughing at myself.

58

Earlier That Day: 0800

Alice finally zips up the body bag, allowing two paramedics to take her father away. She had stopped crying long ago. Her body had become too exhausted to keep quivering. She is now just a woman with a goal, and a son to catch. She'll never forget that look on her son's face when she called out to him. The expression on his face was a pure and honest bullet driving itself right through her heart, staking itself into her soul; her son's eyes showed her that he couldn't recognize his own mother. He didn't understand that the gravity in her life was too oppressive, that she needed him. Those eyes she stared into as she screamed weren't Levi's eyes.

Alice walks away from the ambulance to where Strong and Alfonso are waiting for her.

Strong hugs her. "You sure you're okay? This is insane."

"I'm fine. I need to do this."

Alfonso smiles at her in consolation, not knowing what to say.

Alice tries to smile at her friends but can't, her smile is lost somewhere, some evil thing threw it into an abyss. She turns away from them. "Please keep everything here in check. Thank you."

She hops into her car and drives away, heading for the JNT headquarters. She allows herself some time to process the facts of her situation. Her father is gone, and so is one of her dear friends. How could her son be entangled with such a ruthless group of murderers? Alice will never forget what happened. She'll never forget any of their faces. She needs to keep herself in check. There is no time for tears. She still wants to save her son and get him the proper help he needs, behind steel doors, where she'll ensure Red Fist will never touch him again.

Alice never knew she was capable of so much loathing for one person. She wants Alan. He's taken so much of her time and life away from her that she can only think about one thing when the four letters of his name swim into her mind: death. She wants to kill him. She wants them all to burn; every single member of that awful, deceitful, cruel, inhuman organization needs a special seat in the deepest, darkest, and hottest pits of hell.

Alice makes a decision as she parks her car. This decision is going to carry her forward. It will keep her on her toes because she's lost everything important to her so now, and she must have a goal, an ambition, to keep her alive so at least she can feel like some kind of mother in the end. Her wrath will not be ignored. Not this time.

Alice will get rid of Red Fist.

***

"Sir," Emelia Rose peeks her head into the door, "Alice Rodriguez is in the lobby."

The man is sitting at his desk with his hands clasped together in the middle of a large office that has the barest of decorations. He has never cared to decorate his workplace. His office is gigantic. He has nothing on the walls on either side of him, and only keeps a portrait of his respectable father and mother on his desk. The room might as well be empty. If it weren't for the massive, glass window behind him, the office would be a crude place. He sits straight-backed in his leather chair. He stares straight ahead, deep in thought, making calculations, going through possibilities, and different strategies.

In Nathaniel Collins' mind, he is at war. *Red Fist, I shall destroy you.*

A single vein pulses boldly on the side of his forehead. After receiving a tip from an anonymous source, the JNT had to move and make plans to counter a possible terrorist threat. Collins was put in charge of this task because he's simply superior. He considers everything.

He is so deep in thought that he doesn't notice Rose knocking on his desk until she says, "Sir," yet again.

He stirs from his thoughts, looking up in annoyance at his right hand. "What?"

"The anonymous tipper. She has more information she wants to give to us in person. Earlier you set up a meeting—"

Collins shuts the woman up with a wave of his neatly manicured hands. "I know. Send her up." He stands, straightening his crisp suit. "Sit her right there," he says, pointing to one of two black chairs on the other side of his desk. "Tell her not to touch anything. I'm going to the bathroom."

Rose bows her head as she holds the door open for him. He walks down the hall, once again going into his mind to tangle with the serpent. Collins will think of everything because that's the kind of man he is. He strides into the bathroom and takes a good look at himself in the mirror. If he's to get every bit of information on Red Fist from this Alice, he must look his best. First impressions are everything, and Nathaniel Collins is a master at first impressions.

He stares at himself in the mirror, at the gray suit fitted snuggly to his long body.

Collins is a perfectionist by nature. He has always aimed to be the very best at everything in his life, and so far, he has succeeded. He graduated from Harvard at the top of his class. He wrote a bestseller novel titled *How to Be Perceived as Perfect*, and due to his above-average mind, he's the top agent in this new agency, the Joint Nations Taskforce.

Collins has always got what he wanted in life. His parents spoiled him and made him into a man that looked down on others if they weren't adequate enough to stand next to him. He has made it a rule to not be near anyone that he considers trash long enough for him to smell, too.

He checks his hands. His nails are shining. They are perfect. He believes that a great handshake and stern gaze always make people respect you.

Collins knows all too well that every human is far from perfect, but that doesn't mean that he can't strive to be a God among humans. He smiles slightly and then frowns almost immediately. Collins absolutely despises his smile. He knows his smile is odd. It stretches his face out too much, and the lines on his face make him look like he's wearing someone else's flesh over his head. He rebounds quickly from the depressive moment and resumes thinking positive thoughts.

Collins is taller than average, six feet, to be exact, and his upper body is built like a square, his shoulders appear to be ninety-degree angles. His hair is a thin, whitish-blond color that runs down the sides of his block-shaped face and stops just near his ears. His eyes are dull and sunken; they lack light. They are a sky that is getting ready for an incoming storm.

Nathaniel Collins finally leaves the bathroom, deeming himself immaculate. He believes that anyone gazing at him would assume he was a fighter, an athlete, but that would be wrong. He was—and he hates to admit this to himself—average at those things. Even in his training to be a CIA agent, his shooting skills and physical training were not his best qualities, and that really bugs him, so he conveniently omits those things from his perception of what it takes to be the best. What matters to Collins, and he wrote about this in his book, is the human mind. The mind controls the body, and superior minds are powerful enough to control others.

Collins opens his office doors and smiles that awful smile again, this time even wider, displaying his brilliantly white teeth to no one in particular.

Alice is sitting in the left black chair in front of his desk, just as he wanted.

"Hello there, Ms. Rodriguez," he booms.

Alice turns, standing to extend her hand.

He grasps the small thing firmly, wondering if she's the type of woman to shatter under pressure. But under his malicious eye contact, the woman does not shatter like broken glass onto a floor. She does not squirm. She seems to take every ounce of tension that Collins applies and redirects it back at him. Collins does not let the surprise show on his face, but he is impressed.

He lets her hand go and moves around to his desk, sitting down.

"Sorry for your loss, Ms. Rodriguez. Of course, we've heard about what happened. With the information you'll be providing we can bring those animals to justice."

"I'm fine," Alice says, noting how crushing the man's presence is. There's something about the voraciousness of his gaze, and the way he demands attention. Something about him is off, but she shrugs off her suspicions, getting straight down to business.

"As you probably know," she says, "my son is one of those…animals and has been manipulated by them. I want to save him, and I need your word that you'll agree with my terms before I tell you anything."

The perfectionist glances down at his wristwatch. Time is ticking. He needs to be moving, taking action; this woman will not parade over him. He waves his hand, motioning her to go on.

"I want him to have immunity from harm. Everyone else can be put down. I also want to be at the forefront of the operation. You guys will need me. I've been dealing with Red Fist for a while now."

Collins is irritated. A vein is bulging from his temple. He decides to play her game for now, but he makes a mental note to show her who is in charge. Time is of the essence, and cannot be wasted on ego.

He sighs, and his smile makes Alice recoil on the inside. "Very well then, Ms. Rodriguez. Deal."

59

It could be any of these people here at the museum, disguised as anybody. We're on the second floor, and Ghost pulls me over to the banister, where we look down on the people milling around the sculpture of the elephant. The elephant has its trunk raised. Is it afraid like me? Surprised, maybe? Maybe it knows what's about to happen and is trying to send a warning to everyone to get out, but of course, since it's an exhibit, no one can hear its cry.

Ghost whispers in my ear, "We're definitely being tracked. The guy in the long-sleeved blue shirt at our four o'clock, and there's a woman across from us—sunglasses, headscarf—at twelve o'clock. She's taking pictures of the elephant. There's another as well, I think."

I glance back at the Hispanic guy with the mustache. He's right behind us, texting on his phone. He's with a small woman, dark hair.

"Directly behind us. The couple," I tell her.

Ghost puts her hand to her ear. "Jung, are we ready yet?"

He answers. "Bear said at two forty-five. Remember?"

Ghost curses and looks at me. "Come on. Let's go." She pulls away from the banister, but before I can turn around, she backs into me. It's the couple; they're onto us.

The Hispanic man smiles nervously at us. "Can you please take a picture of me and my wife?" he asks.

"We're actually in a hurry," I tell him. "My parents are waiting for us below."

He nods solemnly and lets us pass. We dive into the crowd, and I pull my hat as low as I can, feeling the needles of anxiety stick into me all over. I take out my phone, the other Levis telling to act like I'm making a phone call. I follow Ghost, who is walking around leisurely, constantly checking her watch. It's two thirty-nine. Six more minutes.

I glance behind us, wondering if anybody is following us. An easy way to tell in large groups, according to the Levis, is to see who makes eye contact with you directly. If someone is staring at you, maybe it's a tail. It's a hit-or-miss game.

We head down the staircase. The lady with the scarf is coming up. She smiles, her red lipstick bright. Something about the way she smiles is familiar, but I can't put my mind around that right now. Why is she going up if we're going down? Does the JNT have a trap for us below? If they're here, why are they not trying to apprehend us?

The old couple in front of us is taking their sweet time, and Ghost rolls her eyes. We finally make it down the steps.

We go stand near the big rock the elephant is showcased on, the glow of the lights all around bright and uncomfortable.

Everybody can see me. I'm so exposed here. The JNT can see us here.

Chill out, dude. Stop being a pussy.

We're almost there. Just last a little longer, buddy.

The Levis are talking back and forth in my head. They're so noisy. That anxious feeling is like a snake now. It's becoming hard for me to suck in air.

Ghost shakes my shoulder. "Dude, what's up with you?"

"I don't know," I answer softly. "Don't worry about it."

The Levis won't shut up. I can hear them. It's like they're everywhere. And everyone is looking at me now. I feel them, their gazes stabbing into what's left of my chaotic existence. Can they see that I'm fucking losing it?

Jung steps up in front of us and takes out his camera to get a picture. A moment later, just as planned, miniature explosions can be heard all over the building, and not even a second later, screams of the unknown and panic lace the entire building. Glass is shattering everywhere, people are gasping. People are already running for the doors as smoke drifts out of doorways and fills the air. Alarms screech to life. Tour guides direct guests towards emergency exits.

We're very close to the main doors, so we jump into the fray of crying people, and I panic. I'm hyperventilating.

Why the fuck is everyone staring at me?

60

It's mayhem. Police are already set up at the end of Madison Drive. They were expecting this. Smoke billows into the sky all over. We go the opposite way, to where the Washington Monument is poking the heavens. There's also police near there, set up on 14th Street, so we make a sharp right onto 12th Street and break out of the sea of people.

"Come on," Jung says. "Bear and Ash should be up ahead."

Just as planned, Bear and Ash link up with us near the Old Post Office Tower. There are people all along the street now, looking in the direction we came from. I keep my head down, like the Levis instruct, and follow the rest of my team. We run across Constitution Avenue and continue until we reach Pennsylvania Avenue.

The road is buzzing with traffic, and Bear is looking for an opening, so we can sprint across. Luckily a red light allows us to jet across the street. I look at the people sitting in their vehicles, knowing nothing of what just occurred. Once we make it to the other side, I glance back and almost bottom out. I see the lady with the sunglasses and scarf, and the couple Ghost and I encountered at the museum.

"Guys, they're already on us," I say into my mic.

Some of the pedestrians give our group perplexed looks, and I figure they're probably wondering how such a random group of people came to be together.

I hear a voice in my small earpiece. "We'll lose them in Chinatown. Sugar and Asha should be headed around the other way. Spread out, act like we're not together."

I drop back from the group, the Levis reminding me to watch my back for our tails. I put my hand up to my ear. "We need to shake these guys."

"They can't do anything here," Bear replies. I search for him up ahead and spot his muscular frame easily among the stream of people. "Turn right onto Pennsylvania North Avenue," he instructs. "Then make a left on 10th Street."

Anxiety is raging fiercely under my skin. I want to run, to sprint away, but I have to ignore that itch. The Levis tell me to act normal, but now I see out of the corner of my eye that our tails are even closer.

I catch up to Ghost, who's startled until she realizes it's me.

"What are you doing?" she says.

"We need to shake these tails," I say quickly.

Calm down. You're even worse than, Beta.

Shut up! He needs to focus. Don't insult him.

Fuck off.

You fuck off.

You're useless.

I drone out the Levis bickering inside me and pull Ghost in closer. "Ghost, we need to get out of here. Seriously. This feels all wrong."

"Dude, chill out. Be cool. We have this covered."

"Ghost..." We're on 10th Street, and I'm fucking losing it.

Ghost pushes me away from her. "Get a grip," she says and stomps ahead.

I look back, and my gut is hollering at me. I feel nauseous. Something is wrong, I know it, but nobody's listening to me. We need to get out of here. How did the police know our moves?

"Guys..." I start talking to myself—to the Levis—who are still arguing. *"Guys!"*

Ghost glares back at me and shakes her head.

What? Both Levis answer, sounding irritated that I interrupted their quarrel. "Something's wrong. Nobody's listening to me."

Because you're not worth listening to. Off yourself, spaz.

Chill out, asshole.

He's the reason the police have us in their cage.

That was us. We were the one's telling Cassie bits and pieces about this op.

"Seriously. You guys said you were going to help me. I'm freaking out."

I know I probably look crazy talking to myself, but I don't care anymore. Fewer and fewer people are walking past us now, disappearing down side streets and into buildings.

Walk straight. That's all you need to do. It'll be okay.

Babying him. Great.

"You're a dickhead."

And you're a giant wuss.

Chill. Out. Keep calm, Levi. You're doing great.

We cross the street. I can see the Martin Luther King Jr. Memorial Library ahead. This block is even more deserted, and there's only us walking down the sidewalk now. I can see Bear, Ash, Ghost, and Jung ahead, directly across from the library. They stop suddenly. I check behind me, to see if we're still being followed. Our tails are gone. Where did they go? All around me, there is nothing but this overbearing stillness. I can feel all the eyes on me. We've been trapped.

"This isn't good," I say to myself, and the Levis ignore my comment.

When I join up with the rest of Red Fist, I see Bear looking all around. Suddenly he frowns.

Ghost catches it, too. "What's wrong?"

"You guys don't feel that?" Bear says. "Having those tails was a good sign. I should've noticed sooner, but I thought we could outmaneuver them." He places his gun on the ground, straightening and standing tall with his chest out. "We're surrounded."

61

My skin feels as if it's trying to jump off my flesh. This isn't right. I told them. I told them. I told them. The whole block is quiet. There are no vehicles. There are no people. The only thing that can be heard is a wind that drops low from the silver sky, threatening rain, playing a sad song in my ears. A round of applause from a single person breaks the silence, and we all snap our heads towards the source.

"Bravo, bravo, bravo." A deep, velvety voice rings out, then out of the shadows comes a proud man dressed in an all-white, from head to toe around the same height as Bear. He has box shoulders, broad and sharp, and his skin is so pale that his lightless, blue eyes look bright. He stops twenty meters short of us. "Any of you have any more weapons I should know about?"

He snaps his fingers. Out of nowhere, from every nook and cranny, people appear holding different weapons. Above us, on the buildings' rooftops, barrels aim down at us.

I have to stop the urge to piss myself. My legs are shaking; I'm trembling so much that the man with the dead blue eyes sees this and smiles. His skin looks rubbery when he smiles, stretching entirely too much; it's definitely the ugliest smile in the world.

"I want to applaud you." He's looking at Bear. "You have my respect for knowing when you've lost."

Bears says nothing. Has he accepted defeat? We can't go down like this.

Stepping up beside the man is the lady we saw earlier with the headscarf and sunglasses. She throws her sunglasses to the ground and yanks the scarf from her head, letting it float gracefully down. When my heart beats, it thumps in reverse. She's staring right at me. Do I know her? Why is she looking at me so intensely?

"Remember our deal?" she asks the man in white.

"Of course."

She looks back at me. "Levi, get over here. This is all over now."

Why is she talking to me? Then I realize the lady is Mom.

Great! This is all just fucking great.

Why is she here? Did she set this up?

She had to, that's how they knew this was happening today. We might as well off ourselves now.

The voices in my head are screaming at each other. I can't fight them, they're too loud.

My body moves on its own accord. Bear reaches out for me, but someone shoots at the ground near his feet. I can't control my body.

I don't know this woman.

I don't want to go. I don't want to go.

That's my mom.

When I get there, I'm going to send her flying.

I don't want to go.

My body won't stop moving. It begins to rain, small drops bursting against everything solid, but I can't even feel the coldness they're supposed to bring to my skin. Everything feels transparent. I feel like a ghost; bullets would phase through me, I am nothing. I can't control myself. I grab my head with both of my hands and apply as much force as I can. I fall to my knees in front of my mom.

Alice? Who is this woman? Mom?

She reaches for me, and I scream. I can't let her touch me.

Mom, I'm sorry. I can't help it! I can't help it! I can't help it!

Stay the fuck away from me.

I scoot away from her, dragging my ass across the wet ground. The people with guns are moving in on my team. I can't see. I can't do anything. I need to do something. I stand, facing the woman, my shoulders square. Alice is staring at me.

I'm going to fucking crush her.

I smile at her and swing. She dodges my punch. I freeze. I can't move. She knees me in the stomach, then forces me on the ground.

"Get off me, bitch!"

Alice pushes my head onto the wet asphalt. "I will save you, Levi," she says. "Don't worry, baby. I'll get every single one of them out of you."

She yells in my ear as she grinds her knee into my back and pulls one of my arms up behind me. I cry out, I can't tell if it's the rain or tears sliding down my face as my mind and body spin in and out of the different Levis' control.

62

Alice gets her son in cuffs. He lies on the ground, seemingly defeated. "Get up," she tells him.

He gets up and then turns to look at her. The regret and pain in Levi's eyes is so vivid that Alice can feel her willpower slipping. No mother wants to see her child in pain. He begins to close the distance between them, for some reason unbeknownst to her, she steps back, afraid. His eyes are different.

She draws her gun. "Stay back. Stand still, Levi."

"Make me," he growls.

She points her nine-millimeter handgun right at his face, her hands quivering. He doesn't stop.

He keeps walking all the way until he headbutts the barrel of the gun softly. Alice can hardly see him with the rain coming down so fiercely. Thunder booms, but she doesn't take her eyes off her son. Right now, he's the devil in disguise.

He headbutts the gun again. "If you pull it out, use it. Do it. Stop me. Make me still, *Mom*."

"Stop it, Levi. Please."

"Shoot me. Do it. Do it. Do it. Do it."

Alice can see in her peripheral vision that something is very wrong. The Red Fist members are no longer standing where they were before. Collins and Rose are gone as well. Thunder? No, it's gunfire. She takes her gun off Levi. The rain stabs at her eyeballs. She blinks a few times, seeing many figures running around the area with guns, wearing black armor, flying through the smoke that is quickly disappearing. She grabs Levi and pulls him close to her. She has to get him out of here. Those aren't JNT agents. Red Fist has reinforcements.

She heads up 10th Street, dragging her sack-of-potatoes son with her. She gets him down the street and shoves him behind a building. She smashes him against the wall. "Levi. Listen to me. I'm trying to save you. Work with me. Concentrate."

"Mom, you need to kill me. Please," he shakes his head, "I can't do this anymore."

"I'm going to help you." She pulls at him, but he shakes her off. "Levi, come *on*."

"I said, kill me."

She reaches for him again, but this time he slides away, falling onto the ground. She can't carry him somewhere safe by herself. He's grown a lot. He's taller and more muscular now. He's not the same thin boy she used to know. She has to get him to work with her. She kneels next to him; he lies there staring up at the sky, taking on the fat drops of rain.

"Levi, please let me help you."

"I want to die. I'm not doing any of this anymore."

She breaks. She can't see him like this. It's too much. The integrity of who he was has gone, stripped away by blood and death and insanity.

He looks at Alice, straining to catch her eyes in the ocean's worth of rain.

Alice grabs her son's head and presses their foreheads together. "I'll help you. I promise."

"Mom, I'm so sorry."

"You don't need to be."

"You need to kill me. It's gonna get worse."

"I can help you, Levi."

"You can't. No one can now."

"I can."

"Mom, it's too late." Levi lets his head smack against the pavement, the film of water cushioning the impact.

Alice stands, and her police instincts tell her to turn around. She twists around, a second too late. Somebody slams into her, knocking her to the ground. Before she can get up, the Tongan towers over her, placing his foot on her chest. She's dropped her gun somewhere during the fall and can't utilize it now.

Shit!

Another person, a small woman with dreads, comes to rummage around in her pockets. She comes out of them with keys. "Bingo."

Asha goes over to Levi. "We're here, little bro."

"Get your hands off of him." Alice wriggles under the bear-like man's insane amount of mass. She claws at his boots. "Get off of me!"

Levi picks up the gun that his mother lost when she got knocked over, cackling like a mad man.

"Let her up," he tells Bear.

Bear drags Alice up while digging his fingers into her brachial plexus, so she won't have the strength to fight. She squeals, her fierceness evaporating. Bear places her near a pole, and Asha locks her to it. Her whole spirit sags, knowing once again that she has lost. She'll never get her Levi back.

He steps up in front of her, his face slack, showing not a hint of emotion. Suddenly he smiles evilly. "I told you to kill me. You let me play you."

And then he looks confused, like a lost child in the park. "I don't know you. I don't know why you came at me, but now you're here, and it's your own fault."

"I'm your mother," Alice cries.

He steps up close to her, so close she can see it in his eyes when he comes back. Alice can tell that this person, right here in front of her, is her Levi, the real one. He touches her face, wiping away the rainwater mixed with tears on her face. "I love you, Mom."

"I love you, too. Levi—"

He cuts through her words, his brown eyes more black than ever. "I'm the Chameleon. And I told you it was too late."

He turns away from her.

Alice knows this is the last time she'll ever see her real son again. He will never be the same. She wants to yell at the heavens to do something, to help her save her son. She wants to scream. She wants to break free of her restraints and tackle Levi to make him stay with her. She does none of this, though, knowing that she can't. Even if she could, it wouldn't be worth trying.

Levi begins to walk away from Alice, but stops, spins, and slides back to her. He whispers in her ear. His breath is cold, his words cutting into her. She winces as he issues his warning with so much gravity that she shatters.

"Next time we meet. You better kill me."

Alice froths at the mouth and shakes the pole violently as she tries to free herself. She needs to be with him. This time when he spins away, he waves at her and continues walking towards Bear and Asha. This is his goodbye.

Alice yanks against her restraints until she's out of energy, until her wrists are bloody, and until Levi, her son, her everything, is nothing but a memory. She wails because she's lost her entire life now. She is a failure. She is not a mother. She is nothing. She tilts her head all the way back and crashes down to her knees, howling at the unforgiving heavens, at all the Gods that might exist that are poignantly boring down onto her as she crouches frozen in place, trapped like some pathetic thing.

63

My mother's pleas to be let free echo in my ears. I don't care. She failed, which means this is what I'm supposed to be. Red Fist won. I will denounce what I was completely. Weak. Naïve. Immature. Rash. All those things are Levi. All those things are old skins that I need to shed. *Levi* is a name that holds too much baggage. I don't need trash where I'm going; I need strength. I need an able mind. I need to let go.

I bow my head to the Buddha statue. Bear's friends in Chinatown are jointly working with Red Fist and giving us refuge until we part this land that leaves a foul taste in my mouth.

Ghost walks in behind me. "Oh, sorry, didn't know you were religious."

I turn to her, smiling. "I'm not. I just need peace."

"Don't we all?"

I shrug.

She gets down next to me and bows to Buddha, lifting her head and smiling. "Did I do it right?"

"Shit, I don't know."

Ghost punches me in the shoulder. "Levi—"

"I'm the Chameleon. Levi is no more."

Ghost doesn't say anything. She just stares at me, her eyes searching for clarity within me. I get up and leave the room. From here on out, I am the Chameleon. I will work for my father, my new family, Red Fist, and the world until my dying breath. I open my right palm; the R is still there, a testament to my oath. I shed blood for this, for Red Fist. I close my palm, knowing that my blood can't sit still within me.

There will be more red to come. There will be more fists raised in revolution. I will not stop my fight here. As much as I wish I could forget the lives lost due to my own recklessness, I cannot wash them away. Devin's blood is on my hands. My grandfather's blood is on my hands. I tried washing them, but all the red was still there, clinging to my skin. And even when I shed, my hands stay scarlet.

The R will always be on my right palm. I don't know what this R stands for. It doesn't do the symbol justice for it to mean Red Fist.

I'm standing in the bathroom now, again scrubbing my hands. They'll never be clean of all this filth. They'll only become stained a crimson that will be with me even after I pass. Scalding water drenches my hands as I stare at them.

Blood. All I can see sometimes is red.

What does this fucking R stand for?

Then it hits me like a truck. I must redeem myself. I am the Chameleon, and I'm in my final form.

The form called redemption.

Epilogue

Ali's shackles ring and chime in his ear as he wakes from his restless coma. *Damn. Guess I passed out again.*

He moves around, suspended in the air, hanging on a wall that is taking every ounce of heat from his body. He's trying to work the kink out of the place between his shoulder blades. His wrist and ankles ache. The thick cuffs are pinching his skin. He smiles, thinking back on the time he had his little brother, Levi, pinned to a wall like this. Ironic.

It's been an entire nine months since Ali's capture. He hasn't told these fuckers a thing except his name. He still doesn't know who these people are who are torturing him. He's crossed the FBI off his list. These guys are way more ruthless. He still remembers the last time he saw Myla, four months ago, when they were locked up across from each other. They dragged her out of the cell by her hair, and all the way down the hall, her cries echoing so loudly that Ali had to shove a rough pillow over his head. He hopes she's okay. Myla is a cockroach. A survivor.

Bear told him a long time ago that Myla's entire family got whacked when the FBI did a raid on her great-uncle. Her mother is the only one who managed to escape, but they found her and "disposed" of her. Myla is the only one left.

Ali hangs here on the wall now, thinking that Myla might just be dead.

He never cared too much for Jefferson, yet he worries. He wonders if Bear and Levi and the others managed to pull off the operation without him. He decides they must have because the torture has gotten progressively worse. The main guy that's been trying to pry information from Ali's mind is a hairless, middle-aged Asian man named Whu, who wears glasses that hang too far down his nose. He reminds Ali of a naked mole rat.

Ali hears shuffling outside the giant, metallic door. He picks up his head, smiling as confidently as he can. He won't let these fuckers break him. Red Fist will come for him. He puffs himself up, tensing his entire body.

Whu walks in, followed by a lanky, block-shaped man with thin blond hair and pasty, glue-colored skin. The unfamiliar man is digging a hole into Ali's face with blue eyes that seem to suck up light. They stand in front of Ali.

The unknown guy is grinning at him, the corners of his lips too wrinkly, his eyes cold. "You are Ali, Levi's older brother?" he asks, his voice loud and resonant.

"Sure am, ugly."

The ugly man balls his fist, obviously trying to keep calm. "You are the previous leader of that group of…degenerate dogs in DC?"

"Of course."

The man takes a step forward and stretches his face into an expression Ali can't distinguish. He wants to puke. "I am Nathaniel Collins. One of the Joint Nation's Taskforce's most superior agents."

Ali doesn't say anything. He wants to spit in this man's face, but he honestly would like to hold off on the pain. It's going to come, sooner or later, and he prefers later.

Nathaniel Collins continues, growling, his extra-white teeth gleaming in Ali's eyes. "I hate you, and I hate Red Fist. They scarred my reputation in DC. I can't find them. Tell me where they are. Tell me *now*."

Ali feels rejuvenated. He can keep this going for years, knowing that his mission has been completed. He begins to cry tears of pure joy. He feels an overwhelming urge to crack up in the repulsive man's face, and he doesn't contain it.

Collins loses it, overcome by an emotion other than cockiness once again. He hates these inferior emotions, this weakness he's feeling. He punches Ali in the jaw, but the man doesn't stop laughing in his face. Collins rages, unable to accept the notion that somebody is looking down upon him, thinking that he is a joke.

Collins rocks Ali again and again, trying to demolish that look of happiness from the dog's face.

Ali feels the pain. He feels the warm blood flowing from his lips. He feels his nose break again, for the second time since he's been captured, and for the third time in his entire life, but he doesn't stop laughing. He can't. He won't. He'll break all these Joint Nations Taskforce agents in his own way.

Ali has decided that when he's free, he will kill them.

He will kill them all.

Coming Soon

Red Fist: Redemption

Acknowledgments

My absolute favorite thing about writing is the freedom it has given me throughout the years. In life, I know we all often feel as if we're trapped in a cage, but there are many different outlets and ways to escape. For me, that has always been writing. Writing allows me to breathe. It is the reason I'm still breathing.

I want to thank you all for reading my book. If you've made it this far, I'm going to assume you loved the read.

There are many people to thank for this major accomplishment in my life. First, I would like to thank my parents, for always, no matter how odd and crazy, *always* reading my stuff and telling me that I can do anything. I love you both, despite our ups and downs.

I want to thank one of my biggest fans and motivators, Mr. Fred Howard, aka "Motormouth". You definitely made sure I kept true to myself, and were always there, supporting me and hyping me up. Honestly, you're a saint, and a simple thank you is not enough when it comes to you.

In addition to Mr. Fred, I want to shout my thanks to the veteran community. You guys always encouraged me and gave me many ideas and suggestions.

I want to say thank you to all the men and women I served with for keeping up with me and for being excited about my book. Your excitement carried me forth. I want to thank three people especially:

my big brothers, Matthew Montalvan, Calvin Lu, and Tyler Carter. You men keep me sane. I'm glad we all talk at least once a week.

Last, I want to thank my beta readers: Andrea Gattis, Melvin Umana, Alexis Green, and Cristian Barcenas. You four made things within Red Fist shift. You four made history. You four are some of my greatest friends, and this book would not be here without you. I'm so happy to have shared my work with such brilliant minds, and I hope we can work together again.

I want to end this by saying thank you once again. This is my life. My dream. I want to tell everyone that dreams can come true; you just have to be willing to put in the effort to make that magic happen. We can all be our own role models. Never stop chasing yourself up the stairs.

Thank you, all, and I hope you're ready for the next one. It's going to get even redder.

About the Author

Jamiel Jones is an author with dreams to write hundreds of books so people can escape and enjoy the other worlds and lives he creates. Jones spends his days writing, dreaming, eating, working out, and playing Xbox. He gets anxiety if he has to cross major highways, and he hates small talk. He has served in the United States Army and now spends his days trying to come up with the next big thing, going to school, and dreaming. He currently resides on the eastern shore of Maryland, but he likes to think of himself as a nomad, so who knows where he will be next?

If you'd like to follow Jamiel Jones and have access to more insiders and his upcoming novels, check out: jamieljones.com

He's also on Facebook: @WritingForLif3

Be sure to follow his blog on his website and his Facebook page.

Made in the USA
Middletown, DE
15 February 2021